Acclaim for Jo

RESER

"So beautifully written and compelling that you can't
will yourself to put it down."   —*The Denver Post*

"This book possesses a conclusion of such power that
it would be a literary crime to reveal it."
                                        —*USA Today*

"A poignant thriller. . . . The novel's resolution is quietly breathtaking."   —*Vanity Fair*

"[Schwartz is] a fine writer. . . . *Reservation Road* is a
page-turner, but along the way there is much to
linger over."   —*The Washington Post Book World*

"A pleasure to read. Suspense is redefined here."
                                        —*Newsday*

"A deeply moving, darkly satisfying novel."
                                        —*The Boston Globe*

"The redemption in *Reservation Road* is unexpected,
compassionate and powerful, making it moving in a
way few novels are."   —*San Antonio Express-News*

"*Reservation Road* is a terrific novel, both a page-turner
and a disconcerting portrayal of the psychic costs of
self-delusion."   —*The Oregonian*

John Burnham Schwartz's

RESERVATION ROAD

ALSO BY JOHN BURNHAM SCHWARTZ

Bicycle Days
Claire Marvel

John Burnham Schwartz

RESERVATION ROAD

John Burnham Schwartz is the author of *Bicycle Days* and *Claire Marvel*. He lives in New York City with his wife, filmmaker Aleksandra Crapanzano.

John Burnham Schwartz

RESERVATION ROAD

Vintage Contemporaries
VINTAGE BOOKS
A DIVISION OF RANDOM HOUSE, INC.
NEW YORK

Sale of this book without a front cover may be unauthorized.
If this book is coverless, it may have been reported to the publisher as
"unsold or destroyed" and neither the author nor the publisher may have
received payment for it.

FIRST VINTAGE CONTEMPORARIES MASS MARKET EDITION,
OCTOBER 2007

Copyright © 1998 by John Burnham Schwartz

All rights reserved. Published in the United States by Vintage Books, a division
of Random House, Inc., New York, and in Canada by Random House of
Canada Limited, Toronto. Originally published in hardcover by
Alfred A. Knopf, a division of Random House, Inc., New York, in 1998.

Vintage and colophon are registered trademarks and Vintage Contemporaries
is a trademark of Random House, Inc.

This is a work of fiction. Names, characters, places, and incidents either are the
product of the author's imagination or are used fictitiously. Any resemblance
to actual events, locales, or persons, living or dead, is entirely coincidental.

The Library of Congress has cataloged the Knopf edition as follows:
Schwartz, John Burnham.
Reservation Road : a novel / John Burnham Schwartz. — 1st ed.
p. cm.
I. Title.
PS3569.C5658R47 1998
813'.54 — dc21   98-14580
CIP

Vintage Mass Market ISBN: 978-0-307-38832-2

www.vintagebooks.com

Printed in the United States of America
10 9 8 7 6 5 4 3 2 1

For Aleksandra

Oh, that I had the indictment
written by my adversary!
Surely I would carry it on my shoulder;
I would bind it on me as a crown;
I would give him an account of all my steps;
like a prince I would approach him.

—The Book of Job

PART ONE

Ethan

I want to tell this right. On a beautiful summer's day we picnicked in a field as an orchestra played under a yellow tent.

The clouds began to gather in the blue sky around five o'clock. Handel was finished and Beethoven was still to come, the Ninth with full chorus, and there were couples strolling across the lush green field and two teenage boys tossing a Frisbee back and forth, the white disc chased by a barking black dog. And then Emma stood up and said she wanted to go home; she was eight years old and didn't much care for Beethoven. Grace suggested a walk instead, and Emma grudgingly accepted, and mother and daughter went off hand in hand, leaving Josh and me alone.

Room was being made for the chorus under the tent. They stood on the grass, in evening clothes, talking or limbering up their voices. Snatches of notes, bits of German, came floating over to us. And for perhaps the second or third time that day, I explained to my son that the final chorus of the Ninth Symphony was in fact Schiller's "Ode to Joy."

Josh merely nodded. He was a thin, private boy of ten, with dark, curly hair like mine. Sometimes he was a mystery to me. He'd been studying the violin seriously since his seventh birthday and was already well acquainted with Beethoven. Countless times he'd sat with me in my study listening to a scratchy recording of the Bayreuth Festival Orchestra and Chorus performing the Ninth Symphony, with Elisabeth Schwarzkopf singing soprano.

Now he reached into the pocket of his jeans and pulled out a flat, putty-colored stone. Staring off into the distance, he began polishing it with his thumb. I followed his gaze and there was the black dog leaping into the air after the Frisbee and the Frisbee floating just beyond the dog's reach. I asked him what he had there, in his hand.

He looked up at me—surprised, as if he'd thought he was alone.

"That stone."

"Arrowhead," he replied, looking away again.

"Can I see it?"

He shrugged, holding out his hand, palm up. I took the arrowhead from him, turning it over in my own hand. It was a fine specimen, the point still defined, the surface at once jagged and smooth. "It's a nice one," I said. "Where'd you get it?"

"Found it."

"You should take it into science class when school starts. You'd be a big hit with that thing."

He shrugged.

"When I was your age, I—"

"Can I have it back now?"

I felt the blood rise in my face. I had a powerful urge to throw the arrowhead across the field and into the trees, but I was his father and did no such thing. "Sure," I said. I gave it back to him. And then we sat without speaking for some minutes, until Grace and Emma returned from their walk, and the four of us were settled peacefully again on our blanket.

"Find anything on your travels?" I inquired.

"A really fat lady," Emma said.

"Emma," Grace said.

"She was."

"Shh," said Josh, "it's starting."

The tent had fallen still, voices and instruments silenced. The conductor in his black tails tapped the air with his baton, and there was a single cough from an oboist in the third row. And then the explosion of the first bars, like the sky opening. I looked at Josh. He'd shifted to his knees to get a better view of the violinists in the first row. His back had gone perfectly straight and his lips were moving.

I will never forget the final movement. How the voices entered forcefully from the first, resonant yet still earthbound, to be joined by a multitude of others. How the sound grew from inside the yellow tent until it became a god, and the conductor's body seemed to beat to its calling. And finally, how my son, alone among us all, got to his feet and remained there, standing and silent, long after the music had ended.

5

• • •

The sun was low in the sky when we started the drive back. It had fallen into a cloud behind the verdant trees and the light emanating from there was seashell pink. In the backseat of the station wagon, Emma had fallen asleep with her thumb in her mouth and Josh was staring out the window, humming.

The next half-hour or so was a disappearance; the light just withdrew, shrinking back behind the curtain. Roadside trees turned ever softer—until, all at once, it seemed, they were granite. I switched on the headlights. Heading south on Route 7, we crossed the state line into Canaan, bumped over the train tracks that ran there, passed the Connecticut State Police barracks on our right and then on our 'left my dentist, Dr. Zinser, and Tommy's Diner. A quarter of a mile further on, I turned east onto Reservation Road, which was the locals' short-cut between Route 7 and our town of Wyndham Falls.

We were twenty minutes from home. It was dark now. Reservation Road was narrow and unlit and flanked throughout by woods on both sides. Above the trees the sky sat like an enormous bruise. We were rounding a turn when suddenly I saw a stirring in the air at the outer edge of the headlight beams, like a small cloud of upward-falling rain. The car punched into it and instantly the windshield was splattered with dead insects. I braked hard but kept the car rolling.

"What was that?" said Grace.

"Bugs," Josh said excitedly. "A swarm."

I corrected him. "Mayflies."

6

"It's not May any more," he said.

I switched on the wipers, but they succeeded only in streaking the glass with dead insects. When I tried for wiper fluid, I found there wasn't any. The wipers were squeaking against the glass and I turned them off. I was irritable; the concert seemed long ago. "Goddamnit."

In a sweet, just-awake voice Emma said, "Don't curse, Dad."

"I could've sworn you were asleep," I said.

"'Damn' isn't a curse," said Josh.

"Thank you, Josh." I tried to find his face in the rearview mirror, but it was angled up for driving at night and all I could see was the smoke-black roof above his head. For some reason the incident with the mayflies had unsettled me, as if I'd been grazed by a hand in the dark.

Grace touched my arm. "Okay?"

I nodded, relaxing a little at her touch.

Then Emma said, "I have to go to the bathroom."

Grace turned and looked at her. "We're almost home."

"How long?"

"Twenty minutes, tops," I said.

"I can't hold it."

Grace sighed. "Yes, you can."

"I can't."

"She's being a baby," said Josh.

"I am not!"

"Josh," Grace said, "that's enough." Then to me: "Ethan, let's just stop."

"Absolutely not," I said. "Anyway, stop where?"

"There's that little gas station just up ahead, isn't there?"

Yes, there was, just ahead. And, I thought, the windshield was dirty with mayflies and we were out of wiper fluid. Perhaps we could buy some there.

Tod's Gas and Auto Body sat on the far side of a deep curve in the road, a break in the trees that might have felt like an oasis if it hadn't felt like a junkyard. The floodlight meant to illuminate the two old-fashioned pumps was broken, and the red neon sign that Tod's father had installed during headier days had been reduced by attrition to the first three letters, leaving a pitiful air of unfulfilled expectations. Half a wrecked car lay abandoned to the right of the low, flat-roofed building. It was a dark and uninviting place to be at night. The only indications of life were the buzzing three letters and a single lighted window next to the garage area, through which we could see, as we pulled in off the road, a young man sitting on a stool reading a magazine.

All four of us got out of the car; we left the doors open as if running for our lives. I got a rag from the glove box and began cleaning the windshield, while Grace took Emma inside. The door was glass, and small bells trilled when they opened it. I stopped what I was doing to watch them. Framed against the gloaming outside, the interior of the office shone stage-bright. And I saw the incongruous beauty of my wife

8

and daughter, their two blond heads set in my mind against Josh's and mine, our coloring so different from theirs. I saw my wife speaking and the young man— dressed in jeans and an untucked plaid shirt—handing over the key to the bathroom, and there was something shy in his manner, though it was all theater to me, the room lit just so. And then Grace and Emma went out, the bells trilling, and they walked around the side of the building and out of my sight.

"Dad."

I turned. It was Josh, behind me, standing in the shadows near the road. Wearing a navy Windbreaker, unfaded blue jeans, and black sneakers, he was almost invisible except for his face, which was colored a faint neon red from the surviving letters on top of the garage. I had no idea how he'd come to be standing so close to the road.

"Move away from the road, Josh."

Josh looked at the ground and stuffed his hands in his pockets; it was clear that I'd let him down yet again, had, at some fundamental level, failed to respect his sense of himself. My face grew warm. "Hey," I said with false lightness. I extended a hand out into the air for no reason, a professorial affectation. I missed the feeling of the concert, sitting in the field with my son and listening to music.

"I'm not a baby, Dad," he said to the ground.

"Of course you're not," I said. "You're my son. And I'm just being your father the best way I know how. Forgive me?"

He was silent, looking at his feet. When he finally

looked up again, I almost smiled with guilty relief. "What about the bugs?" he asked.

"Bugs?" Then I remembered. "Ah, the *mayflies*," I said declaratively, as though I were not here with my son but at the college teaching The Novel Since the Second World War. A new literary movement, perhaps. Just then I felt certain I was a fool. "We're out of wiper fluid. Why don't we go see if they have any?"

He hesitated, then shook his head.

I wanted to warn him to stay clear of the road, but I'd learned my lesson. "Hold the fort," I told him instead, and walked toward the lighted window, where the young man was again reading his magazine.

At the door to the building, I turned to check on my son. His back was to me. He was standing where I'd left him, staring across the dark curve of road. He seemed someplace else, as though he were still back at the concert. And I wondered if it was music playing in his head, notes like shooting stars.

The small bells trilled when I opened the door. The young man looked up from his reading but didn't stir from the stool. He was younger than I'd thought, with lingering acne and an attempt at a goatee. He had shuffled his feet and gone shy in the presence of my lovely wife, but before me his eyes betrayed a quick hard judgment followed by withdrawal; his remove was daunting. Perhaps he had me pegged for a rich weekender. He couldn't have guessed that I was worse than that, an academic. I wasn't rich, but my life was secure. That had always been its fundamental premise.

He said he wasn't sure he had any wiper fluid left,

he'd have to check. He went through a door into the adjoining garage and turned on the light. In the middle of the grease-stained floor a car was raised on cement blocks, the engine sitting beneath it like a fallen heart. The odors of oil and gas were overpowering, and suddenly I felt the onset of a headache. I wanted to be home, reading a book, with a drink in my hand.

The young man reappeared carrying a gallon jug of blue wiper fluid. I handed him the money and took the jug. The weight of it surprised me; I didn't feel strong. The bells trilled, and I started back to the car with my head down, studying my left knee, which was inexplicably sore, musing on my tennis game and my body and my age.

I want to tell this right. I was thirty-eight years old. I had spent my entire adult life reading meanings into other people's stories, finding the figure in the carpet, the order in things. God in the details and no place else.

The car came from nowhere. No, it came from the left, racing around the bend in the road. The tires screamed and I looked up. The car was dark blue or green or black. Only one of the headlights worked. It broke from the trees like an apparition. And my son was standing in the dark road. My son's head was down as if he were looking for something. I shouted his name and his head jerked up, and then he saw the light coming at him. And in that light as it climbed him from the feet up, his eyes grew wide and his mouth dropped open but made no sound. The right front of the car struck him dead in the chest. It sounded like ice cracking. His body flew thirty feet.

Grace

The gas station appeared up ahead as they came out of the turn. And without warning the words were ringing inside her, signaling a sudden change of heart: *Not this, not here.* The place dilapidated, decrepit, abandoned, dark; the sign partially blown out; a car wrecked like a ship and left to rot among the weeds. All wrong, not at all what she'd ordered. But Ethan was already braking, pulling over; it was already happening. To try to change his mind now would be to admit to the same old fear. He'd complain that it was time, finally, just to let it go. Yes, of course. But how? Not so easy. *All my life,* she thought. The car slowed still more and then, distinctly, it was the tires she heard, tread by tread over the road, pebbles and sticks, slower and slower, the car listing to the right, while she berated herself, castigated herself, and thought: *This is ridiculous.* And was eight years old again.

• • •

The grass had been watered that morning; the feel of it cool and still wet between her bare toes. She could hear them by the pool, behind her as she went into the house: Daddy laughing loudly, like a happy horse, at something one of the guests had said. In the kitchen Gloria was standing at the counter slicing tomatoes for lunch. She held up the pitcher with both hands, and Gloria, smiling down at her, filled it with iced tea from another pitcher, and then she went back outside. The pitcher was heavy and made her arms hurt. She stared at it hard as she walked with small quick steps back across the lawn, trying not to spill; but the more she stared, the more she seemed to spill. The bright sun made her blink a lot, and the grass came up again, cool and still wet, between her toes.

She never knew how she dropped the pitcher; it just tumbled onto the lawn, landed upside down, and before all the iced tea had disappeared into the grass, she was already crying. And then a loud crash near the pool made her look. Her first thought was that Mother and Daddy had dropped something, too, and for a moment she felt relief so strong it was almost like joy. But then, looking over, she witnessed a strange, frightening scene: Daddy was lying on his back on the ground, and one of the guests was pounding him on the chest. And Mother, who was always so polite, was screaming for God to help her. . . .

Ethan turned off the engine, the doors opened: she was getting out, they were all getting out, she was taking Emma's hand, leading her off toward the little lighted office, trying hard, with a soldier's discipline, to focus her attention on anything but the awful gasping image lingering in her mind or the cracked, weedy pavement under her feet—the sound of the crickets singing across the road, all around, the music of any summer's night; that would do. Anything. Anything but this fear that had entered her life so long ago and yet still clung to her memory like cobwebs in an attic. Opening the door to the office, she was startled by the jingling of little bells. Thinking, *Why bother to do that, with the bells, in a place like this?* She wanted to go home now. *Let's just pee and get out of here.* A young man in a plaid shirt—beard, sort of, pimples, clear blue eyes—blushing and looking down at his feet as he handed her the bathroom key, attached to a four-by-three-inch rectangle of plywood to deter thieves and loiterers; his cologne home-grown, tangy, his attentions to her physical person welcome right then, as far as they went. *I've had enough of my mind for one day.*

She took the key and, leading Emma by the hand, walked back out into the warm, dark, pungent evening, the little bells jingling behind her like a broken song.

Ethan was cleaning the windshield with a rag, Josh standing a few paces off, bored, hanging out, both his mood and his clothes somber, evening-colored. And this: standing there he seemed hauntingly a spirit, a shadow, not a boy. She made herself turn away.

Enough. It was time. Around to the left with Emma, a kind of blind alley there. The light bulb out. She could see it stuck on the side of the building, useless, and beneath it a large metal Dumpster. Creepy place, all right; she had to smile to herself when she felt Emma's hand slide into her own. Past a couple of pulled-apart wooden crates and a mangled hubcap stood the bathroom door: unisex, apparently. She opened it with the key and, pulse surging, reached in a trembling hand and flipped on the light.

They stood there, peering in, trying to breathe through their mouths.

"It's gross," said Emma.

"It's a gas station, Emma."

Emma turned her head away, refusing even to look. "It's still gross."

"Would you like me to come in with you?"

"I can hold it."

"We stopped just so you could go."

"Mom, I know, but . . ."

"I'll come in with you, if you like."

"Okay."

She didn't want to go in with her; the bathroom stank to high heaven. But she'd offered. She couldn't afford, in her own eyes or anyone else's, to be less adventurous than her eight-year-old; there were limits to everything. She pushed the door open wider with her foot and stepped inside. Emma followed reluctantly; suppressing a shudder, Grace toed the door closed. There was no stall—Emma stood in front of the naked toilet, crinkling her nose and looking as if she might gag any second.

"Can't we keep the door open?"

"No, Em. We can't."

"Why not?"

"Because it's not a good idea. Now don't talk, okay? Pee. I want to get out of here just as much as you do."

Emma unzipped her jeans, pulled them and her white underwear down to her knees, and stuck her bottom out over the toilet seat, making sure to keep several inches between her skin and any hard surface—at her height, a feat of willful gymnastics. Standing by the sink, Grace glanced at herself in the streaked mirror, then away: crow's-feet around the eyes, she saw, already, and her blond hair looking limp and dulled; she did not know what the young man in the office had gotten so worked up about; she did not care. She was tired of feeling death everywhere, this private, lifelong battle against a fragility that only she seemed to feel; tired of lugging around her bag of pet psychological tricks to make everything seem safe, when nothing really was. She wanted to go home now and take a hot bath.

The sound came. Finally Emma was peeing, eyes fixed, oddly as an adult's might have been, on the wall in fierce concentration. Grace found herself both surprised and moved by the faint evidence of muscle quivering along the outside of the thin bare thighs; by the tan line that must have developed only yesterday. It had been weeks, perhaps months, she realized, since she'd been in the bathroom with Emma. It was just the sort of motherly chore that when the children were very young she used to despair of ever being free of, and now here she was missing it. And the hand holding: one shouldn't have to be frightened to death to have such things in one's life, she thought. She dreaded, simply dreaded, Emma being thirteen.

Dwight

There's the truth in there somewhere; there's the beginning. I took my ten-year-old son to Fenway to see the Sox play the Yankees, Clemens dueling Key. We drove two and a half hours to get there. I'd gotten box seats, and Sam spent most of the game standing with his chin just above the railing, looking down over third base, his hands clenched into fists. It felt, for a while, like a perfect day.

But the game didn't end when it was supposed to. The pitchers dueled and nobody won. It went into extra innings. Sam's fists clenched tighter and I started looking at my watch. His mother was expecting him back by seven; his mother, who was my ex-wife. It was five, then five-thirty, and I could feel trouble waiting for me there, the way you can feel rain before it happens. I could almost hear Ruth's foot angrily beating time on the front porch that I'd built myself, in Bow Mills, where she still lived, two and a half hours away.

The game nearly ended in the bottom of the thirteenth, but the Boston base runner was thrown out at the plate. I couldn't believe it. Now I wonder if there wasn't a kind of pattern to it all, or something like that. Things lined up just for me to knock them down.

At five minutes to six, the Sox finally clinched it with a grand slam. Sam said it was the best game he'd ever seen. Afterwards, the hands that had been fists for hours were turned loose, and as we made our way out of the stadium to the jammed parking lot, one of them found its way into mine. It took him a minute to realize what he'd done and take back his hand. I acted as if I didn't know anything about it—didn't know what I'd had, didn't know what I'd lost. We got in the car and inched our way out to the Mass Pike.

The sun was still in sight, angled low through Sam's window and reflecting off his sand-colored hair. For some reason the color of the light then made me think about Buzzards Bay, where he and Ruth and I had spent a long weekend once when he was five, just before the accident. The memory came and went, no place for it to stick. And I drove as fast as the traffic would allow, talking baseball with my son.

I could tell he was tired. It had been a big day. Eventually I stopped talking, to give him a chance to sleep. Sam yawned a couple of times and grew quiet. The prospect of his dropping off then seemed like a good thing to me. I saw it as a kind of savings plan, a way to insure that he'd remember our day together fondly. As if a nap would make time stop on a dime for him, and the day would be encapsulated, wrapped like a gift, worth enough to hold on to till next Sunday, when I'd get to try again.

I turned on the headlights around eight o'clock, just as we were leaving the pike. The tolltaker told me my right headlight wasn't working. He mentioned also that it was against the law to drive with a broken headlight. Something about his tone irked me. Pocketing my change, I told him in a friendly way that I was a lawyer and no doubt knew the law better than he did, and was on my way directly to get it fixed. I didn't say anything to him about my ex-wife. It was none of his business. The headlight could wait, but Ruth Wheldon, formerly Ruth Arno, could not. As it was, I'd be lucky to get Sam back by nine o'clock, two hours late. I'd be lucky if Ruth didn't already have a cop or two waiting on the porch with her (the porch I'd built with my own two hands), all of them keeping time with their feet. I thought about calling her from a pay phone somewhere, but that would have just seemed weak. I lit a cigarette and drove faster.

There'd been a time when seeing my son had nothing to do with the rights of law. It's nowhere in the history books—the trouble-free times never are. Ruth and I were still married. The three of us were a family. Sam was five when all of that came to an end.

A lot of people said afterwards that I used to beat him. That was a lie, and Ruth knew it was a lie, but she didn't say so. She let people think it. The fact is I'd

never laid a punishing hand on my son until the night
I nearly killed him.

He was in bed asleep when I came home from
work. I was with a hotshot firm in Hartford then, doing
wills and trusts and the like, working hard and getting
home late. A career going upward, that's what it was
called. I went into his room and kissed him in the
dark. I sat a moment there on the edge of his bed, part
hoping he'd wake up and talk to me. But he was out
like a light. All his days were full at that age, I guessed.

Ruth had my dinner on the table when I came out
of Sam's room. She'd already eaten. I said, "He's sleeping like a log," and she didn't say anything. I opened
a can of beer and ate the food she'd cooked. She sat
down across from me and started talking in a rush
about one of her piano students at the school, some
little boy. Then it was as if she just ran out of things
to say. We sat there in silence. And gradually, as the
dead minutes started piling up between us, and while
I drank a second beer and then a third, I began to
feel there was something wrong in the house, a kind of
stillness that I didn't recognize or care for. To me right
then she looked not like my wife but like some woman
alone in a roadside diner at night; some woman who
was waiting for anything or anyone but the usual
scene she found staring back at her. And I realized
that for weeks now I'd hardly seen her or Sam; had, in
fact, not a clue what she might be thinking as she
sat across from me with her mouth closed and her eyes
fixed on the table. Boredom? Indifference? Resentment? I had no idea. Which, finally, was the only thing

I could think to say to her. That I didn't know. And that was when, still looking down at the table, she told me that she was having an affair with a man named Norris Wheldon.

From here it all looks simple. I'd always had a temper, though for much of my life I'd kept it hidden away, safe and out of sight. My father was a violent man who used to beat me with a stripped-down juniper branch he'd taken from our yard. He had his method. Each time, he'd raise that branch and pause, hoping to catch me flinching or, better yet, raising my own hand against him. Any sign of fear or anger from me gave him the right to thrash me like some runt in a bar. The happiest summer of my childhood was when my body finally started turning into a man's. If I hadn't gone off to college, I might have killed him. I was a freshman at U Conn when he dropped dead of a heart attack. I didn't go home for the funeral.

My wife told me that she was in love with Norris Wheldon and planned to divorce me so she could marry him. She said she intended to keep Sam with her. I could visit him when I wanted, she said, as long as when I wanted wasn't more than one day a week. It was a canned speech, as if she'd prepared it while making the meat loaf. I was a lawyer. I should've been calm right then, calm and already building my case against her. What I felt instead was something else. My old friend Jack Cutter, who later represented me before the state, made a big deal to the court about the five beers I'd drunk that night (he included the two I'd had while still at work). He called what happened a "double impairment" of my senses brought about by alcohol and jealous rage. That essentially was my defense. It sounded plausible to me. I wanted someone to explain to me and for me how I could have done what I'd done, and Jack obliged. I had been impaired. The court agreed, up to a point.

To this day it feels the same to me; it feels no different. I see it all. Ruth gives me her canned speech about her and Norris and my son and our future, her eyes darting away like minnows. Then, all done, she waits for me to react. And when I don't, when I sit there with my cleaned plate and my three empties and do nothing, she starts getting nervous. Too quick she says, "Well, okay, Dwight. Okay then. I thought I should tell you myself, and now I've told you. It's over. Bob Jamison's going to be my attorney. I'm sorry." She gets up, taking my plate, clearing my place like it's any old day, and goes into the kitchen.

She's halfway to the sink when I hit her. Hit her with my fist as hard as I can, my knuckles striking around her right ear and drawing blood. She cries out and crumples to the ground. My wife. The plate shatters on the linoleum. I take a look at her on the floor, but it hasn't registered yet, hasn't happened yet. It was somebody else's fist. I don't feel released or relieved. And I turn to go. It's not my house any more. Not my wife. Every bit of it is a mistake. I get to the front door and am putting on my coat.

She grabs me from behind by the hair and pulls, screaming, *"Bastard!"* Rips a clump of my hair out by the roots, scalp too, like somebody sticking hot pins into my brain. It makes me crazy and I lash out blindly, a roundhouse punch for her stomach. To end it.

I hit my son in the face.

He had arrived, running, to protect us from ourselves. It had never occurred to me he'd do that. The bones in his jaw were fragile like a bird's and I felt them break under my fist.

He was unconscious for a little while. He had a concussion. His jaw was wired, I was told, for weeks afterwards.

Jack Cutter, old friend, did his legal best and got me two years' probation, during which time I was suspended from practicing law. It was strongly advised that I move to another part of the state, which I did. I got counseling. Every week I wrote a letter to Sam. Once in a while, he wrote back. He said he was feeling okay, school was okay, he didn't like his stepdad so much. His spelling was bad, and sometimes I worried about permanent damage. It was four years before I was allowed to see him again.

I moved back to the northwest corner of the state, to a town about ten miles southeast of Bow Mills called Box Corner. So I could see my son again—Sundays, home by seven, nice and easy now. Ruth Wheldon looking at me. It was hard at first, but it was a life. Jack Cutter was good enough to take me on as a partner in his small-town practice in Canaan, and was patient when I was slow to bring in business. Not everyone was so friendly. There were some people around Bow Mills who still remembered all too well what they thought happened that night. But Sam wasn't one of them. He never mentioned what I'd done to him, or seemed to be chewing on it. If you didn't already know his history, I thought, you wouldn't know it. He was a pretty regular boy.

We went to ball games and things. And for a while, that was my life.

It was a quarter to nine and we were still twenty, twenty-five minutes from Ruth's. How had it happened? I had us on the shortcut that I knew like my own birthday, and we were zinging along in the dark without a right headlight, the trees standing dense as pitch on either side of the road. It was hard to see. I threw a smoldering butt out the window and lit another cigarette. We were late. Sam was asleep with his cheek pressed up against the door and I was starting to talk to myself. *Sorry I'm late, Ruth. The game went extra innings. Sam says it was the best damn game he's ever seen, Ruth. Go ahead, ask him. . . . See? Right, okay then. Take that fucking noose from around my neck.* It was tricky when my thoughts got going to keep my foot from pressing too hard on the pedal; just my brain trying to shape what was happening in a more favorable way. I switched on the radio—low, so as not to wake him. A little bit of country music to take the edge off.

But I couldn't keep from thinking: in the light of day you could see the faint scar on Sam's smooth face, a thin white tributary mapping the line of his reconstructed jaw.

I don't remember checking the speedometer. Reservation Road was too black for that speed. I was thinking about Sam, hoping he'd remember the day for what was good in it, when I drove us too fast into the first of the two sharp, tree-packed turns leading to Tod Lovell's gas station. The car started shimmying across the midline and too late I tried to adjust, cutting the wheel hard to the right. But I cut too hard. The front wheels were already on the near shoulder of the second turn before I jerked the wheel sharply back to the left, the tires screeching, quick and pinched, until I cut the wheel again and the fishtail straightened though the road did not, but still I felt control coming back and almost sighed with relief. And then suddenly on the right the trees opened and the three glowing red letters of Tod's sign appeared.

I don't know how a single frame could have held so much: two old-fashioned pumps and a flat-roofed building with one bright-lit window but no other lights, as if the planet right there was underwater. A station wagon parked in front with all its doors open, looking like a winged flying machine. And a man, a tall, dark-haired man with little round glasses, coming out of the office carrying something in his hand. He was looking at me and I was looking at him, through the dimness. I saw his mouth open wide, and then his eyes moved off me, his head snapping around to see the road ahead.

And then I saw what he saw.

The boy standing in the road as if he'd sprouted from it. Dark-haired like his father. And the father's shout suddenly making a kind of sense: "Josh!" The front of my car hit him in the chest. The useless headlight popped like a gunshot. And he flew away into the darkness.

The impact made the car shudder. My foot came off the gas. And we were coasting, still there, but moving, fleeing. Unless I braked now: *Do it*. My foot started for the brake. But then Sam started to wail in pain and I froze. I looked over and he was holding his face in both hands and screaming in pain. I went cold. "Sam!" I shouted, his name coming from deep down in my gut and sounding louder and more desperate to my ears than any sound I'd ever made. He didn't respond. "Sam!"

In the rearview mirror I saw the dark-haired man sprinting up the road after us. His fury and his fear were in his half-shadowed face, the frenzied pumping of his arms. He was coming to punish me, and for a moment I wanted him to. My foot was inching toward the brake. But suddenly I felt Sam warm against my side, curling up and holding on and bawling like a baby. I put my foot on the gas.

As we began to pull away, I checked the mirror one last time: the man had veered off our path and was bent over in the thick roadside shrubs. Where his child was. About my son's age, maybe still alive, though I knew he wasn't.

The car kept picking up speed. Then we were gone from that clearing, swallowed up by the trees.

Ethan

Explain this to me: One minute there is a boy, a life thrumming with possibilities, and the next there are marked cars and strangers in uniform and the fractured whirling lights. And that, suddenly, is all the world has to offer.

It is cold beyond believing. A hand holding a black metal flashlight. A hard mouth saying who, what, where. My son covered by a sheet.

They came. They came quickly, I'll grant them that. They all seemed to know where Tod's was. It had, after all, been there a long time. The ones in white swarmed like paparazzi over Josh's broken body; flashbulbs popped in the night. They zipped my son into a white plastic bag, and then into a red plastic bag, and then wrapped him in a sheet. They took him away from us.

Grace followed in our car. She hadn't seen anything and the police suggested she go home. I was worried about her driving. I'd held her as tightly as I could until her crying grew less uncontrolled, almost rhythmic, but the expression of shock and denial on her face now belied all that. She took Emma with her. Emma didn't cry. She trembled and that was all.

Hit and run: it was enough to bring the state police from Canaan. Sergeant Burke was our man. Ken Burke. Perhaps forty, with close-cropped brown hair graying at the temples. Broad-shouldered, a square-jawed, square-nosed, determined face. A deep voice, basso profundo. I distrusted him on sight. And after a few terse exchanges—at no point would I have described it as a conversation—I got the impression that he felt the same way about me.

I was leaning against one of the gas pumps. Leaning against it or I would have fallen down. The smell of gas, which I hated, was the only thread tying me to the world I now found myself in: Sergeant Burke with his official notepad, his badge catching the weird, warping reddish light from Tod's half-broken sign, and the cruiser lights still turning at the side of the road, though turning now without sound or purpose—the accident had already happened.

"Sir?"

What? It was Sergeant Burke getting the ball rolling, starting the process. It turned out there was indeed a system to uncovering the truth, a way. I looked through the window into the lighted room where, not twenty minutes earlier, I'd been musing on the state of my life, and saw Burke's young partner questioning the flannel-shirted gas-station attendant. Who had seen nothing.

Out on the road a couple of police types were scouring the area for evidence. There was broken glass, yes. Blood, too. Jittering flashlight beams and voices calling to one another: "Anything?" "Negative."

"Sir?" It was Sergeant Burke again. "I'm afraid I need to ask you some questions."

I didn't know what to say, how to do this.

"How you and your family came to be here, what you saw. So we can get after whoever did this to your son, not waste any time."

"I'll make things easier for you," I said, pushing myself to an upright position. I could taste the bile rising in my throat. "My name is Ethan Learner. I'm a college professor. My wife is Grace Learner, she's a garden designer. We live in Wyndham Falls. Our daughter is Emma. Our son is—was—Josh. He was ten years old. He was very good on the violin. And we loved him. Excuse me." I walked briskly to the edge of the asphalt, where the scrub brush began, and vomited my guts out.

When I was upright again, Sergeant Burke raised his notepad to the ready position. "Sorry," I said, wiping my mouth with the back of my hand.

He nodded. There was compassion there—or some stiff-lipped incarnation of it—but I did not want it.

"Let's start by you telling me exactly what you saw," he said.

I took a deep, acid-smelling breath. "We stopped so my daughter could go to the bathroom. We weren't far from home, but she said she couldn't hold it, so we stopped. My wife took her inside." Sergeant Burke gave a quick nod. "I stayed out here, with my son—with Josh."

I stopped speaking and Sergeant Burke waited. He had the patience of a hunter or a psychoanalyst. I looked across the road and tried to lose myself in the black trees, the dense nothingness. I didn't want to vomit again. This was harder than I'd thought. I hadn't thought. Had had nightmares, certainly, bad daydreams about the safety of my children. But not ever in my life had I really thought about this.

"He was—he was by the road. There. And it worried me. I told him not to stand so close to it. But that hurt him. Hurt his feelings. He has—had—a lot of pride. I shouldn't have said that to him. So I kind of took it back. I went inside."

"Inside the office?"

"Yes."

"For what reason?"

"What? To find—we were out of wiper fluid." Sergeant Burke squinted slightly. "Look, back on the road we drove through this swarm of—I thought they were mayflies, but Josh didn't believe me. Now I don't know. They were all over the windshield. I tried to clean them off, but there wasn't any fluid."

I noticed that Sergeant Burke wasn't jotting any of this down.

"So you went inside the office to purchase a container of wiper fluid. And where was the—where was your son at this time?"

"I told you. He was by the road."

"Can you tell me what time this would have been?"

"Time? I don't . . . it must have been close to nine. I checked my watch when we pulled in. I was impatient. I wanted to get home. It must have been about a quarter to."

Sergeant Burke made a note on his pad. "How long did you spend inside the office?"

"I don't know. He had to go get the stuff. Three, maybe five minutes."

"Did you see your son during that time?"

"I . . . no. No, I did not."

The breath went out of me. Time went from whirling to stillness, and suddenly where the question had floated between us, hanging in the air, there was an impenetrable black silence, which was my guilt; nothing else was real. I saw Josh standing by the dark road, his back to me. Slowly, I saw myself turning away from him, discarding him, until he was behind me, and gone.

"It's my fault," I whispered. Without knowing it, I had fallen into a crouch, a kind of squat, my hands touching the hard ground.

Sergeant Burke gave no sign that he had heard. He looked away, into the brightly lit office, where, in a terrible pantomime, his partner was busily writing down something the gas-station attendant was telling him. Sergeant Burke shifted his feet. I remained where I was, almost on the ground, not quite.

"I saw him just before I went inside," I said. "I checked, and he was just standing by the road looking at nothing. Thinking. I thought maybe about music. And I'd already hurt him by worrying. So I left him alone."

"When did you see him next?"

"When I came out."

"What occurred then?"

"What do you think?" I snapped.

The skin on Sergeant Burke's face tightened and he looked away. I made myself get to my feet. "Excuse me," I said. "That was rude."

"Yes, sir."

"This is hard."

"Yes, sir."

"I was looking at the ground when I came out. I was—I was tired and I was thinking about myself—about nothing—when I heard the sound of the tires. . . ."

"From which direction?"

"There. To the left."

"And then?"

"I looked for Josh. I looked where he'd been, but he wasn't there. He was in the road. Just standing there. I called out. . . ."

The car was coming again, striking him in the chest, his body flying into the bushes. A line of blood leading from his mouth, a dent the size of a fence-post hole in his chest. Crushed. When I lifted him up, his head dropped back and his mouth gaped open. His teeth were painted with blood that looked black in the darkness.

"Can you tell me anything about the vehicle?"

I closed my eyes. Inside the dark, racing car there

was a glowing orange pinpoint: a cigarette. A man driving. "There was a man," I said.

Sergeant Burke grew very still. "Driving?"

I nodded.

"Anyone else there with him?"

"No." I had raised my head, and for a moment, as the car raced by, it had felt almost as though he'd turned his face in my direction. "He looked at me."

"Could you describe him?"

"He was smoking. There was a lit cigarette in his mouth."

Sergeant Burke waited. I tried to see something, anything, more about the man who had killed my son, but I could not. "No," I said bitterly. "Nothing."

Sergeant Burke stood quietly, staring at the notepad in his hands. Then he said, "Let's move on. Can you tell me anything about the vehicle itself?"

Now I felt an edge of panic. Trying to picture the car in my mind, I saw just the glowing tip of the cigarette, the man hidden in shadow. "I don't know."

A barely audible sigh escaped Sergeant Burke's lips. He turned his head five degrees to the right and looked at me from there. "Anything."

"Let me think." I made myself go back to before. Tires crying out. An apparition out of the trees. "One of the headlights was broken."

Sergeant Burke touched the pen tip to the paper. "Right headlight or left?"

"What?"

"Right or left headlight?"

"Left—no. Right."

"Which is it? Right or left?"

"Right."

"Is that a definite?"

"Yes."

He jotted it down in his notebook.

"Okay," he said. "Type of vehicle."

"A . . . I guess you'd call it a sedan."

"Make?"

"I don't know. I don't know much about cars."

"Four-door or two-door?"

I tried to think. He looked up sharply from his notepad. "It was dark," I said.

"Yes, sir."

"Four doors. It was a four-door."

Sergeant Burke studied me. "That's a definite?"

"Yes."

He jotted it down. "Okay. Color of the vehicle?"

"Dark."

"Could you be more specific?"

"It could have been black. Or dark blue, dark green. It was going fast, and you see what kind of light—"

"Let's talk about what kind of dark. Was it matte or shiny?"

"I think there was some light on it."

"You mean reflecting?"

"Yes."

"What I'm trying to get at here," Sergeant Burke said, "is whether it might have been old or new, flat or metallic paint."

"I told you. There was some light on it."

He didn't write this down.

"I don't know what else to tell you," I said.

He shook his head imperceptibly. "Let's move on. Did you catch the license plate?"

"No."

"None of it?" Sergeant Burke sounded disappointed. "How about state of origin? Was there a picture or design on it? Or any other distinguishing marks on the vehicle you might have noticed—bumper stickers, decals?"

"No. I don't know."

Bells trilling: the glass door to the office opened and the two young men walked out, their questioning session completed. Sergeant Burke's young sidekick paused to put his gray felt state trooper's hat back on— with two hands, just so. The gas-station attendant had tucked in his flannel shirt.

"Anything else you can tell me, sir?"

I was remembering something, if he would just be quiet: sprinting down the road after the car, hearing nothing but the blood in my heart and the gathering thrust of the engine, seeing nothing but the small dim shadow of the back of his head above the headrest. Then . . . what? He took his foot off the gas, there was no mistaking it—the engine seemed to die, suddenly the car slowed, and then I was gaining on him. I heard him shout something. His window must have been open, because I heard the sheer force of his voice, but it didn't make sense, a single word or sound. "Sham!" it sounded like. "Sham!" And through the rear windshield I saw the shadow that was the back of his head and shoulders lean across the front seat toward the passenger side. The car swerved slightly and he shouted it again: "Sham!" or "Sam!" or "Slam!" None of it making sense. And I was still gaining, there was still the possibility of catching him. And then he stopped shouting, and the car pulled away.

"Sir?"

"What?"

"Anything else you can tell me?"

I made myself focus on Sergeant Burke. "Yes. He shouted something. The man in the car. I was running after him. I heard him. Some sound— 'Sham,' maybe, or 'Slam,' or 'Sam.' I don't know. Some word. I don't know what it means. He might have been shouting it to himself or to me. I don't know. All I know is he said it. He said it twice. I heard him. Then he got away."

"'Sham'?" said Sergeant Burke.

"Or something like it. Something that rhymes with it. I heard him."

Behind me, a car started up and drove away. It must have been the gas-station attendant. Going where? To a bar for a drink. Home to his girlfriend or his mother. Then the police radio crackled and I saw Sergeant Burke's eyes dart sideways to the cruiser where his partner sat waiting. Sergeant Burke wanted to leave now.

He folded his notepad and stuffed it in his back pocket and clipped his pen to his shirt pocket. He took his time about it. And then he was ready to go.

"Sir."

"I just told you something important."

Sergeant Burke's expression was impassive; he

might have been a statue. "Important, sir?" He gave his head an apologetic shake. "No, sir. Sorry."

"I just told you something important and I want you to write it down."

"No, sir. Sorry."

"Yes, goddamnit. Yes!"

I was breathing hard, starting to shout, pointing my finger at him.

"Easy now," Sergeant Burke said.

"We're not done here. We're not even close to done."

"My partner and I are going to take you home now," he said. "We can talk some more in the a.m."

"You listen to me. There was a man driving that car. There was a man smoking a fucking cigarette and he looked right at me before he ran my son into the ground. I *saw* him."

"Yes, sir."

"And why don't you guys cut the 'sir' crap? Why don't you talk like human beings?"

Sergeant Burke took a small step back from me, as if he didn't trust what he might do. "I'm going to let that pass. You're upset."

"You're fucking right I'm upset."

I found I was trembling uncontrollably. And I fell again into that crouch, that ungainly squat from which I could place my palms flat on the ground to steady myself. Anything to touch the world as it had been before. But it would not go back. I kept trembling. Thinking now about my Emma, the waves of grief and fear rolling through her, and no end in sight.

Dwight

Black land rushed by. Finally the woods opened as if they'd been split by an ax, and this car with us in it ran out under the moonless night past stone-walled fields still and dark. We passed a farm, or its shadow, the silo rising like a prison guardtower.

Leaving that boy behind.

Eight more miles to Bow Mills. I kept my speed, cornering with white-knuckled hands. Now and then the tires squealed out, but lightly, nothing like before. I was sweating as if a fever had just broken.

"It hurts," Sam whimpered. "It hurts."

He was pressed against me, curled up, still crying, holding a hand over his right eye. I couldn't stand it. "Is it your eye?"

"I hit it," he whimpered. He seemed five years old again.

"Here, let me see it." I took a hand off the wheel and tried to pull his hand from his eye, but his crying climbed an octave, so I quit. "Let me," I said.

He took his hand away. It was too dark to see anything. I leaned over him. Before I knew it the car was drifting to the left again and my heart kicked. But it went no further than that; I cut the wheel and we were back on the right side of the line. "I can't look at it right this second, Sam," I said.

With my eyes on the road, I groped in the dark for the top of his head, put my hand on his soft hair. Then with my fingers I trailed down his smooth brow and lightly touched the eye where he was hurt. I felt the wet trace of his tears and the swollen flesh and bone all around his right eye. He cried out and tried to hit my arm. "Stop it," I said, and he stopped. "I needed to know. You're not bleeding but you're going to have a bad shiner. We'll get you some ice as soon as we get to your mother's."

There was a silence; he'd stopped crying. "What's a shiner?"

"Black eye."

"Black?" he said, quizzical.

I almost smiled.

Suddenly, Sam sat up. "Dad?" His voice was nasal from crying. It was strange. He seemed twice as old as the boy who had spoken just before.

The question was on the way. And it came down to this: What did he know? What had he seen? I had to get there first. "Sam," I said. "Listen to me."

In the dark of the car my son looked at me. Whatever he'd been about to ask, he let go.

"We hit something back there on the road," I said.

"I know."

"Do you know what we hit?"

He didn't answer.

"Do you?"

"No."

I breathed out. "We hit a dog."

Sam was quiet.

"Was it big?" he said finally.

"Yes."

"Did we kill it?"

"Yes."

"How do you know if we didn't stop?"

"I know."

"It could still be alive."

"No, Sam. I'm telling you. I saw it happen."

"But—"

"No, Sam. Believe me. Okay?"

"I believe you, Dad."

That was the end of it. I felt numb. Dead. My son's imagination had my dirty footprints all over it. We crossed the Bow Mills town line and drove down quiet tree-lined roads filled with people I used to know. I turned onto Larch Road and there at the end was my old house.

The porch light clicked on the second my headlight showed in the driveway. The door opened and Ruth came rushing out to the edge of the porch. She had on a cardigan thrown loose over her bare shoulders and a long gingham dress and a pair of reading glasses dangling from a chain around her neck, banging against her breasts as she moved about.

Not long after marrying Norris, Ruth had started dressing strangely, sometimes like an old schoolmarm and sometimes like a suburban beauty queen who'd once had a guest spot on *Hee Haw*. Norris was in insurance and seemed to appreciate it. Personally, though, when I thought about my ex-wife at night, which occasionally I still did, she was wearing Levi's if she was wearing anything. That was how it had been when we'd met in college, and for the first few years of our marriage. Ruth had looked as good in an old faded pair of Levi's as any woman I'd ever known.

I pulled to a stop, facing the porch, and immediately turned off the headlight. Darkness was what I wanted. But not Ruth: in her hand, I saw, was a footlong Mag-Lite—heavy enough to double as a club should things get rough. She was down the porch steps in a flash and hurrying across the little lawn. I had run over one man's boy and was holding on for dear life to my own, but as I watched her I couldn't help thinking about how I'd laid the sod for that lawn and built that porch, how all of it had come from me and once been mine. It was petty and shaming.

"Norris!" Ruth called, over her shoulder. "Norris!"

Norris appeared at the door and hesitated. I had threatened to kill him once and maybe he was thinking about that now. Backlit from inside, in his Sunday casual mode—a madras short-sleeved shirt and high-waisted slacks—he looked like one of those fun-park cardboard figures you throw baseballs at. He took a few more steps before stopping again.

"Norris!" yelled Ruth. She was coming fast. Neither Sam nor I had moved to get out of the car. We were frozen men.

"Looks like your mother's a little upset," I said.

"Yeah."

"When she sees that eye she's going to be a lot upset."

"I know."

"You and I will just have to weather the storm together."

He nodded. His face was pale in the darkness except around his right eye, where the skin was already coloring up pretty badly. I reached out and took his jaw gingerly in my hand. He winced and almost pulled away.

"How's the eye?"

"It hurts. Is it a shiner?"

I smiled. "Right. You're a tough kid. Don't forget about the ice."

"Okay."

"It was a good game, huh?"

Before he could answer, Ruth yanked the door open on his side. I pulled my hand off Sam's face as if he'd bitten me. She gathered him in her arms, saying, "Come here, baby," and at the same time managed to shine the Mag-Lite directly in my eyes.

"Ruth, get that light out of my eyes."

"Go to hell, Dwight."

"Ruth, goddamnit, turn that light off."

"He'd better be okay," she said. "If he's not okay, you're in deep shit. Do you hear me? You're in deep shit anyway."

"The light," I said.

But she wasn't listening. She'd pulled Sam out into the open to better embrace him and check for damage. I got out of the car—I didn't want to be sitting when she caught sight of his eye.

"Hello, Norris," I said.

"Hello, Dwight."

"Sorry I'm late. The game ran sixteen innings."

Norris was a serious Red Sox fan.

"Sixteen? No kidding. Who won?"

"Sox. Mo Vaughn hit a grand slam."

"No kid—"

"Shut up, Norris," Ruth snapped. She had the Mag-Lite trained on Sam's face. He was squinting painfully, not liking it one bit but staying quiet. The light was bright and hid nothing. The eye was swollen almost closed and the skin around it looked as if it had been inflated and then injected with a black-and-purple dye. I looked away. "Norris," Ruth said. "Go call the police."

"What?" I said. "Don't do that."

"You take my son to a ballgame and bring him back looking like he's been mugged. But he hasn't been mugged, has he? No, he's just been out with his good old dad. You're sick, Dwight. You've got a problem and should be separated from the rest of us who don't get a thrill beating the daylights out of our children. Go call the police, Norris."

"Norris," I said. "Don't do that."

"Ruth . . . ," said Norris.

"Mom, it was a dog," Sam said.

Everybody looked at him. And my son with his eggplant eye calmly reached up and pushed the Mag-Lite aside, so it was no longer blinding him. "We hit a dog, Mom. We killed it. It was terrible."

Ruth just stared at him. The expression on her face was a mix of so many things I remembered in her from our marriage: relief bordering on happiness; petty disappointment at having her moment stolen; anger at me that went, finally, way beyond words; a mother's unbearable love for her son. After a moment she noticed the Mag-Lite beam shining uselessly across the lawn and switched it off. We settled into calmer waters, lit now by just the faint edge of porch light.

"That doesn't explain your eye."

"I got hit," Sam said.

"*What?*"

"He means he was sleeping against the door," I said quickly, "and got thrown into it when we hit the dog."

"Where was the dog?"

Ruth was asking Sam, but he shook his head. He was ten and didn't know the names of the roads too well. So Ruth reluctantly turned to me. "Where was it?"

"Cantwell Road," I said, naming a road about half an hour's drive from Reservation Road. A road I was sure she knew: one afternoon years back, we'd pulled off Cantwell Road and made love in the car. That was fact. But if Ruth remembered the details of that day, she showed no sign of it.

"What were you doing on Cantwell?"

"Coming home from the game. Taking a new shortcut. Driving like hell, in fact, because, as I just told Norris here, it was extra innings."

"I'll bet it was."

"It was, Mom," Sam said.

"Lay off, Ruth," I said.

"I'll lay off when I'm good and ready. Your headlight's busted."

"It was the dog," Sam said.

"That's right," I said. "I heard the light pop when we hit."

The Mag-Lite came on suddenly, found first me, then the front of my car, the busted right headlight. Ruth studying it all as if it was just another symptom of the mess my life had become after she'd stopped loving me.

And then my heart nearly quit.

I was standing about a yard from the front of the car. A tiny fragment of dark cloth, about the size of a dime, was caught on one of the shark's teeth of glass along the rim of the crushed headlight. In my shock I half expected to find signs of the boy's blood, too, but there weren't any. I stole a look at Ruth, who was standing with Sam about ten feet away. But her expression—hard, reserved—was impossible to read.

I waited.

A moment later she switched off the Mag-Lite. I breathed again, hearing her say, "Poor thing." Her tone was soft for the first time all evening. She had a great fondness for animals, dogs especially. When, the year after Sam was born, our first dog—a retriever named Sanford—died, Ruth had cried for three days straight.

"It was black," I said. "Good-sized. It ran right in front. There was nothing I could do, Ruth. I don't really want to think about it." I paused. "And my guess is Sam doesn't want to think about it, either."

Ruth nodded then. There was a brief, tired silence between us. I saw how some of her hair, sand-colored like Sam's, had fallen out of the bun she'd put it in, and lay now across her cheek like a silk ribbon.

"I'm sorry, Ruth. What can I say? I tried. It was a good day when it started. I just got a step or two behind, that's all."

"Old Dwight," Ruth said almost sadly, shaking her head.

I sensed some long-ago tenderness in her voice; if not for the darkness, I would have sworn she was looking me straight in the eyes. For a second I forgot what kind of day it had been.

Then she broke the spell. My ex-wife. She brought our son extra-close, held him by the shoulders with his back against her front, as if to keep him from running anywhere dangerous he might want to go. "Well, Dwight," she said. "You're a free man, I guess."

"Free to go, you mean."

"That's what I mean."

"Till next Sunday."

"That's the rules."

I looked at Sam. "What'll we do on Sunday, sport?"

He shrugged; it had been a long day. "I dunno."

"We'll sleep on it. Okay?"

"Okay, Dad."

"I love you," I said.

I got in the car without waiting to see if he'd say it back. My strength was down and I could feel the panic rising not so far off, about to flood over the dam. I keyed the engine and switched on the headlight.

"You should get that light fixed, Dwight," Norris said through the open window. "It's against the law."

"Thanks for the tip, Norris. I intend to."

Ruth already had Sam on the porch steps. Norris hurried after them.

I tried to bring myself to drive away then, but couldn't. I watched my son enter the bright sphere of porch light, his battered eye come to shocking life.

Norris caught up with them. Ruth opened the screen door. The three of them were just about to go inside when Sam turned suddenly and gave me a small stiff wave so fraught with the tragic circumstances of life that tears sprang to my eyes.

I stuck my head out the window. "Don't forget to ice that eye!"

But the door was already closed; the porch light went out. It was just my one headlight now, climbing the house, rearranging space. Bad magic. I put the car in gear and turned around, leaving tire tracks on the lawn.

Grace

She sat curled up on the worn green-velvet chair in her studio, holding her knees in her arms as if they constituted a whole person, a love.

The room was full of shadows. The carefully nurtured plants standing in clay pots and hanging by long weblike wires from the ceiling—the plants she had watered and looked to for inspiration and sometimes even talked to like people—were gathered around her now as always. But in the lack of light the leaves and flowers that had always seemed to her like the natural forms of words, a kind of living poetry, were suddenly just dead shadows like everything else, everyone else, the dark absent space where something of value had once been. As if, she thought, someone had just told her how the magic trick worked and ruined everything.

It was a sham. It was loss, just loss.

Something came nudging now against her shin, warm and insistent: Sallie. Shepherd-collie mix, eight years old. Same age as Emma. She reached out and stroked the noble head, fingers working behind the fine, upstanding ears. The two-tone-brown dog eyes fixed on her, one ring of color softer than the other; a universe there, impossibly soft and liquid. And fur the color of tortoiseshell, like something pulled from a sultan's treasure chest.

"Sallie," she whispered.

Then, closing the door in herself that had come ajar, she pushed the dog away. Sallie took a few steps back and hesitated, eyes searching. But Grace was inward, unseeing. Soon just the paws padding on the rug and clicking on the wood floor, and then she was alone.

Thinking: *Where is Ethan?* He should have been home by now.

Thinking: *Drink. Go ahead.* She released one of her knees and found the glass sweating in the dark, took a gulp of Scotch made watery from too many melted ice cubes.

Thinking: *Pills, too.*

But there was nothing to do. She saw that with a godlike clarity. *Goddess*, she suddenly thought: what Mattie Gilmore had called her in high school. Mattie Gilmore, who'd been envious of her; who was still envious last year when Grace brought Ethan and the kids back to Durham for a family visit, and Mattie dropped by the house. Grace hadn't spoken a word to her since the senior prom. She was Mattie Tucker now, mother of three and a good forty pounds heavier, casting that burning eye over them all, reaching way back for a southern pleasantry that was more like a Halloween apple with a razor blade in it: "Well, don't y'all make just the *perfect* family of four?"

It hadn't hurt then. It had been funny. She and Mother and Ethan had had a good laugh about vindictive old Mattie that night, sipping drinks by the backyard pool, in the very spot where Daddy had dropped dead of a heart attack. But it hurt now. It hurt, and it would go on hurting. Perfect family of four. As if Mattie Gilmore were some kind of witch and had put a curse on them. Why? What had she ever done? What had any of them ever done? To give a child only to take him away. To make and then unmake, as if a family weren't built of lives but of things that could be broken, returned, thrown out—

She was holding her knees again. Weeping. Grief as a way of living, she saw now, like breathing. The price of being a parent.

There was a sound at the door.

"Mom."

Emma's pale legs and white underpants and luminous face and blond hair shone out of the darkened doorway; her sleeping T-shirt was navy blue and made her torso nearly invisible, as if some creature had taken a bite out of her in her dreams. And suddenly, against her will, Grace thought: *What if it had been Emma instead of Josh?* Emma who was gone, and Josh who was here now, whom she must hold and love and console? Josh standing in the doorway, calling her? For a moment it felt so real she thought she saw him. He was wearing his red-and-white-striped pajamas and the curls of his dark hair fell down over his ears, and as he came toward her she saw with a kind of humorous pride how his feet were slightly pigeon-toed, and when he opened his mouth to call her again it was in his familiar night voice, his nasal stuffed-up sleepy-boy's voice that made her smile, and she reached for him—

"Mom?"

She blinked hard: it was Emma standing in the doorway, it was Emma. Josh was gone, and here was Emma. "Oh," she whispered, as if she were filled with air and had just punctured herself by mistake, as if she were leaking. She felt sick with confusion and guilt.

Emma was standing in the doorway, needing her. Letting go of her knees, she quickly wiped the tears from her face as best she could. "Sweetie, you can't sleep?"

"I was having bad dreams."

"Come here and tell me about it." She patted her lap, and without a word Emma came over and climbed up on her; a little girl again. She placed her hands around Emma's narrow waist and shifted her along her thighs, Emma facing her, so that the thin, newly muscular legs she had seen earlier in the gas station bathroom were locked now around her waist, joining them together.

"I'm glad to see you," she said. "I really am."

Emma was looking into her eyes. "Were you crying?"

"Yes," Grace admitted. She tried to smile but realized immediately that she would lose control again if she did. So she cut it out, felt her face lock, frozen and contorted. She took a hand off Emma and wiped her own swollen eyes. "Sorry," she said. "It's the only thing I seem to be any good at right now."

"I couldn't," Emma said.

"Couldn't what?"

"Cry."

"Oh, Em." She hugged Emma to her, feeling threads of silken hair against her cheek.

"I couldn't. I tried but I couldn't."

"Your heart's just telling you it hurts too much to take it all in right now. That's all. It will happen. And when it does, Em, when it does it will be very sad, but the world won't end. You'll be all right. I promise you."

But she was weeping again, her breathing ragged and hideous to her ears. She was foundering. And it was Emma trying to save her, not the other way around. Emma touching her hair, saying, "Don't cry, Mom, don't cry." Over and over again. Until minutes had passed and this mother could breathe again like a human being. Until she could think. Until she could know, indisputably, irrevocably, that she was no kind of mother. *Not like this.* One child still left but not the strength any more to do what is necessary. That strength is gone.

"Ow," said Emma, pulling back a bit. "Not so hard."

"What?" Squeezing too hard, hugging too tight; she eased up. She was trying to grasp the sequence of events, trying to figure out how it could have happened.

"That's better," Emma said, as though she were the one in charge here.

Always a mistake, looking for guilt, Grace thought, always a one-way street, heading over a cliff: *Then just don't do it.* She had told Ethan to stop at the gas station; perhaps she had made him. Four doors flying open . . . *Why?* Emma in the bathroom, the yellow light, the stink. Ethan with Josh by the car, the dark road—

"There," Emma said, almost satisfied. "You've stopped crying."

Somehow, it was true: suddenly she was a field without rain, drought-ridden, cracked. It was rage. Rage had dried her up, redirected her blood. She saw Ethan wiping the windshield with a rag, blind, never once turning around—

Emma stirred in her lap; Grace looked down and there she was.

"I think we should get you back to bed," she said.

"Promise you'll stay until I go to sleep." Emma's blue eyes, suddenly fear-struck, roamed her face, seeking reassurance.

"I promise."

But, promise made, she didn't move. Thinking, *Every promise now must necessarily be a lie.* Seeing now how nothing, not the slightest act or gesture or word, would ever again be simple or easy, or even possible.

"Another minute," she murmured. "I'll give you another minute."

A minute: perhaps it was less, perhaps more. The point was holding each other with an imperturbable stillness; the point was survival.

Then Emma shifted, stirred.

"Is Dad in trouble?"

"What kind of trouble?" Grace said.

"I saw him talking to that man. The cop."

"Say 'police officer,' Em." The correction came out automatically—*If I was Emma*, she thought, *I'd laugh in my face*. It was all meaningless now. Still, it felt good to say the words without thinking, to be a mother again for even a second, obsessed with the normal, small-minded punctuation of daily life. "Daddy was just answering some questions. Trying to help."

"Did he see what happened?"

"Yes, Em, I think he did."

"Was Josh in pain, Mom?"

"I . . ."

Ethan had told her not to look. Carrying the weight in his arms, coming toward her along the road: it was her son. And the world did not stop. Ethan kept coming, staggering almost. Then she was running at him. She was screaming Josh's name. She was right on top of Ethan when he turned his back, trying to protect her. All she could see of her son was two splayed feet. She was pounding on Ethan's back with her fists and he was begging, begging her not to look. . . .

"No, Em. He wasn't in pain."

"Is he dead?"

What had she told Emma? About death. What had Ethan told her? Grace couldn't remember. She would have to explain it all over again, or for the first time.

But not now. So all she said was, "Yes."

Emma hugged her more tightly. Her perfect young

body pressed against Grace's breasts like a hand over a bleeding wound, temporarily stanching the flow out. Grace closed her eyes and imagined living.

"I'm scared," Emma said.

"I know you are, darling."

"Josh was in my dream."

"What?" She almost pulled back; it took all the self-control she possessed to keep from jumping to her feet and dumping Emma on the ground.

"It woke me up and I was scared."

"Just now?"

Against her shoulder Emma's head moved up and down.

"Your brother loved you very much," Grace said.

She no longer knew how she was getting the words out; it was like surgery, a bloody excision; perhaps it would help, perhaps it would be fatal. Thinking: *What am I, then?* And knowing now the answer: *A victim, not a mother.* In her arms Emma had begun to sob, slim body shaking as if from terrible cold. Grace felt the child's grief enter her own body like a current.

"Oh, my baby," she said.

Suddenly Emma's grip tightened frantically around her neck and from her throat came sobs like convulsed words; she was trying to say something: "W-we . . ."

The sounds were terrible. *She is dying,* Grace thought; *she is dying, too.* "Emma, sweetheart, tell me. . . ."

"W-we stopped because of *me*," Emma sobbed.

Grace felt a chill run through her. "No, sweetheart, no—"

56

"Y-yes. So I c-could go. Because of *me*."

"No," Grace protested. "No. It was an accident, a terrible accident, terrible, but dear God, no. . . ."

But her voice was too weak and the words that might have given comfort died within her. Destitute and hateful without them, she rose, bolting, awkward as a foal, to her feet—and felt how, even so, Emma tightened her grip and held on: a child's indomitable love and weight. Grace nearly staggered beneath it; until, somehow righting herself, she found, if not balance, then a way to move forward nonetheless. Holding her daughter tightly against herself, she carried her out of the room that way, and up the stairs to bed.

Dwight

The house I was renting in Box Corner was a pale-blue two-bedroom ranch-style with a free-standing two-car garage. There was nothing in it—not a windowpane or sheet of dry wall or bathroom S-pipe—that was more than five years old, that had any history or soul. Until I came around waving my rent check and the flag of my desperation, no one had ever lived in it. The developer who'd built it had had high hopes, I guessed, but what he'd thought was a big fat windfall turned out to be just a two-bit S&L. Bankruptcy followed, America's gold rush in reverse: foreclosure, a failed auction, the need to find a tenant until the market picked up. Around that time my probation was lifted and I came back, looking to be near my son. This was the place I found. Perfect nothingness. The first thing I did was to make up the second bedroom for Sam, preparing for the day when, thanks to the courts, I'd no longer have to have him back at Ruth's by seven p.m. or else.

It was nearing eleven when I put the car in the garage. The fragment of dark cloth was still caught on the broken headlight, but I did nothing about it. I left it there, pushing a button as I went out, hearing the pulsing hum of the electric door descending from above. Sealing up the evidence.

A man can convince himself of anything, for a little while. I tried this now. I let myself into the house, tossed wallet and keys on the pale-blue Formica counter that separated the kitchen (unused; the latest appliances) from the den (where I lived, mostly), and went straight to the fridge for a beer. I turned on the TV in the den and sat down on the gray leather sofa that had, like most everything else, come with the house. Waiting for the local eleven o'clock news to start, I drank the beer. Then I got another out of the fridge and polished that off, too. I lit a cigarette.

The world was suspended. I hung in it like one of those buzz-haired astronauts filmed in deep space, trying to drink a mug of Ovaltine, eat a freeze-dried dinner, before it, too, floated away. It was possible— between, say, ten-fifty and eleven o'clock—to feel as if nothing had happened. To feel nothing. To see no images besides the sweating green bottle, the burning cigarette, the TV commercial for Pizza Hut, the furniture that would always smell as if it was wrapped in plastic.

Was that peace? A cool blank ten minutes before the news came on. A blond-haired anchorwoman named Kyle. I knew her well from just such tidy domestic scenes as now, sitting here on the gray leather sofa with beer and cigarette in hand. I leaned forward. Unless war had broken out somewhere—and it had better concern at least one country that was damn Big and Important—the eleven o'clock news in this corner of the state usually began with a local tragedy of some sort. And the truth is, they were rarely without the kind of juicy material that made men like me—solitary, beer-drinking, failed dads who knew more than a little about the workings of the criminal-justice system—sit up and pay attention. Forget football. Every night somebody out there lost control of car, body, mind, and somebody else suffered for it. Blood was spilled. People went missing and were never found. Children died.

Tonight it was a three-car pile-up on Route 8 coming out of Waterbury. Two boys, both seventeen, were dead; another, eighteen, was listed critical. Names were being withheld. Drinking was strongly suspected. Behind the TV reporter—not Kyle any more, but some hardier, at-the-scene type—red lights whirled. A police squawker could be heard clearly through the open window of a parked cruiser, a single word: "Negative." After that, gibberish.

Police, Fire, EMS: red lights whirling like a cheap light show. A few bystanders were standing at the edge of the cordoned-off stretch of hardtop, drawn to the scene first by mayhem, or even worry, then by the hallucinogenic lights of television. Where were the victims' parents? Send your boy out on a Sunday evening for sandwiches and bumper pool, get him back in a bag. Hear all about it on the eleven o'clock news. . . .

The spell was broken. I found myself in the den, sitting on the gray leather sofa with the same old beer and cigarette (or maybe, by now, a different beer and cigarette), when gravity returned.

Coming out of the second turn, the car had been mine again. I had regained the touch, found the road. Tod's three-letter sign came shining out of the trees like a fractured beacon, and I saw the tall, dark-haired man with glasses step out of the bright-lit office into a night he knew nothing about. I saw him look up, right at me, felt the connection of surprise and dread and pain draw tight like a noose around us both. Forever.

The boy's name was Josh.

On the news at this moment, sudden and pointless, the week's lottery pick; Ping-Pong balls with numbers written on them were being shot up out of a modified popcorn popper into a clear plastic tube. I got up from the sofa, went to the fridge for another beer. Half of it was gone by the time I reached the Formica counter on which my keys and wallet were sitting. There, too, was an empty cigar box (from headier days) in which I kept important odds and ends, such as the spare garage-door opener. I lifted the lid of the box and pressed the rectangular white button on the opener. Through the far window of the den, above the TV, I had a view of a section of lawn and driveway, and I watched as an expanding chunk of light appeared in front of the far side of the garage, the grass there suddenly turning yellow in the surrounding darkness, the pavement suddenly turning brown. And then I knew my car was visible from the road, lit up like the spectacle it was.

Still, it wasn't enough. I took the car keys and went outside. Light spilled through the open front door onto the lawn that I kept mowed short and crisp (I was a good citizen and neighbor). Anybody driving by then would have been struck by the odd light show of my existence, this formerly uninhabited house and garage exhibiting such atypical life, doors open and lamps beaming into the night, lottery balls coming up all the right numbers. There was dew on the grass. It might have been any other night. I entered the bright coffin of the garage. On the empty side (it had been designed for a two-car family) sat the usual detritus: a file cabinet; a charcoal grill; a hand-push Honda mower; a floor lamp that had short-circuited months ago; a ten-year-old set of golf clubs; wax-encrusted, rock-scarred skis; a makeshift worktable (a plank on two sawhorses) with vise and lamp, tools spread on and beneath it; snow tires; a deflated football; two Louisville Sluggers, one big and one small, and three grass-stained base-balls; my old outfielder's glove from law school, and a newer, stiffer, smaller glove for Sam.

I didn't look at the headlight, the fragment of cloth. I didn't have to. I got in the car, behind the wheel. It smelled different, hard to describe, some scent sharp and metallic, ozone after lightning. I started up the engine. The sound filled that boxy, nearly enclosed space with its reverberations, product of the five-year-old Ford exhaust system, the eighteen-month-old Midas muffler. Time to change? Trade in? Too late. Live with it. The half-drunk beer was still in my hand. I'd brought it, so I drained it. Thinking, for the first time, about my case. I was a lawyer, after all. There was the illegal broken headlight, and my failure to stop at the scene. There was my record and my life. There was the dead boy on the side of the road. In the eyes of the law, there was no such thing as an accident.

The engine was running. If I pushed the white button clipped to the visor above my head, the garage door would slide down. The opener was also a closer. All that CO would enter me like a long, last dream at night and send me to permanent sleep. So I wouldn't have to see anything more, how it would all play out. The dumb pain of living. It could end like that, if I willed it to.

There are so many kinds of failure in a man's life; an Olympiad of humiliation. Maybe this was just another variation: I put the car in reverse and backed out of the garage. I turned it around and switched the engine off and got out. I left my car sitting in the driveway, its busted nose pointing at the road, bright as a neon sign, saying Punish Me.

Ethan

I was driven home by Sergeant Burke and his partner, whose name was Tomlinson. It must have been around eleven o'clock. The roads were empty and quiet. I sat in the back of the police car, listening to the intermittent silence and crackle of the CB radio; for twenty minutes no actual human being spoke a word. It was dark in the backseat, not even the glow from the dashboard. I sat with my knees aligned, my hands tightly clasped—as if, with this hand and that hand, I might somehow hold myself together. I heard Tomlinson, behind the wheel, sniff the air twice—there was dried vomit still on my shirt, and its stink had infected the car. He rolled down his window. Burke glanced over at him, murmured something that I didn't catch, and then Tomlinson rolled up his window a couple of inches and left it like that.

We turned onto Pine Creek Road. In a little while lights appeared up ahead, on the left, a yellowish wash like a faint stain reaching out through several windows of a handsome old Colonial house, white with painted shutters, onto a broad rectangle of yard, a split-rail fence: the house I lived in. As we pulled to a stop by the mailbox, the precise delineation of the fenestrated light came clear: the upstairs landing illumined; the kitchen downstairs; and from Grace's studio, at the lower back corner of the house, there emerged just the faintest suggestion of a glow, like a candle flame in a church. From here the house appeared empty, a nest of vacancies.

And to this quiet, anesthetized scene add now the headlights and brakelights of one police cruiser, and the war-zone cacophony of radio static and belch. Tomlinson shifted gear into park. And suddenly I was home.

Burke, in the passenger's seat, slid an arm along the seat back, turned, and regarded me with what I took to be intended kindness.

"You'll be okay?"

How to answer? The question not a question but a generic encouragement, a euphemistic hand on the shoulder; not at all, really, about revelation. And so, hunched like a felon in the dim backseat of the cruiser, I nodded. And then I opened the door and got out.

"Mr. Learner?" Burke was getting out, too; with a little sigh, he rested his hand on the top of the open door and looked at me earnestly. Then he pulled a business card from his shirt pocket and offered it across the roof of the cruiser. I took the card but did not look at it. "We're on the case here, sir, I want you to rest assured of that," he said. "And if at any time you feel like getting in touch with me, you can give a call over to the station. I'll get the message and get right back to you. That's a promise. We'll be in touch."

He stood waiting for some response, but when I remained mute, he seemed to come to some decision about me. With a nod of his head, he murmured, "Good night, sir," and ducked back into the cruiser.

I watched them drive off.

I didn't go in right away. I stood at the edge of the lawn, by the split-rail fence and the mailbox, looking at our house. The night was warm, moonless dark, and still; the crickets had stopped singing. In the air was the damp, lush, private scent of the garden without the sun: lilac, lavender, mint, thyme. I saw the lighted windows of our house—this which was to have been our place of permanence, our home and hearth inviolable: Build and it will last, was the idea; reap and ye shall sow. This place to which we'd moved ten years ago, with Josh still in his bassinet; this sagging old house we had lovingly shored up and restored; where, bit by bit, Grace had made this garden. She had planted trees—dogwoods, junipers, Japanese maples, peach, apple, cherry. Carrying Josh with her wherever she went, pointing out plants and flowers to him, talking to him, sometimes voicing ideas aloud as they came to her. On the western side of the house, where the land climbed to a rise, she had stood one day imagining a garden of perennials. At the end of every summer they would bloom, she had promised him, and the butterflies would flock to them, wave after wave of monarchs. She said she could see it all as if in a dream: it would be Josh's garden.

Upstairs, a window was opened: Grace stood on the landing, in the artificial light, cupping her hands against the upper panes and squinting, like someone looking into the sun. For perhaps a minute we simply stared at each other. Then she went down.

Grace

She had the impression, when he first came through the door and put his arms around her, that he was embracing her simply because she was standing there, because she would do; that he did not recognize her. But the feeling passed. His grip on her tightened with a sudden and awful need; he seemed to come apart in her arms, and then she felt herself holding him together in some way she'd never imagined would be necessary. She could feel his heart beating violently against her breast. He smelled of vomit. There was nothing to say.

Wordlessly, like a woman with her tongue cut out, she made him a drink and another for herself. Standing in the living room by the sideboard, she heard a rushing sound in her ears and pressed the cold sweating glass against her forehead. Then she gathered herself and the glasses and joined him in the kitchen, where he had wandered listlessly, like a ghost. The kitchen: butcher-block table, two chairs, two stools.

Stools for the children, she thought, watching him sit down heavily, selfishly, on Josh's stool, and felt a bright star of outrage burst in her chest: *How dare he*. But then she retreated, telling herself, *That world is gone*. There were no boundaries any more. Everything was broken. Things were simply done to you.

She sat on one of the chairs.

Across from her, Ethan had his glasses off and was rubbing deep into his eyes. "Stop it," she wanted to scream at him. He was practically blind. Without his glasses, he looked too young, all the scholarly wisdom and self-assurance gone; she wanted to shake him, and looked away.

"How's Emma?" he said.

His voice had no strength; it was the voice of a victim. She looked at him. His glasses were back on. Behind clear round lenses his eyes were shot through with red. A stunned, beaten expression on his face, his lips parted as though he were having trouble breathing. And now, with pathetic heroic effort, he reached across the table for her hand—yet she did not feel touched, or better.

"How's Emma?" he asked again.

Emma. "Asleep. She woke up and . . ." She could not finish.

Ethan nodded dully, as if she'd actually said something. He swallowed half his drink and said nothing more.

She made herself ask the question. "Do they know anything?"

She had meant to say "the police," but found

...ly that she didn't want to use the word; language was a minefield now.

Ethan took back his hand. He opened his mouth but no words came out. He shook his head.

"Ethan?" she said.

He wouldn't look at her.

"I need to know what happened. What you saw. Because I just . . . I don't understand. He was there alive. And then . . . I just don't understand."

She stared at him; she waited. But he had no answer, or would not give her the one that he had. Nor did he have the courage even to look at her. He got to his feet and left the room.

He was gone only a minute. She watched the clock on the wall because it was not life. And then it was over, and he was back, walking slowly, unsteadily, carrying the bottle of Scotch. He put this on the table in front of her but did not sit down.

"I can't really talk about this now. He was . . . he was standing by the road. It was dark. I left him there." He stopped talking. He turned his face away from her. She could see his throat contracting, over and over, as though he were trying to swallow something that would not go down. Then he turned back to her and his voice came again and it was a small, lifeless thing, pushed as far from the pain of his heart as he could manage. "I turned my back on him. When I saw him again, it was too late. I saw the car. I saw him get hit. But I don't seem to know anything. And because of me the police don't know anything, either."

There were tears in his eyes, trying to get out. The

fact that he wouldn't let them out made her feel as if she were suffocating. She closed her eyes and saw Josh standing in the dark road—alone, afraid, without protection or care. A groan of pain escaped her, like an animal in a trap.

Then she felt Ethan's head touch her lap, and heard him sobbing: "It's my fault. Oh my God, it's my fault."

Dwight

Something woke me. Maybe it was the birds. I was sitting on the gray leather sofa with my legs propped on the glass-topped coffee table. Predawn light. Green empties standing all around—I counted five—and the ashtray overflowing with butts and gray matter. I tried to sit up but my knees felt as if someone had taken hammer and chisel to them. The TV screen was fuzzy gray with a violet stripe down the middle. It almost looked pretty.

The light came through the den windows and struck me in the face, dragging with it a new day. I wanted to run somewhere, and keep running. I got myself on my feet and went to the window. My car was sitting in the driveway. The dew had formed a kind of caul over it, and the sunless light was starting to shimmer over the dark wet skin. It seemed alive. Around it on the lawn a couple of mourning doves were poking for worms, their cooing the only sound at this hour. Everything else was still.

Why hadn't they come for me? Box Corner was not so far from the rest of the world that it couldn't be found. The police could easily have passed through here in their cruisers and spotted the car sitting in the driveway, facing the road. They would have seen the piece of the dead boy's jacket stuck in the broken headlight, the last thing anybody took from him while he was alive.

I'd gone back inside the house, last night, to sit on the couch, to drink more beer and smoke more cigarettes, to wait for them to realize who I was and what I'd done. I'd made it in time for the end of the eleven o'clock news. In time for sports, baseball and Fenway Park and hot dogs. I'd watched a replay of Mo Vaughn slugging a grand slam in the bottom of the sixteenth to win it for the Sox. The camera took in the crowd surging to its feet at the crack of the bat, a sea of heads rising as if synchronized to follow the ball's flight across the green field and over the monster left-field wall. Then the cheer exploding upward through bright rings of raucousness — a war cry, a fertility rite, a dance for rain.

And there the videotape had ended, the news ended. Good night. In just a few minutes we'd witnessed the deaths of teenagers, a lottery winner, a life-altering home run. And I had remembered my son's hands bunched into fists during the game; then released, happy, loose, and trusting. Mine for a minute.

I went down the hall now. Pale-blue synthetic carpeting thick and feisty under my feet, like walking on foam rubber. The realtor had referred to my bedroom as the Master Suite. All the furniture here had come with the lease. The bed was round. The bureau and bedside tables were made of a white wood-laminate that spoke of cheap hair salons and big-chested women in pussycat pajamas. Most of the things I valued I kept in this room, tucked away in furniture I couldn't stand the sight of. My treasure chest of memories, my Ode to Life. Sam's letters I kept in the top drawer of the left bedside table, where I could reach for them while lying awake at night, while remembering, while trying to explain to myself, like a shock victim, the how and why of things. I found them now, took out the bundle and peeled off the rubber band. I pulled one out at random and sat down on the bed to read:

DaD
    i aM LeRNiNG To pLay TRuMpiT at sCooL. MoM WaNTs Me To pLay peaNo LiKe HeR BuT i DoNT WaNT To. i LiKe TRuMpiT BeTeR. oK?
    My sTepDaD says To CaLL HiM THaT BuT i DoNT WaNT To, He TRys To pLay BaLL BuT Hes NoT GooD LiKe you. i ToLD HiM aND MoM GoT MaD. sHe sTaRTeD To yeLL aND say sTuFF aBouT you. soRRy.
    BoGGs GoT FoR HiTs. i Mis you. SaM.
    MoM DiDNT ReeD THis.

There was no date, but I didn't need one. He'd been eight years old when he'd written that. Ruth was married to Norris by then. Norris, in fact, was living in my house. (For some reason, Ruth had been anxious about our coverage, and had gone to the offices of Wheldon and Peterson Insurance to get more information about the vast array of protections available to the American family unit. What was most available, it turned out, was Norris.)

I read the letter over again. The spelling was worrisome. Sam had since been diagnosed with dyslexia. He was getting some extra tutoring at school, and spelling a little better these days. Still, he was behind the normal rate of development for boys his age.

In other respects, though, the letter stood out as a happy bulletin. I even smiled once: Norris would not be much of a ballplayer, no. Mr. Stepdad. Sam knew what was what, all right. He would never call a nickel a dime. He would not settle. Ruth had wanted him to play the piano. That was natural enough—teaching it to children was what she did for a living. But being part of a phalanx of piano-tinkling upstarts was not Sam's dream. He was an individual, and individuals played the trumpet.

I had written him back, of course. To tell him I was proud of his decision to learn the trumpet. To say that though I could see his point about his stepfather's limited skills with bat and ball and glove, sometimes the truth could hurt more than he realized, so he should be careful how he said things to people about themselves, since people—adults especially—were often blind to their own faults. I'd gone on to say that Boggs possessed the best pure swing in baseball. But everyone knew that, I admitted, so maybe I was no wiser than most. What, if anything, separated me from the pack was my love for my son. Your mother will say bad things about me sometimes, I'd written. She's mad as hell at me for a lot of things, and right about most of them, too. I've made some terrible mistakes, and you know I'm sorry. But nothing anybody says about me is as true as this: I love you, Sam. I'll write again next week. We'll see each other sometime soon. I'll hear you play that trumpet. Dad.

I folded the letter in half along its well-worn crease and stuffed it back in the envelope (on the flap: "saM aRNo"). Like a player returning a lucky card to the deck, I slipped the envelope back into the pile with an obsessive's attempt at recall; it had told me something, and I already counted on seeing it again. Then I twisted the rubber band around the letters, closed the bundle up in the drawer, and went outside.

The sun had risen above the stand of trees across the road. The light was weak but still strong enough to have burned the dew off my car. The '89 midnight-blue Ford Taurus sat dry as toast, all its secrets exposed.

I climbed in, started it up, turned it around. I put my car back in the garage and listened to the machine hum of the door going down.

There are heroes, and there are the rest of us. There comes a time when you just let go the ghost of the better person you might have been.

PART TWO

Ethan

A fuel truck was parked in front of the Canaan State Police barracks when I arrived the next morning, its pump droning and its hose half buried in the ground. A black man in gray coveralls stood in the sunlight with his hand resting on the pulsing hose, testing the pressure, a transparent, heat-stoked cloud of fumes shimmering just above his head as if he were being baked.

The front door of the barracks opened directly into a small waiting room with three plastic chairs, a drinking fountain, and a low table supporting a cardboard rack of Alcoholics Anonymous brochures, "A.A. at a Glance" and "Is A.A. for Me?" To my right, through a Plexiglas window, I could see into a larger room in which three policewomen dressed in pale blue uniforms with dark blue trim were sitting at their desks and talking. One of them—thickset, with small eyes and an auburn perm—nodded soberly when I gave her my name. She informed me that it was only eight-fifteen

79

in the morning and Sergeant Burke wasn't in yet, though he would be shortly, if I cared to wait.

I sat down on a plastic chair. The waiting room had no windows. After a while, I got up to take a drink of water. Next to the drinking fountain was a steel door marked Authorized Personnel Only. Finally I sat down again and stared at the facing wall, which was covered with bulletin boards papered with xeroxed messages like "Lost Dog 'Moby'—Last Seen in Sheffield," and "Wanted by CT for Failure to Pay Child Support," and "Fugitive Alert," complete with grainy mug shots of rapists and killers. It was a wall of crime and shame and suffering, and I stared at it a long time, until the many names and pictures and deeds began to blur, becoming indistinguishable.

Sitting there beneath it all, the point was not so hard to grasp. They made it easy for you. It was a message anyone could understand, if you'd been hurt badly enough. It said that you who were suffering, you who'd been the victim of an unthinkable crime, the loser of a life, the man who couldn't find his wife, the parent robbed of a child—that you were not, as you assumed, unique in the world. Far from it. There were many just like you, many worse off, even. Consequently, special treatment was out of the question. An impartial system existed. The scales were already set. It was a question of protocol, etc. You got in line, took a number. Your turn would come, not before, not after. Everyone was equal.

And now, as I sat in the windowless room reading these bulletins, images of my own guilt began to reel

behind my eyes like a Zapruder nightmare: images of
the car bearing down on Josh and his absolute, knowing stillness, his silent terror—but everything seen
now through a darkened prism, the muddied geome-
try of my negligence: seen over my turned shoulder,
through shadows and night, from an angle, at a remove
too great to be measured or bridged or helped, as if I
had not just turned my back on him but fled, and now
could not get back—

My heart was pounding. I was sweating. The A.A.
brochures lay on the floor at my feet and I was staring
at them; I'd kicked the underside of the table, upset-
ting the cardboard rack. I got down on my knees and
began gathering them into piles.

Distant beyond the Plexiglas shield, the policewoman who'd spoken to me earlier was looking in my
direction. I could see just the top third of her, as though
she were a bust. She kept me pinned with her small
eyes until I'd gotten the brochures back in the rack and
safely on top of the table, the titles hopelessly mixed
up, and I was seated again on the plastic chair, and
then she turned back to another policewoman, a broad-
shouldered brunette, who was saying, apropos of I didn't
know what, "That is so cute." And then they all turned
when a trooper—some sergeant, not Burke—walked in
and began telling a story, something amusing about last
night that I didn't catch because just then the steel door
opened and I stood up, thinking it would be Burke.

It wasn't Burke—just a tiny gray-haired woman
wearing a green smock who smiled at me, before ush-
ering in a red-haired man with a mop and bucket. The

man had the large head, small eyes, pallid skin, and slightly unhinged smile of a Down's child; he looked like an adolescent, though he was probably close to thirty. Seeing me in the room, he stopped, and an expression of intense anxiety spread over his face. I sat down again. The woman put a hand on the man's shoulder. "Go on," she said softly. "It's all right."

He entered the waiting room and began mopping the floor with broad, slow strokes, and after a moment the woman went out through the door marked Authorized Personnel Only, and I lifted my feet so the mop could pass underneath my chair.

In the dispatch room, the sergeant was finishing his story: ". . . And just when the son of a bitch opened the door, I was pulling the biscuits out of the oven!" The three policewomen laughed. The floor was opening up under my feet and no one seemed to realize it but me. The red-haired man was drinking thirstily from the water fountain, water running down his chin onto the freshly mopped floor. There were pools of water all over the floor anyway. He looked up when the old woman returned.

"Finished?" she asked.

He nodded, wiping his mouth on his sleeve.

"It'll dry in no time," she said, looking satisfied. She went to the entrance and pushed the door open. I tried to prepare myself for the fuel truck parked there, and the sickening smell of gas and the hard thrumming of the pump. I saw how bad memories were buried everywhere and would be forever.

To my surprise, though, the truck was gone and

the air coming through the open door smelled clean and fresh. Morning sunlight spilled in with it. For a moment I thought I was going to cry.

Sergeant Burke must have entered the barracks through a rear entrance; when he finally came to get me it was through the Authorized Personnel Only door, and he was carrying a half-full mug of black coffee.

He asked me if I'd been waiting long, but I didn't know; I'd forgotten my watch that morning, something I never did. Not that it mattered, any of it. I followed him down a water-streaked hallway (the red-haired man had been here, too) and into a large, windowless, fluorescent-lit room with half a dozen metal desks in it. A clock on the wall read 9:10. Three of the desks were occupied by short-haired uniformed men talking on the phone, their gun belts causing them to sit unnaturally tall. Burke's desk stood in the far corner, its surface cluttered with phone books and stacks of papers and framed photographs of two little girls and an attractive woman who must have been his wife. The frame of this last picture had a chipped corner and a long diagonal crack in the glass and I wondered what had happened to it.

Burke pulled a chair over from one of the unoccupied desks and motioned for me to sit down. I did, and he settled himself behind his desk, placed a stenographer's notebook on the blotter, unclipped the ballpoint pen from his shirt pocket, took a sip of coffee, and looked at me.

When I didn't begin immediately, he said, "You want some coffee or something?"

"Okay. Please."

"Milk? Sugar?"

I shook my head, and he went off to get the coffee. The wall above his desk was composed of bare white-painted cement blocks. A Disney World poster was taped to it like a Magritte window, and directly beneath the poster there was a plastic plant on the floor. The artificial leaves of the plant were reaching up toward the sun in the picture—a posture of false desire, it seemed to me, a cold perpetual sunniness. My eyes trailed back to the photos on the desk, Burke's smiling children and wife, the chipped and cracked frame, and beside them this time I saw what I hadn't before: a small tear-away desk calendar with "Tod's Gas and Auto Body" printed in red ink across the bottom of the page. The name didn't register at first. I sat calmly observing the red ink and bold typeface, the grid of days and dates, until I felt a chill so deep I shivered. Then I lifted the calendar off the desk and crumpled it between my hands and, with a quick check around the room, stuffed it deep into the wastebasket under Burke's desk.

When I looked up he was at the far end of the room, coming slowly toward me with a Styrofoam cup in his hand, staring at it, trying not to spill. He had seen nothing. He looked perfectly human then, an awkward, decent man in uniform, and I badly wanted to feel some connection to him. But I felt little—empty, far away even from grief, aware of everything and nothing.

Burke set the cup of coffee down on the desk in front of me and settled himself again on his chair. His face was tanned in the way of someone who spends considerable time outdoors, with faint white squint marks at the corners of his eyes which looked like tiny scars. *He is not the enemy*, I told myself. I pictured him standing in his backyard, holding one of his daughters up toward the sun.

"So," he said. Now he looked me in the eyes. "You and your wife probably didn't sleep much last night."

I shook my head, thinking about the calendar in the wastebasket beneath his desk.

"Did you remember something you wanted to talk to me about? Something from the accident, maybe. Something you saw."

"I had a dream last night," I said.

"A dream?" he said.

"That's right."

A light seemed to go out of Burke's gray eyes. "A dream," he repeated.

Suddenly I felt a terrifying rush of adrenaline through my arms to my fingers; I took hold of the tops of my thighs and squeezed as hard as I could. "You don't believe in dreams, Sergeant Burke?"

"No, sir, not in police work."

"It's Learner," I said. "Not 'sir.' Ethan Learner. That's my name."

"I'm aware of that, Mr. Learner."

"I'm a person just like you, in case it hadn't occurred to you," I said. "And I'd appreciate it, I'd really fucking appreciate it, if you would listen to what I have to say."

But I'd lost him. His gaze had slipped off me and fallen on someone or something over my shoulder, another trooper probably. His face was a kind of code, unreadable by me, and I became aware then of a weird silence in the room (except for a single ringing phone no one would answer), and the feeling of people watching me.

The light falling from the ceiling was cold and white. I felt close to sick, and bent over and looked at the floor between my knees.

Sighing, Burke stood up. "Mr. Learner, I'm going for more coffee. By the time I get back, either we'll have ourselves a talk or we won't. Either way, I've got a lot of work to do on your son's investigation. I hope you understand that."

I looked up at him. "I apologize, Sergeant."

Burke reached down and straightened the photographs on his desk, though they did not need straightening. He did not seem to notice the missing calendar. His thumb was working the top of his pen furiously, clicking the point in and out.

"I'd like to start over," I said.

"I'm doing my job, Mr. Learner. This is my job."

I nodded without looking at him, and then he sat down, sighing again. "All right," he said. "I'm listening."

"Thank you."

"All right."

"Last night I told you I heard him shout something," I said.

"The perpetrator."

"The perpetrator. I woke up in the middle of the night. I'd been dreaming about it. A nightmare. It was 'Sam' he shouted, not any of the other words. It was 'Sam,' somebody's name. I'm positive now. He shouted it twice."

"Sam?" said Burke, studying me skeptically.

"Yes."

"That's a definite?" He did not sound convinced.

"Yes. Definite. I heard him."

"Sam," he repeated.

"That's right. Sam."

"Hmm," he said.

I waited. Then, slowly, deliberately, Burke folded back the cover of his notebook and clicked down the point of his pen and printed the name Sam.

"Thank you," I said.

"Questions," he said. "One: You're sure there wasn't anybody else in the car? The suspect was definitely alone?"

"I told you last night. I didn't see anyone else, but it was dark."

"So you're not sure."

"No. I guess not."

"Two: Did your son have any nicknames?"

"No."

"I'm not talking about just at home. Is it possible he might've had a nickname at school you wouldn't've known anything about?"

"It's possible, but I doubt it."

"Nickname like Sam, maybe."

"No."

"Three: The name Sam mean anything to you? Do you recognize it? Know any Sams? Anything?"

"No. I thought about it all night, but no, it doesn't mean anything to me."

Burke paused to take a sip of coffee, wincing at the cold and bitter taste. Afterwards, he sat thinking, as though alone, and a few moments later he refolded his notebook and played again with his pen. Somewhere a phone was ringing—whether the same caller as before or someone new, I couldn't have said. And then I saw another man, a man like me, sitting hunched and broken over a desk on the far side of the room, talking to a sergeant.

I said, "It's not enough to go on, is it? It's not enough."

Burke cleared his throat and drew himself up on his chair. "Mr. Learner, I'll be straight with you about what kind of case this is shaping up to be. At the moment we don't have a lot to go on, but that doesn't necessarily mean too much. Things can turn up. We've already sent out teletypes with the current information to every police barracks in the state, and any time now we should have checks established on the main roads. If the perp's trying to flee or just out there driving around like an idiot, odds are we'll know about it. In the meantime we'll be trying to home in on the vehicle any way we can. In cases like this the vehicle's usually the perpetrator's weakest link, as good as fingerprints if we can tie man and machine together. Along those lines we've got glass samples already in the lab, and cloth from your son's jacket—could be some paint on there, smaller than the eye can see. Any vehicle characteristics we can identify that way will help get us a lead on the make and model. And get make and model, we'll be that much closer to the man. Then there's the autopsy. Should be done by this afternoon. Things can turn up there—paint, glass, plastic chips. You never know. A fast-moving vehicle almost always leaves some kind of trace behind on the victim. I'm sorry to say it like that, but that's my job."

"What are the odds?"

"Of getting him?" Burke shook his head. "I don't give odds, Mr. Learner. You understand. I'd have to be crazy to do that, and I'm not crazy."

"I'm asking for your professional opinion."

He considered this, his eyes scanning his desk while his mind worked the angles of the question. Where the calendar used to be, his gaze suddenly grew fixed. But to my surprise he made no mention of what was missing, and when he looked at me again his eyes were clear.

"Mr. Learner, I'll be straight," he said. "Hit and run is among the toughest of all cases to prosecute. Problem is, at the end of the day it's not just evidence. You can have all the goddamn evidence in the world and still be smack in the woods. Let's say we identify the perpetrator, all right? The man you believe you saw driving the car. Let's say we find him and bring him in. It's still our responsibility to prove in court that he was aware of hitting your son, that the son of a bitch left the scene with full knowledge of having fatally hit someone, not an animal or an object but a living, breathing human being, that he was fleeing and not just driving on. You see what I'm saying? That he knew what he'd done. How do we prove that? That's hard. I'll be straight with you, sometimes it's damn near impossible. And without that proof there's not a whole hell of a lot we can do to him. Even with it, we're pretty much hamstrung when it comes to sentencing."

"What are you saying?"

"I'm saying even if we convict him, it's unlikely he'd serve much time."

I felt the hole already opened beneath my feet suddenly opening wider, deeper. And then I was falling into it and something like a wind was in my ears. "How long?"

Burke looked down at the pen in his fingers. "I'm probably more cynical about it than most."

I slammed my fist down on the desk, knocking over the Styrofoam cup and spilling the black coffee onto the floor. The room fell quiet at once, but Burke did not flinch.

"Easy now."

"You fucking tell me, Burke. How long would he get?"

"Maybe a year."

"No."

"Maybe six months. You've got to understand—"

"No," I said. "Jesus Christ, no."

Then I was on my feet, no idea how I'd gotten

there, and Burke was rising too, his hand out to settle me down, put a hold on me.

"Mr. Learner—"

I heard light footsteps behind me and saw Burke make a single deft shake of his head to whoever was there, and then the footsteps and the wide blue shadow behind me faded away across the room.

"Sit down," Burke said. "Please."

I sat down. There was a strange heaving in my chest that had nothing to do with exertion, and I put my head between my knees and closed my eyes.

"Mr. Learner," Burke said, "I think we should see about getting you and your family some counseling." A new note of temperance had entered his voice, one man talking another down from a ledge. "We have a professional here, a nice lady."

"I don't want any counseling," I said. "Talk to my wife."

"You're in a tough place," Burke said. "A hard place. I know that."

"No, you don't. It was my fault. Do you understand what I'm saying? My son is dead because of me."

"Your son's dead because a man in a car ran him over, Mr. Learner. Vehicular homicide. And I promise you—"

I was on my feet. The room was not spinning, but it was not stable either, and I set my legs against the possibility of its tipping. Then I was halfway across the room.

Burke called to me. "You'll hear soon as we know anything, I promise."

I walked away under the cold white light past the troopers behind their desks, eyeing me warily, and the man like me seated in the corner, hunched over and whispering to his police confessor, then down the hall and through the heavy steel door marked AUTHORIZED PERSONNEL ONLY. In the dispatch room, behind the Plexiglas shield, the woman with the auburn hair was doing a crossword puzzle in pen. She did not look up as I passed.

Dwight

I left the car in the garage, all closed in, and took a taxi to a Chevy dealership in Winsted, where I leased a white Corsica on a month-by-month. Then, dressed for work, blue summer suit and red tie, black wing-tip shoes, I drove the new car out Route 44 through Wyndham Falls and on into Canaan.

The law offices of Cutter & Trope occupied the first floor of a handsome two-story Greek Revival situated to the east of the tiny center of Canaan proper. There were neatly clipped box hedges out front of the house and a paved lot behind. The lot was just big enough for five cars to get in, park, and get out without running into each other, if you were smart about it and looked where you were going. Today especially I tried to be smart. It was late morning already when I stepped out of the car, and the July sun was beating down. I walked around the side of the house and between the hedges and up the steps to the porch. Through the door I could hear Donna Kabrisky, the secretary I shared with Bob Trope, talking on the phone. Donna was a large-boned, pretty woman of thirty-four, divorced with no kids, and we'd been sleeping together, haphazardly but not unsuccessfully, for about six months.

"Mr. Trope's on vacation this week and next," she was saying. "Sorry, Mr. James, it's a secret. . . . Right, two weeks. . . . Okay, I'll tell him. . . . Thank you too, Mr. James. . . . Okay, bye." I walked in just as she was hanging up, and her expression changed. "Well, if it isn't Dwight," she said.

In her mouth this morning my name didn't sound like my name but like some disease, a blight that had come down on the heads of good farmers and folk all over the county. People were dying, livestock too, and it was my fault. (She couldn't have known how right she was.) My mouth was dry and I ran my tongue over my lips.

"Morning, Donna."

"It's almost noon," Donna said coldly. "Catching up on your sleep?"

"As a matter of fact, my transmission's completely shot and I had to take my car to the shop. The guy over there says it's so bad I may have to scrap it altogether. So right now I'm leasing."

I'd planned this little speech on the drive over. It was about facts and alibis and the way life was going to be from here on out. I was sweating, and took off my jacket and loosened my tie, undoing the top button on my shirt.

"Poor old Dwight. You're having a tough time today, aren't you?"

Donna didn't sound sympathetic. If not for the low-cut summer blouse and the large breasts and the long African earrings (none of which, including the breasts, Ruth would have been caught dead with), it might have been my ex-wife talking.

"As a matter of fact, I am."

Donna shook her head, and I noticed wisps of gray in her curly brown hair that hadn't been there when we'd first started together. She plucked an emery board from a Garfield pencil mug on her desk and began filing her pinky nail with brutal, expert strokes. "I don't know, Dwight. Maybe it's age. Closing in on forty, right? Maybe you have Alzheimer's."

"My problem is the opposite," I said. "I remember too much. Are there any messages?"

Donna stopped filing and studied her pinky, then started in on her ring finger. "Actually, Dwight, I'm good. Doing well. Thanks for the concern."

I sighed. "What did I do, Donna?"

"Nothing. You did nothing. Last night was fun for me. I didn't miss you at all." She stopped filing and looked right at me. "Am I wrong, or did you say you were going to call last night?"

I remembered then. "You're not wrong."

"Are you even sorry?"

"Yes. I am. I'm sorry."

"Something better come up?"

"I took Sam to the ballpark," I said. "I must have told you about that last week."

"Oh, that's right. I forgot. Men and boys and sports, rah rah. You still should've called."

"Anyway," I said, "it was a mistake. I thought I'd be back in time and I wasn't. The game ran till six and I had to drive like hell to get him back to Ruth's before she went crazy." I paused to gather my wits. I was still sweating and my mouth was dry again. "And then coming home we hit a dog on Cantwell Road. The whole thing was just a huge mistake."

I looked closely at Donna. She had closed her eyes and lifted her head in a pose of lamentation. "A dog? Oh God, Dwight, how awful. Was it dead? Did you kill it?"

"Yes."

"Jesus," Donna said. "Poor Sam."

There was a window to my right, not big, but it was open and a faint breeze was coming through it, blowing in over the porch, carrying the green scent of the hedges. I turned and looked out at the road. A Ben and Jerry's truck passed by, heading east toward Bow Mills and my old life; for a moment I pictured Sam eating ice cream and smiling. Then the truck was gone. A family wagon came next, country-club mother driving and three blond daughters in back, the tops of their tennis dresses showing white above the car window like flags of surrender—then they were gone, too, and then a police cruiser drove by and I stopped breathing. (Which, even at the time, I understood to be pure instinct, a natural act of self-preservation by a body that is on the verge of drowning; like a man thrown into a swimming pool while asleep.) As the car went by, I could see the trooper in the passenger seat. He was no one I knew. He had his hat off and his trooper's shades on and his blue shirtsleeves rolled up fair and square, bare forearm hanging out the window like any old teenager in summer, and he did not appear to be looking for anyone like me. Then he too was gone, and I rose again to the surface of my life and breathed.

I found Donna studying me, her expression neither hard nor soft, just curious, watchful. We were not close friends, but we were intimate in a way. In six months of sleeping together once a week or so we'd necessarily caught the kind of intense, momentary, self-regarding glimpses of each other that only sex provides. Along the way we'd gone to sleep touching and woken apart and had managed to mutually confess a few important things. She knew what I'd done to my son, not to mention my ex-wife, and I knew what her ex-husband had once done to her, how she still occasionally dreamed about it and woke in the night crying.

"Dwight?"

"What?"

"Are you okay?"

"No," I said. "I'm sorry about last night."

"Me, too," Donna said.

For a second I had an overwhelming desire to tell her the truth. But just then the phone rang and she picked up and said, "Cutter and Trope, Attorneys at Law, hold, please," and put her hand over the mouthpiece. "Dwight, Stu Carmody's been trying to reach you all morning. Says he wants to change his will again. And Jack wants an update on the Peckham estate."

And then she took her hand off the mouthpiece and began talking again, and I walked into my office and shut the door.

I sat down behind my desk. It was made of cherrywood and expensive and I'd brought it with me from my old days on the rise in Hartford. The old days of doing estates and trusts and wills for the wealthy. People who'd paid my firm an abundance of green for my services. The old days of tidying up the packages and stroking the legacies. What I remembered most was that people died anyway. They died rich and then they weren't rich any more because they were dead. They paid me to cut the corners, make the square peg fit into the round hole so that everyone could sleep better at night, and then they died and I died with them because the client is always right. In the end it was all about money. And the fact that the thing I had chosen to do with my life was the one thing I couldn't abide. I'd had a corner office and a spot for my car in a garage. I'd billed entire lifetimes and driven home late, listening to the first few innings from Fenway on the radio, and found my only son asleep, incommunicado, and my wife in love with another man. I had always been late, behind, playing catch-up. The boy was standing in the road and I was driving too fast to see. I heard his cracking bones, his life gone to pieces, and saw him flying off the road.

There was a knock on the door and Donna stuck her head in.

"Mr. Carmody's here."

"Carmody?" I looked down and saw the three fresh pink message slips on the blotter, the name Carmody on each one. "Is he scheduled?"

"No."

"What's his problem?"

"Like I said. He wants to change his will."

"Again? I just settled it for him last week."

"He says it's urgent."

I sighed. "All right. Send him in."

I waited for him behind my desk. I had stopped thinking about the boy flying off the road. There was a faded leather blotter on the desk and a stack of blank yellow legal pads and a pencil cup full of yellow Ticonderoga #2's. And there were two framed photos of Sam, one from before the accident and one from after. In both he was a serious-looking, sandy-haired, small-for-his-age boy with green-and-gold eyes. You had to know where the scar was to notice it, I thought, to see the difference—aside from height and weight and a curious, sad questioning behind the eyes— between the later photograph and the earlier one. You made for the left earlobe and dropped down an inch, followed the jawline with care and maybe even a magnifying glass, and there it was, pale as a thread of sun. Anybody could see it if they knew where to look.

I took a blunt-tipped pencil from the cup and inserted it into the bright blue electric pencil sharpener I'd kept from my law-school days. The engine chugged like a toy locomotive and the hidden blades whirred. When the pencil was sharp, I snapped it in two. Then I put the pieces back in the cup with the other pencils.

Stu Carmody appeared in the doorway. He was a tall, gaunt man of sixty-nine, with short white hair and cutting blue eyes and an Adam's apple the size of a fig. He owned a good-sized farm out toward Falls Village and never wore anything but the same checked gingham shirt, pressed blue jeans pulled up high with a western belt, and spit-polished leather workboots. I stood up and came around the desk to shake his hand.

"Stu."

"Dwight. I was callin' all morning."

"Car trouble," I said. "Have a seat."

Stu sat down on one of the two straight-backed chairs I kept for clients, and I went back around the desk and took my usual seat. I saw him glance to his left, at the leather-bound law books that lined the wall of shelves. There were not enough books to cover the shelves, so that gaps were conspicuous and it looked as if the place had recently been robbed.

"What's on your mind, Stu?"

"Dyin'," Stu said.

"You're not even seventy."

"I had a checkup Thursday, Dwight," Stu said. His eyes were so blue that it hurt to look at them. "Routine, the doctor said. Well, don't you believe it, mister. By Friday a.m. I was down in New Haven with my veins chock-full of needles. They crammed me into one of those MRI contraptions and turned the switches on. Juiced me up pretty good. Cost a good goddamn fortune too, even with insurance. And all for what? Cancer."

The word didn't mean as much to me as I knew it should. I tried to think about Stu but instead found myself thinking about the will I'd drawn up for him. His wife was dead and both his kids had moved out west. He was leaving them his farm anyway, knowing they'd probably sell it the very day he was gone. The fact was, he didn't have any other options. Though he wasn't the type to get sentimental over it, and the will had not been difficult to draw up.

"I'm very sorry, Stu."

"I hate doctors," Stu said matter-of-factly.

"Where is it?"

"Here." He touched his neck just below the Adam's apple, where the lymph nodes would be, swollen and malignant, beneath the dull wrinkled skin. "And here and here." He touched both armpits.

"Lymphoma?"

"You're smarter than that doctor," Stu said.

"There's treatment."

He shook his head. "Treatment maybe, but no cure."

"Treatment'll buy you time. Maybe a lot of time."

"No, thank you."

"Why the hell not?"

"Because I'm lookin' ahead, Dwight, and I don't have to be a medical genius to see what it'll be like. Pain and pissin' and drugs and the rest. And I don't want it. I flat out reject it. And it's my life, goddamnit. That's what all this legal stuff's about, isn't that right? So that I got these papers say it's my poor life and this is what I want done with it. I want us to be clear on that, Dwight." He was breathing hard, his rib cage rising and falling.

"We're clear, Stu," I said.

"Good."

"What is it you want me to do? We already drew up the will."

"I want to know something," Stu said.

"What?"

"Is the will still good if I don't die natural?"

I looked him in the eyes. "You mean if you kill yourself?"

"That's what I'm gettin' at."

"It's still good," I said carefully. "It's your life and your will, Stu. That's what the law says on this."

"Good. All right, then."

"All right, what?"

"Nothing," Stu said. "Just all right."

We sat there a minute more. I tried to think about Stu and what he was facing, but the feelings weren't sharp or clear or about him or anything real. It was as if there'd been an amputation, my heart flying off with that boy on the road, my body left behind. And the body is nothing. This man was going to take his life and I was going to say nothing to him about it because that's what was in me. Because he was going to die anyway and there was no such thing as help. There were only the yellow pencils standing in the pencil cup and the broken pieces with them. There was my son, too, there was Sam, two photographs on a desk.

Stu cleared his throat and I glanced up and found him looking at me. I could see on his face that he knew my mind had drifted. My failure to help him was all over the room.

"I'm sorry," I said. It could have been for a hundred things.

"You're my lawyer, Dwight."

"Yes."

He reached into his back pocket and pulled out a white envelope, crisply folded, and placed it on the desk. "This is a letter for afterward. I want to know things're in order, Dwight. I don't want my kids and people talkin' about what a mess I left. I was never like that."

"I'll take care of it, Stu. If you're sure that's what you want."

"I'm sure."

"All right."

"So we're clear, then?"

"Yes, we're clear."

"Then I'll be going."

He stood up, and I came around the desk and we shook hands. His hand was thin and callused and dry and couldn't have been mistaken for a young man's hand. Our eyes met, until I looked away. Then he went out, closing the door behind him, and I sat at my desk again, swiveling my chair so I was looking out the window to the little parking lot. Behind the lot stood a field, soft and green in the summer with daisies growing there, and a jungle gym at the near side. In a few moments I saw Stu Carmody climb into his pickup and drive away.

I tried to think about him. But with each new thing I looked at through the window, each thought I had, I just seemed to get farther away. As water rises in a flood, so memory fills in the empty places, covers all that is dead.

There'd been a jungle gym, too, in the weedy yard in front of the house I grew up in in North Haven. I remembered my old man making a big deal out of it when he brought it home, pulling the new parts from the long cardboard Sears box and holding them up ceremoniously for my mother and me to see. As if there was some secret there. It took him so long to put it together that it got dark, even though it was summer, and he made me hold the flashlight while he worked. When my arm got tired and I couldn't keep the light where he wanted it, he screamed at me. Later, after he died, I went back and pulled the whole thing apart and hauled the pieces to the dump. And later still, after I was married and Sam was born, I went myself to Sears and bought a jungle gym and put it together with my own hands. Sam used to play on it. Then, some time during the years when I wasn't allowed to see him, he stopped. I never asked him why. Maybe, in the way of all growing boys, he simply lost interest, moved on to other things. In any case, I never saw him on it again.

Ethan

We buried him. We buried our son on a Tuesday, in a stone-walled cemetery, under a sky the color of ashes. He would have been ten years, three months, and nineteen days. It did not rain. There were two dozen people, a minister, and a rabbi. I have no recollection of what was said. What I remember is the smell of damp earth, and that Grace held one of Emma's hands, and I held the other.

Afterwards, people came back to the house with us. Friends, good neighbors, bearing food; they brought their children who had known Josh, gone to school with him, played with him. They stayed as long as they could stand it, and then they left, taking with them their bewildered, frightened children, to whom they must now try to explain.

We stood in the front hall, in our funeral clothes, with no idea what to do. Grace's mother, Leila, finally took charge, suggesting to Emma, with painfully forced enthusiasm, that they go upstairs to her room to change, and then perhaps read a book together. Emma did not say no, but she refused to climb the stairs; she sat down on the ground and began to cry.

"Come on, sweetie," Grace said desperately. She picked Emma up like a baby and carried her upstairs.

The sound of her crying faded; soon a door closed.

Leila put her hand on my arm and looked me in the eyes. "She will be all right, Ethan," she said tenderly. "In time, you will all be all right." She was her daughter, only older: a fine-boned beauty with wonderful white hair, which she kept short and always well arranged. Perhaps she was more innately genteel than Grace, being a southern woman of a certain age. She had lost her husband, many years ago.

I wanted to acknowledge her kindness, but no human gesture occurred to me. Seeing this, Leila leaned over and kissed me on the cheek. "I'll go make us some tea," she murmured, and went off in the direction of the kitchen.

Outside, it had begun to rain.

I stood there, confused for too long, starting to pat my pockets as if I'd lost something I needed, pocketknife or pipe—a sad joke of an addled professor, I realized dimly, through a haze of even sadder truths. It was not just the moment that paralyzed, but the vast circumference of time ahead; I could imagine no way of filling this picture, or keeping away the silence that lay behind it. My fingers found a small hard oblong object in my pants pocket and began to worry it through the cloth.

Some of Josh's things had been returned to us that morning. His shirt and Windbreaker were being held for forensic testing, but everything else he'd been wearing or holding on Sunday had come back in two brown paper bags labeled with his name. Trooper Tomlinson had delivered them to our house, just as we were preparing to leave for the funeral. Some enterprising soul at the coroner's office or the morgue had come upon the arrowhead in Josh's blue jeans pocket, had slipped it into a clear plastic evidence bag, only to discover, to his professional disappointment, that it was not evidence at all, or at least not of the kind that would mean anything to him.

Here it was. I pulled it out, looked at it: putty-colored, smooth, wondrous, ancient, thumb-shined, collected, secret.

Can I have it back now?

I could not remember hugging him that day.

What other things? In his room alone I could name these by memory: peacock feather, sparrow's nest, sheet of mica, chunk of pink quartz, hockey puck from a Hartford Whalers game, comb with missing teeth, rail spike, harmonica, the inside of a baseball wound like the earth. And his violin in its case under his bed, the sheets of music.

This is what my son loved: tidal pools, abandoned train tracks, the sound of woodpeckers, the movement of turtles. And hated: brushing his hair, the taste of eggs, the feel of wool socks, lies.

A clap of thunder outside, low, close by: the wind had picked up and was blowing rain against the windows. I went to the front door and out. The rain was a torrent.

Dwight

The paperboy drove by in his pickup just after six Friday morning. I lay awake in bed with the windows open and the breeze riding in sweet and not yet hot, and heard the light *whump* of the rolled-and-rubber-banded weekly *Winsted Register-Citizen* hitting the driveway. Then the truck went past and I heard what had been there just before, the birds again, the doves cooing on my lawn. Just another sunny summer morning.

I lay in bed and tried to ignore the paper, the sound of it landing on the driveway, the fact of its existence. But this was impossible. There's a feeling you get if you live in the country but find yourself in the city one day, any city, walking around and minding your own business and believing yourself not just alone but one hundred percent anonymous, when suddenly from out of the blue, and almost always from behind your back, somebody calls out your name. The heart starts to go crazy. Whether you're innocent or guilty doesn't matter. It's the sound of your name in a place where you expected no one to know it that's enough to tip you over the edge, and for a moment you know exactly what it's like to be the wrong person in the wrong place, spotlighted, picked out of the lineup. And even if it turns out to be just a big fat mistake, everything afterwards feels personal. So I tried to forget about the newspaper sitting in my driveway, but I couldn't.

The article would be under "Crime Watch" or under "Accidents" or maybe even on the front page. There'd be facts, names and places. Last Sunday night the so-and-sos from such-and-such lost their son Josh. Car did not stop. The funeral was held on . . . Suspect still at large. Reward offered.

The father was tall and dark, thin, with glasses. I could see him clearly. I would always see him clearly. Without question he'd have a wife, probably other children. Now or in an hour they'd go outside for the newspaper—this paper or a different one, it didn't matter, there were crime watches and accidents and unsolved tragic incidents in every local weekly—and then over coffee, if they could stomach it, they'd see their own names in print and where they lived, and the name of their son who was dead and how he'd died. And it would all seem like a sick joke to them; as if they didn't already know their own names and where they lived and the name and age of their son and how he'd died.

A breeze eased in through the open windows. Outside, it was starting to heat up, it was going to be a hot day. The doves had stopped calling to each other and to me. A car drove by and in the silence afterwards there was a loneliness that wouldn't go away. I pulled the sheet off my naked body and lay there on the bed, imagining the tall, dark man sitting at a wooden table in some kitchen somewhere, reading the newspaper. His glasses were round and reflected light. I imagined him getting to the word "suspect" and not knowing what to do. Not knowing anything about me. Where my name should be he'd find just that word; and where my photograph should be he'd find nothing.

I imagined knowing him and him knowing me. I imagined telling him the truth about myself, filling in the blank places.

This suspect was thirty-eight years old. His body was of the burly, chunk-a-lunk variety—six feet tall, two hundred pounds. Big enough to hurt somebody. He'd played football in college (second-string tight end) until injuries knocked him out; there were operation scars on his right shoulder and left knee, and those joints ached in the cold weather. He'd broken his nose, too, or his old man had, long ago, and it had set wrong and there was a permanent bump there. It gave his face "character," people always said. His eyes were green if they were anything, and he had a cleft in his chin as if a little piece of him had fallen out during birth. His hair was brown and straight, with the first signs of gray, and he wore it short, lawyerly, though by now it was generally known in the area that his best days as a lawyer were behind him.

What else? He could remember an afternoon sitting in a graveyard with his back against the curved gray stone wall. The wall stones were large and round and they pressed against the bruises his old man had made earlier, and with the pain there was the smell of fresh-cut grass and turned soil. Then skip a few years and he could remember being big and strong for the first time, lifting weights in the gym at school and learning to hit the heavy bag and the speed bag. There was the smell of sweat and leather and the sound of his taped fists smacking against the bags, a different music from each, and the magic, rock-hard, lactic burning in his arms. He could remember people being afraid of him, and how his old man started looking like just another little man to him. He could not remember crying, ever.

What else? We were getting close now, the tall, dark man and I, making our way through the history. This was important. I wanted to tell him that the newspapers didn't give a shit about him. They wouldn't listen. Listening was a lost art and they weren't about to dust it off just for his sake. No, they'd tell him how it really was, who had been there on the dark road, what he and his family'd been through, the name of what they'd lost. The article would be maybe two inches long. It would be in a section like "Crime Watch" or "Accidents" or "Deaths," or maybe it would even be on the front page. It would contain all the necessary names but one.

He should throw the newspaper out. I wanted to tell him. He should take his wife's hand. He should talk and be listened to. He should know the whole story.

What else? Tell the truth now, don't lie. There were the elements of a life, yes indeed, basic things, rock-paper-scissors things, and then there was what you did with them. In the end it was only what you did with them that mattered. This was important. (Somehow, though, the suspect had not learned this.) Was the tall, dark man listening? There was love and marriage and then one day the suspect had hit his wife. There was a child, his only son, and the suspect had hit his son, too. And there was the rest of life, there was trying to be a father and a decent man, and the suspect had driven his car into another man's son and killed him and had not stopped.

Outside, another car went by. Maybe it was seven by now, neighbors going to work. Maybe it was already hot out there. Somewhere the tall, dark man was drinking coffee and reading the newspaper. I could hear birds again, not doves but chickadees and blue jays. And something else, too. What I heard was like ice, like ice cracking in the heat, and I brought my hands to my chest. Between the dense, mounded pectoral muscles there was the breastbone, thin and brittle, and I put my thumb against it, on the spot where the right front of my car would have hit his boy, shattering the bone, and I pressed.

Ethan

I left Grace sleeping. The early morning light came in through the half-curtained windows, and I left my dreams by the side of the dark road with my son, and climbed out of bed. Every night now was a graveyard visit.

Grace didn't even stir. I wondered if she'd taken something, some drug, so steady was her breathing. The light fell across her. Her closed eyelids looked swollen. Her jaw was clenched, a muscle working there, over and over. Still, she was beautiful. My beautiful wife. She lay on her back with the sheet fallen and her nightgown slipped off one shoulder, her breast exposed. I looked; I wasn't dead. I remembered the first time I'd seen her skin like this, unprotected and unadorned, as she lay on a thin mattress on the floor of my university apartment. She'd been twenty. Her eyes had been open then.

Suddenly I wanted to cover her; I reached down and tugged at the sheet. She didn't move. I smelled

the warm-laundry scent of her sleep and saw up close
the areola not perfectly round, the tiny bumps on the
raised pale pink luminous skin, as though she were
chilled. And the pinpoint indentation in the center of
the nipple, through which her milk had flowed. And I
remembered how she'd carried Josh around the garden with her day after day, feeding him as she went.
Talking to him. Telling him the names of things.

I finished covering her and turned away.

Knowing this: It was all still his. Belonged to him.
Everything he'd touched, needed, every place he'd
been.

The door to Emma's room stood open; she wouldn't
sleep with it closed. Her room was on the west side of
the house and the light within was gray. She'd kicked
the covers off during the night: tanned, thin legs; navy
T-shirt; blond head; thumb in mouth; long neck of
Twigs, the stuffed giraffe, held fiercely in the crook of
one arm, as if she were trying to love him to death. I sat
down on the edge of the trundle bed and put my hand
on her hip.

"Emma. Time to get up."

"No." A sleepy whine, she curled up double, folding Twigs's neck in two.

"It's Friday—camp today. Remember?" I shook
her gently until, finally, her eyes opened and blinked
at me. "Come on. Get some clothes on and I'll make
breakfast."

"Where's Mom?"

"We're letting Mom sleep in today."

"Why?"

"Come on now, hurry up."

I went out of the room, found Sallie getting up from her dog bed at the end of the hallway. She yawned, showing every tooth, and then stretched, forepaws straight out, bending low as a praying Muslim.

"Mecca's *that* way," I said, pointing to the east.

Raising herself, Sallie looked at me.

"Look, I don't care," I said. "Do what you want."

She followed me down the stairs.

Standing in the afterworld light of the refrigerator, staring into it, I saw half a package of English muffins, one egg, some skim milk, a jar of Dijon mustard. No cereal, no fruit. Nothing of any interest to a child. The freezer contained three sticks of butter, a bag of French-roast coffee beans, and a stack of empty blue ice trays.

Upstairs, the toilet flushed. Emma getting ready, doing what I'd asked. While I stood looking at the emptiness, trying to decide. Breakfast for my child. What would it be? Either choose or forget the whole thing. But I could not choose.

A noise freed me: Sallie scratching at the inside of the back door. I'd completely forgotten about her. I let her out and she raced over to her favorite tree, a big sugar maple, where she squatted and peed like the lady she was, looking at the heavens.

I stood in the doorway. Sunlight was visible, though

no sun. The morning air held just the remnants of the night, the dew already leaving the ground, becoming sky again. Good, country air. Mourning doves stepped gingerly across the grass, their heads bobbing in the manner of wise men, their throaty, ruffling calls speaking of safety and peace, proclaiming this land we'd come to, the life we'd chosen—away from danger, from noise, the reaches of artifice, the probing hands of strangers. Our children had never known cities.

Sallie raced around the tree and over the grass. The doves scattered into the air.

There was my own growing up. The only child of older parents, intellectuals both, who lived in fear. My father who watched in a kind of disbelief as year by year our neighborhood near the University of Chicago, where he taught linguistics, turned into a dangerous, unfamiliar place. Yet he was a stubborn man and would hear no talk of moving. As if the city— and by extension the world—had a responsibility to do right by him and he would hold his ground until that responsibility was met.

And then one night, as he walked home from the campus, he was mugged and badly beaten. I was ten years old. And I saw how after the incident he grew too afraid to walk home from work; too afraid, eventually, to take the bus. I saw how, though he still refused to talk of moving, every evening without fail my mother drove to his office and brought him home. And then at dinner he would rage to us about the violence of the world. It was for him a form of personal betrayal, and his feelings of helplessness were such that he could only intellectualize them.

And so as he aged, my father became a living paradox. He joined the movement of nonviolence and took to quoting, with Old Testament fury blazing in his eyes, Gandhi and King. He declared his hatred of guns and the people who used them. When I turned twelve, he told me that he would punish me if he ever heard that I'd been fighting at school, whatever the cause. Violence was weakness, he said, and neither he nor his son would ever be weak.

I left as soon as I was able. Found a life far from home. Married a woman with fears of her own but with strength too. And here we raised our children and taught them not to be afraid.

Sallie was sprinting across the front lawn. Happy dog after a pee. She was by the red garage, circling Grace's station wagon parked in the driveway. She disappeared behind it.

"Here, Sallie!" I called. I didn't want her wandering out to the road.

She reappeared a moment later, carrying a newspaper in her mouth.

"Sallie," I said. "Come here."

She let me take the paper from her. The *Lakeville Journal* that was thrown, freshly printed, onto our driveway every Thursday evening. This time we hadn't seen it. Grace had been in her study all evening and I'd been in mine, and Emma had been watching a video of *Beauty and the Beast*. I'd read for twelve hours yesterday, because that was what I could do. Never thinking that the paper had come.

It was damp now, from the dew. I didn't look at it. I took it inside, leaving Sallie to run around as she pleased. Emma was not in the kitchen, which was a relief. I dropped the paper on the table, took the coffee from the freezer and ground it and put it in a filter in the coffeemaker and turned on the machine. My heart was hammering inside my chest. When the coffee was done, I poured myself a cup and sat down at the table.

I found him first on page A2, under "Obituaries":

JOSHUA B. LEARNER

WYNDHAM FALLS—Joshua B. Learner, 10, died July 24, 1994, from injuries sustained when he was struck by a passing automobile on Reservation Road in North Canaan. He was the son of Ethan and Grace Learner.

Joshua Learner was born April 7, 1984, in Wyndham Falls, CT.

He was to enter the sixth grade in September at Sherman R. Lewis Public School on Route 44 in Wyndham Falls.

In addition to his parents, he leaves a sister, Emma, in Wyndham Falls; and a maternal grandmother, Leila Spring of North Carolina.

Funeral Services were held July 26 at a private location.

There were fourteen other obituaries on the page. My son was the youngest. The oldest was a woman ninety-six years old, who died in a nursing home of natural causes.

I took a sip of coffee, scalding my tongue. My hand shook, coffee spilling over the rim onto page A2 of the *Lakeville Journal*, soaking through to the end. The paper already damp anyway. I set the mug down on the table.

So clean, the obituary. A time-honored literary form. Move on, then. Get it over with.

On the next few pages the familiar section headings, so strange today as to seem like a series of surreal jokes: "Senior Menu"; "Salisbury Calendar"; "Canaan Chronicle"; "Kent Briefs"; "Northwest Corner." Then, on A6, under "Regional," I found him again:

BOY'S DEATH MOURNED IN WYNDHAM FALLS

WYNDHAM FALLS—Family and friends said their final goodbyes to Joshua Learner during private services at the Learner home last Tuesday.

The 10-year-old Pine Creek Road resident died at the scene of a hit-and-run accident July 24, as he was standing by the side of Reservation Road in North Canaan.

According to state police, the fifth grader was standing in front of Tod's Gas and Auto Body shop at about 8:45 p.m., presumably waiting for his parents, who were inside the gas station.

The identity of the driver remains under investigation.

Joshua Learner recently completed the fifth grade at Sherman R. Lewis Public School in Wyndham Falls, where he was in the school orchestra.

"Josh Learner was a prize student, and the most talented musician to come through this school since I've been here," said Lawrence Briggs, principal of the school since 1988.

Plans are under way by the school orchestra to plant a tree in his memory.

The boy's father, Ethan Learner, is a professor of English at Smithfield College in Great Barrington, MA. The boy's mother, Grace Learner, is a local garden designer.

Emma Learner, 8, sister of the deceased, is to enter the fourth grade at Sherman R. Lewis Public School in September.

There was nothing more.

I finished the coffee, staring out the window at the dog running there and the morning rising with relentless disregard for all souls alike. It was not any longer a question of theory or interpretation; of course, it never had been. I had left Josh standing by the side of the road because I lacked the courage to tell him not to. I turned my back on him to save myself the trouble. That was the truth. And it was beyond forgiveness. And the papers with their fastidious regard for fact had missed the truth.

And they had missed the other guilty party. The unknown man under investigation. The killer in his car. Who did not stop.

I got up, went into the pantry. The room was tiled

and cool, always cool, smelling of flour and soup cans and dry dog food. A familial smell, the smell of our house. The safe smell of stores in waiting, nourishment in reserve. Pancakes today, French toast tomorrow.

It required not thinking. From here on out. It required a state of suspended disbelief. Otherwise you might go insane. You might want to take the fucking house apart beam by beam, until it was spread all over the lawn, as if exploded, no more and no less than the pieces it came from.

You might want to kill yourself.

Grace

She was still sitting in her studio Friday afternoon when Ethan came in. She'd been there all day, listening to the phone ring, hearing the answering machine pick up, as if her only remaining power lay in this stillness that was like death. She did not move, did not speak. The machine took care of all that, marshaling the disembodied voices of friends and relatives into their respective corners of the room, where they stayed quiet and tame. Still, she listened, because any words were less poisonous than her own. As when Judy Aronson called for the second time: "Grace? Grace, are you there? Call me, honey. Please. I know how hard this must be for you." And Pam Foster too, to say that she and Dick had just heard from Judy, and how sorry . . .

Then the machine was full. Which was a relief. And she could sit curled on the green-velvet chair as the afternoon shadows lengthened from the world outside to the floor at her feet, and count the messages, each call a tiny red blink of light: *So sorry . . . So sorry . . .*

Until here, now, was Ethan. Standing before her, his face dark with stubble, wearing the same khaki pants and blue work shirt he'd worn since the funeral. The shirt had a hole in one elbow and the pants a black ink stain on the right front pocket. Though she could not judge him for this, she thought; she looked just as bad. Unkempt. Her jeans too long unwashed, a white T-shirt with a rust stain down the front, her feet bare.

He stood a few feet in front of her, crossed his arms over his chest. And something in the gesture made her feel unkind, as if he were a visitor and she were being rude to him. It was true: she had designed the room to be like this. It was hers and not for other people. It wasn't a sitting room. There was nowhere to sit but at the worktable or on the green chair.

"Where's Emma?" he asked.

"What?"

"Emma."

"Emma?" For a moment her heart stopped beating. *Emma*. She'd completely forgotten. Emma was at music camp. Three days a week, working on her piano technique with Mrs. Wheldon. Had stayed home this past Monday and Wednesday, but then after the funeral the parents had decided that it was important, probably it was important, for Emma to keep up with her life, to keep busy in spite of everything. So this morning Ethan had resumed the old schedule and driven Emma to school, where the camp was. It was her job to pick Emma up at the end of the day. It had always been her job, but today she'd forgotten about

Emma and now, realizing it, she felt frightened and ashamed. She felt angry. She wanted to hit something.

"She's at camp where she's supposed to be."

"And you're planning to pick her up?"

"Of course I am."

"What time?"

She didn't like his tone. It was a test of some kind and she knew already she would fail. "When do you think, Ethan? When it's over. Four-thirty."

"Grace, it's five-fifteen."

Now she was not curled up on the chair any longer but standing on her feet. Still, though, she was determined to sound firm, not to show him what a lost cause she was. "Is it? Well, then I guess I really blew it, didn't I? I guess I'm awful."

"That's not my point."

"No? So what is it, then? Your point."

Ethan sighed angrily and rubbed both his hands hard over his face. "Grace, just listen to me. It's all right. But one of us needs to go now and pick her up. That's all. Right now."

"I'll go. I'm going right now."

She was not going to cry. She picked up her shoes from the floor and walked right by him. They did not touch.

"Grace."

She turned around.

"What have you been doing all day?"

"Sitting here. Listening to the machine. It's full. It won't take any more messages. And you know what? I've decided I'm not going to listen to it any more."

Then she turned and walked out and left him standing in the room alone.

On Route 44 at the east end of Wyndham Falls stood the modern red-brick building with gray stone trim and raised gray stone crosses on its facade that was the Sherman R. Lewis Elementary School. The lobby was empty, cool; classes were long out for the summer. At first Grace could hear nothing but her own footsteps echoing on the tiled floor. The sound was haunting to her, full of Josh, and she was relieved, after she stopped walking and stood quietly in the square, empty space, to hear rising up from the basement the first blurred edges of a woman's voice, and then the high-octave tinkling of a piano.

She walked to the back of the lobby. The stairs leading down to the music rooms were there and the sounds were stronger. She heard piano notes. Then the notes ceased and Emma said, "Like that?" and Mrs. Wheldon answered, "Still too strong, Emma. Remember, *pianissimo*," and right afterwards the same notes could be heard again, climbing the stairs, only softer than before, and Grace leaned her back against the wall and stared across the lobby to the front entrance.

The gray stone crosses on the facade were visible from inside the building too, she saw now. She counted six of them. They were set into the red brick, they must have been three feet deep. All but the central overhead light was off in the lobby, and the walls were in shadow, with the crosses shining through as in a church, and as she stared up at the walls she felt something stir inside her chest and then fall away. She thought how these crosses had always bothered Ethan. He had even gone so far once as to say that he was glad his Jewish father hadn't lived to see his grandchildren going to a school with crosses built into its walls. He'd made no mention of his WASP mother's feelings on the matter, or about the fact that she was dead, too. Not that it mattered in the end. God had never meant very much to Ethan except as the protagonist of a long, imperfect, beautifully written work of literature called the Bible. It was not God's laws or proverbial wisdom that attracted him so much as the novelistic questions of individual character and motivation. Faith for Ethan could be distilled down to words, and words he could revere all right, but only through the ruthless lens of criticism.

She stood remembering how at the beginning of their relationship they had debated endlessly over the nature of faith. He kept trying to pin her down, make her say definitively what she believed in, where God lived for her, as if it were a house with a street number and mailbox. He couldn't accept her answer that she didn't know, that certainly she believed in Him and there had been moments in her life when she'd thought she'd known precisely where she lived in relation to Him (eight years old and finding in the attic the box of Mother's love letters to Daddy during the war in Korea), but that those moments had passed, and what remained was a constant wondering why and where and when it would finally be revealed to her, and that this, probably, was the imperfect faith she had come to live on.

They had talked and debated and argued, but they hadn't necessarily accepted or understood. And then, around the end of their first year together, as quickly and completely as it had risen the subject had dropped from their shared lives; they had moved on to other things.

Downstairs, there were still voices, but the music had stopped. Now the voices were growing louder. She pushed herself off the wall she'd been leaning against, and gathered herself, and started down the stairs.

"There's a room here where we can talk," Mrs. Wheldon said.

Grace followed her into one of the empty white music rooms. It was simple and small. There was a black upright piano and a lacquered black piano bench and beside it a folding metal chair. As in all basements, she thought, the light felt deathly.

"It's private here," Mrs. Wheldon said.

She was probably forty but looked younger. She wore a knee-length summer skirt and a white blouse that was oddly prim for someone so pretty and young-looking. Half-glasses hung by a chain from around her neck. The blouse was closed at the neck by a black ribbon tie, tied in a bow, and her sand-colored hair was pinned to her head in a kind of bun. It was an odd effect, Grace thought—noticing, at the same time,

that where Ruth Wheldon's calves came out of the
skirt they were shapely and young-looking and so were
her ankles.

"I'm sorry I'm so late," she murmured. She'd gone
and said it twice already, and now she'd said it again.
She felt a need.

"Don't be sorry," Mrs. Wheldon said. "Emma and
I had some extra scales to work on anyway."

But Grace was sorry just the same. She thought,
just before Mrs. Wheldon shut the door, that she
could hear Emma's footsteps on the tiled floor of the
lobby; she hoped Emma would wait there, where
she'd been told to, and not wander around. And then
the door shut and the room was suddenly, absolutely
quiet. The door was thick, for soundproofing, and
there was carpeting on the floor. Mrs. Wheldon sat
down on the corner of the piano bench and motioned
Grace to sit down too, on the folding chair, and Grace
sat down.

Mrs. Wheldon said, "I was hoping to get to talk to
you today."

Grace nodded but didn't say anything. She thought:
I am here. The folding chair was hard and uncomfortable, the metal seat unpadded and still faintly warm
where Mrs. Wheldon had been sitting just minutes
before, teaching Emma how to play the piano.

"Your husband left this morning before I had a
chance to say anything to him," Mrs. Wheldon said.

Grace nodded again, thinking that this woman was
the first stranger she'd seen since the funeral—though
not a stranger, exactly; Mrs. Wheldon had been giving

Emma piano lessons for close to a year. And for a few months her son, Sam, had even been a classmate of Josh's in the first grade—but then Josh was pushed ahead a year. Grace had seen Sam now and again since then, caught bodily in the throng of kids pouring out the doors of the school in the afternoon, after classes let out, and into the arms of anxious waiting parents like herself; a small, sad-looking boy with hair the color of fine yellow sand, like his mother's. He played the trumpet once in a while at school assemblies, not very well, and his name was Sam Arno, she remembered now, not Sam Wheldon. She felt almost as if she'd been thinking about the boy without knowing it. But that was impossible.

"I wanted to tell you how sorry I am, Mrs. Learner," Mrs. Wheldon said. "Everybody I know is so sorry. Josh was a wonderful boy. It was an unthinkable tragedy."

It wasn't the word "tragedy" that got through, or even her son's name on the lips of this woman, but the word "unthinkable": it pushed a button in her brain she didn't know was there, and the next thing Grace knew she was saying, in something close to a normal tone of voice, "Thank you, Mrs. Wheldon."

"Please. Call me Ruth."

"All right."

"I wanted to talk about Emma."

"If you want."

"Something like this is hard enough for grownups, but for kids . . . I've been worried about her."

"Of course."

"Can I ask if she's getting any counseling?"

"She isn't."

"Do you and your husband have any plans?"

"No," she said. "Not yet."

Mrs. Wheldon looked as though she were about to say something else, but then didn't. Silence started edging into the room. It was like smoke and not the relief Grace had thought it would be. Without her being aware of it, Mrs. Wheldon's left hand was reaching for the closed lid of the piano, a couple of her fingers nervously dancing, but then she noticed it and withdrew it onto her lap. Grace saw that Mrs. Wheldon was afraid. Afraid of what had happened to a ten-year-old boy on a dark road at night, afraid of accidents and death and another woman's pain, another woman's guilt. Watching other people fall apart was a lousy business, Grace thought—and she reached over and did what the other woman wanted to do herself but wouldn't: she opened the lid of the piano, exposing the long, dulled row of keys, ivory and black. She was sick to hell of talking about her life.

"Mrs. Wheldon?"

"Ruth," said the other woman.

"Ruth, how's your son? How's Sam? I haven't seen him in a long time."

Mrs. Wheldon let her fingers touch the piano. She played two of the keys, middle C and F-sharp, in quick succession, and the quick probing notes filled the room and then died. Then she was embarrassed, her face coloring up. "Sam's fine. He's okay," she said. "Thanks for asking." Her accent had changed slightly, it seemed to Grace; let go of something, turned linear and flat.

"Does he still play the trumpet?"

"Oh, yes." A smile began to appear on Mrs. Wheldon's face but was pulled back. "He plays all the time. He makes a racket."

"I remember hearing him play at assembly."

"Of course," Mrs. Wheldon said quickly, "Sam's isn't the kind of talent Josh's was with the violin. I was always sorry I didn't have the skills to teach him."

"Would you say hello to Sam from me when you see him? He won't remember me, but I'd like you to anyway."

"Okay." Ruth Wheldon was looking at her strangely. But Grace didn't care. She no longer expected to be known or understood. She had all kinds of memories, too, and they were all around her now in the little room, and it was impossible to speak about them with anyone who was alive.

She stood up. "I'd better be going. Thank you, Ruth."

"Don't go." Ruth Wheldon hurried to her feet.

"Emma's waiting for me."

"Sure," the woman said. "I'm sorry. Stupid of me."

Grace shook her head and turned to go. She was almost to the door.

"Mrs. Learner?"

"Yes?"

"Wednesday is the last day of camp. We always end with a concert in the gym here, so all the kids who want to can play for their parents and friends. It's less pressure than you'd think. Really, it's about family and showing appreciation for how hard the kids've practiced. Emma's worked really hard this month, Mrs. Learner. She's a good girl and she's improved a lot and we're all proud of her, and I have to say I think it's important for her now, given everything, to get up and play for everybody and for everybody to listen."

"Does she want to?"

"I asked her today and she said yes."

She tried to picture Emma playing the piano up on a stage, but she could not. Somehow, her vision of things got stuck in the audience, all the people she knew, who were full of pity and whispers.

"If she wants to play, I wouldn't stop her," she said.

"I'm glad," Ruth Wheldon said. "So I'll see you all there Wednesday evening?"

"I guess so."

She said good-bye then, and went out of the room and up the stairs to the lobby. Emma was there, beneath the high wall of stone crosses.

Dwight

It was my policy, for the weekly pickups and drop-offs of my son, to arrive unannounced when possible. On the Sunday mornings when Ruth didn't have Sam already waiting for me out on the porch—his hair combed and his teeth brushed and, for all I knew, flossed; looking every inch like somebody else's child—I liked to sneak in the front door without knocking, a practice which drove Ruth up the wall because she knew perfectly well what I was up to, how my real goal was just the gathering of evidence. A sly glimpse, maybe, of the family troika sitting around the breakfast table; of Sam perusing the Sunday comics while ignoring every attempt on the part of his stepdad (whom he thought was just plain dull, if not stupid) to make conversation and "bond"; of Ruth ignoring Norris, too, for not dissimilar reasons (that she thought he was just plain dull, if not stupid); and even of Norris himself, dressed in madras and verbally flailing, on the verge of tossing up the white flag and beating yet another hasty retreat to the green peace of the country-club golf course.

What was also true, though, was that for all my guerrilla tactics to see *her* life, Ruth didn't know or care a whole lot about mine in return. So long as my smallish child-support checks showed up on time (they were voluntary, not compulsory, on my part since she'd married Norris), and I didn't fudge my hours with Sam, her curiosity about my daily existence was minimal. She'd never been to my house in Box Corner, although it was only ten miles away. She never asked me about my work or how my friends were. Which was okay, in some ways, because my house was not worth seeing and my job not worth talking about and my friends were few. Because much had been diminished since the old days, and, like many whose lives are fueled largely by regret, I'd come to feel that what was diminished was better left to the dark, in private.

Either way, now that our history together had been written and tossed out, Ruth didn't seem to care two cents what I did outside of my dealings with our son. It was as if she could not forget my past and could not remember my present.

Maybe it was sad, the fact that I meant so little to her. I knew it was lonely. Still, I counted on it making the lying I had to do easier.

I went up the steps to the porch and into the house. Nobody saw me. From upstairs I heard Ruth's voice in a nagging vein; it sounded as if she was after someone about something. I turned left from the foyer and went through the dining room (I remembered the Sheffield antique shop where we'd bought that wrought-iron chandelier for $138) and into the kitchen, where I found Norris sitting alone at the breakfast table in his green and yellow golf clothes, drinking coffee and reading the *Litchfield County Times*. He nearly knocked over the mug when he saw me.

"Dwight!"

"Hello, Norris. Don't get up."

But Norris was already up, pumping my hand, and wouldn't sit down. "When'd you get here, Dwight?"

"Just this second."

"How'd you get inside?"

"Just walked in."

Norris nodded vigorously but seemed at a loss what to say next. Color had suddenly appeared in his cheeks, and I had the feeling that if he'd had a crowbar in his hands and been a different sort of man, he'd have gone for me.

"Is Sam here, Norris? How about Ruth?"

"Upstairs," Norris said.

"Maybe I'll just go up and let them know I'm here."

"You mean go upstairs?"

"Either that or yell."

"I don't think Ruth would go for that at all, Dwight, to be honest," Norris said—a little nervously, I thought. "Why don't you have a seat? How about some coffee? We've got a fresh pot right here."

Norris poured me a cup of coffee and refilled his own, and we sat down across from each other. He seemed a little wired all of a sudden, blowing unnecessarily on his coffee and drumming his fingers on the table. And I thought, not for the first time, that my evidence-gathering tactics were a sham. I wasn't learning anything I didn't already know, and all the old news was bad news at that.

Norris cleared his throat. "So, Dwight, how's tricks?"

A solid *thump* came from upstairs, something chunky and serious, like a bowling ball, hitting the floor right above our heads. Norris made no sign that he'd heard anything unusual. It was Sam's room up there, and right afterwards I heard Ruth's shrill warning cutting through the timbers: "Don't play with that in here!" And I tried to imagine what it was she could be talking about, what piece of sports equipment or farm machinery Sam was chucking around up there. But it had been a long time since I'd seen the inside of his room, and I was no longer well acquainted with his inventory.

"Not much to tell, Norris," I said. "You know, same old life."

"I do know that, Dwight, I certainly do." Norris did a little more finger drumming on the table, then abruptly stopped. "Say, how's the car?"

"What?"

"I said, how about the car?"

I was careful to take a sip of coffee then and not to spill. "What about it?"

"Get that headlight fixed?"

"Headlight? As a matter of fact—"

"You know, the cops're rough on that one. They'll ticket you for sure—hundred, maybe a hundred and fifty buckaroos—and then to top it off they'll haul you in and treat you like a bona fide criminal." For some reason, Norris found this funny and laughed, showing some silver in the molars. "It's a double whammy."

"As a matter of fact, Norris," I said, "my car's in the shop. It turned out the headlight was just the tip of the iceberg. The transmission's totally shot. The guy over there said it's so bad I ought to think about scrapping it." I paused. "So I'm leasing."

Norris whistled. "That was one expensive dog you hit, huh?"

I made myself smile. "It's all right. I got a real good deal on a lease. Zero money down."

"Well, that's good, I guess," Norris said. "But you know, Dwight, hitting a dog is just plain bad luck. Just about the worst luck there is. And a *black* dog?" Norris shook his head. "Whoo, boy. Glad it wasn't me."

"It was an accident."

"Not according to the police," Norris said, taking a sip of coffee. "You hit a dog and don't report it, they'll fine you for that too, you know. One way or another, they get you."

I studied him for a moment, to see what he might be getting at. But he was just holding up his cup and looking into it, turning it this way and that, and didn't seem to have meant anything.

"I reported it the next day," I lied.

"Well, lawyers know best," Norris said without conviction. He got to his feet, poured himself another mug of coffee. Then he sat down again.

"I've been worried about Sam, Norris. Since the accident. Has he seemed upset to you?"

"Upset?" This didn't seem to have occurred to Norris; he shook his head again, pursing his lips. "Not especially, no. Not to me he didn't. No screaming nightmares, if that's what you mean, Dwight. Of course, there's that eye. More coffee?"

Before I could answer, I heard light, quick feet on the stairs and then on the old floors in the dining room, and in a moment Sam appeared in the kitchen. The first thing I noticed was his eye. It was still blue and purple in places but starting to turn yellowish all around, which was less shocking maybe, but uglier. And the eye itself was blood red from the broken vessels. It was a jeweled ruby eye and he wore it like a young prince, as if he knew its true value all right but couldn't have cared less. He smiled a little shyly when he saw me, and I felt my heart lift for the first time in a week.

"Hey, sport."

Sam looked from me to Norris and back to me. "Hi, Dad." Now his voice was quiet, quieter than his footsteps running through the house, and he was looking down at his sneakered boy's feet, which he had stacked, one on top of the other, like a flamingo's. He was wearing cutoff jeans and a white T-shirt.

"Is your mother coming down?"

"I guess so." Staring at his feet.

I was experienced in this sort of shyness and tried not to let it bother me. If you don't see your son for four years and then see him only on Sundays for eight hours at a pop, and there's a new man in the house to boot, then there is a shift in the numbers, the natural math of loss and gain. Compare it to anything you want—the ocean carrying sand away to another part of the beach—but don't expect what you left behind one week to still be there exactly as you left it the next. At the start of every Sunday my son was shy with me again. Yet each time I tried to have confidence. I told myself that we'd been through worse than this in the past, had closed more distance than this.

"I thought we'd head on over to my place for a little while," I said. "See what you and I can kick up. Sound okay?"

"Yeah."

"Good. All right." I stood up and so did Norris—immediately, as if he was attached to me by a string. "Thanks for the coffee, Norris. We'll be back at the usual time."

"Um, actually, Dwight, I think Ruth wanted to have a word with you."

"With me?"

"That's what she said."

"Well, that's fine, Norris, as long as she shows up by the time Sam and I get out to the car. That sounds fair, doesn't it?"

"Well, I don't know, Dwight. . . ."

I put my hand on Sam's shoulder and led the way out of the kitchen. Norris followed. We were just stepping out onto the porch when I heard Ruth coming down the stairs behind us. A moment later she came out onto the porch. Today she wore a little denim vest and plaid short-legged cotton pants that looked as if they'd been in the deep freeze since the Eisenhower administration, and white bobby-type socks and a pair of Keds. The whole thing put me at a loss.

"Well, Dwight."

"Hello, Ruth."

"Did Norris tell you I wanted to talk?"

"I told him," Norris said.

"He told me."

"So can we talk?"

"All right," I said. "Sam, why don't you and your stepdad go check out the new set of wheels while your mom and I have a little talk. Okay?"

Sam nodded, and he and Norris went down the porch steps and across the little lawn to the Corsica. Ruth and I stood side by side watching as Norris opened the driver's door and Sam climbed in behind the wheel, and then Norris went around and got in the passenger's side. It looked like a driving lesson.

"You look good, Ruth," I said. "Your figure is as fine as it ever was."

"I'm glad you like it," Ruth said coolly.

"I mean it."

"That's nice. Listen, Dwight. I took Sam to the doctor Tuesday. For that eye."

"And?"

"Nothing's broken."

"I could've told you that. In fact, I did."

"I wanted a professional opinion."

"So you got one. What else?"

"Insurance won't cover the visit."

"Is that what this is about?" I sighed. "Just send me the bill, Ruth. Okay?"

"Thank you." There was color in her cheeks. Embarrassment, I guessed. She was not beyond it after all.

"Well, if that's it, then we'll be going. The clock's ticking. I'll have him back on time. Promise." I turned to go, but she stopped me with a hand on my arm.

"Dwight?"

"What?"

"I saw Grace Learner the other day."

At the mention of the name I went still. A sudden meltdown in my bowels caused a rush of heat up to my face. "I don't know who that is," I said.

"Didn't you see the papers?"

"No."

"Her son was killed last Sunday night. A hit-and-run over by Tod's Gas on Reservation Road. They have no idea who did it. Can you imagine that? There couldn't be anything worse than that."

"They don't know who did it?"

"No idea."

I breathed out privately, as relief spread itself through my body like a tonic. "How'd you happen to see her?"

"Her daughter's at the camp and she came to pick her up. I tried to tell her how sorry I was, how sorry everybody is, but I'm afraid it didn't come out right.

141

She looked—I don't know, she looked just kind of broken."

There were tears in Ruth's eyes, something I hadn't seen for years.

"Dwight, their son was Sam's age. He was only ten years old. I just can't stop thinking, What if it'd been Sam instead? It could have happened to anybody, but it happened to them, not us. I don't think I could live through something like that."

Ruth was standing close to me, closer than she had for a long time; then in a moment she was leaning closer still, as if she wanted to be held. So I did just that. There on the porch in plain view of our son and her husband, I put my arms around her and felt the old feeling well up briefly between us, old and familiar and gone. For those few moments it didn't matter what I'd done, I felt our shared fear for Sam and what the world might do to him; we were his protectors. Until in my ear Ruth whispered "Okay" and opened her arms. I stood back and we separated. Before I knew it, I was walking across the little lawn to the car.

Getting out from the passenger's side, Norris gave me a Charles Bronson staredown that would have flattened a weaker man. He was justly aggrieved that I'd laid hands on his wife, and maybe he was even a little confused. But hard as I tried, his feelings had no effect on me. I looked at him as if I'd never seen him before. And then I drove my son away from that house and over to my own.

Ethan

Sunday: Josh had been dead a week.

Our house the site of a wordless, internalized diaspora over a landscape riven with fault lines: Emma in her room and Grace in her studio and me in my study. Silence.

Take away the ritual of meals from a family and what you have left is a way station; human contact is not guaranteed, even by love. It must be fought for, earned, desired, fed. Hope and courage are required. The last time we'd all eaten together had been at the concert, the four of us gathered on the blanket, sublime music in the air. Josh sat Indian-style and ate the only food he ever truly enjoyed eating, which was a bologna-and-cucumber sandwich on white bread with the crusts cut off, no mayonnaise, no mustard, and a pint of Hershey's chocolate milk and cookies. A bubble of self-containment around him, of private serene concentration, like a child mystic, oblivious to his father's probing gaze, the old man's hungry, thwarted desire to know his son's innermost thoughts, intent upon just this: the long thin fingers pulling the carton open into a wide square brown mouth, dunking the cookies one by one into the milk, until they were perfect.

I was in my study now.

Seeing his hands, which were beautiful.

Remembering his hands, seeing his hands holding a rope swing when he was nine.

Remembering the rope hanging from a tall elm by the Connecticut River, and his hands holding on to it, and the sunshine filtering through the leaves.

He is afraid. He does not want to. He stands on a low wooden platform that looks down the sloping field to the gray-green river. I stand with him. I tell him to place his feet on the knot at the bottom of the swing, to squeeze the rope between his knees. I take his hands and place them around the rope, which is rough-hewn and three inches thick; and I tell him to hold on tight, he will be fine, it will be fun; and I say "Ready, set, go"; and I give him a hard fatherly shove that sends him sailing out over the platform into free space, over the ground sloping away, and the rope with his hands locked around it rising into sky; and I watch his body rise and soar, and he is soundless. And then, at the apex of the rope's flight, I watch him fall like a stone. He just seems to let go. It is about twelve feet to the ground. He lands in a brittle little heap. And I run to him.

He is unhurt. It is a miracle. He picks himself off the ground, dirt on his knees, and walks past me without a word. Because I have lied to him.

Dwight

The ball game was on the radio. Sam and I listened to it as we stood on the lawn playing catch—Sam in his cutoffs and white T and me the old man in ancient semi-athletic gear: knee-length Bermudas and a U Conn sweatshirt with the sleeves hacked off at the shoulder (the Spartacus of the senior league). The sound of the ball hitting our mitts was constant but different each time. It was music, more complicated than you might have thought, and more pleasurable too.

I threw the ball and Sam caught it a little south of the webbing, pretty much dead center, and the ball went *smack!* against the oiled leather and his palm, calling back in some unexpected way my growing up, raising those years between us in the warm summer air, leather and sweat and the smacking sound of my fists hitting the bags in the gym at school, long ago. "Ouch!" I said, trying at the last second to make it sound comical.

"Ouch!" Sam yelled back, imitating me, and then he laughed a happy laugh, yanking his hand out of the mitt and shaking it as if it was on fire, which made me laugh, too. We were not bad clowns after all, the two of us.

"I thought you were supposed to be a tough kid," I said, smiling.

"I *am* tough!"

"Could've fooled me."

"I'm tougher than you, Dad! Why'd you say ouch?"

"Empathy," I said. "Now toss me the ball, sport."

But he wasn't ready to throw the ball just yet. "What's 'empathy'?"

"'Empathy' is a word that means . . ." I paused to consider. "I don't know, I guess you could say it means I'm thinking about you. That's all. Thinking so hard about what I think you're feeling that I start to feel it too."

Sam didn't say anything. The look on his face said he was working through my explanation and possibly growing skeptical of it.

"Your hand doesn't hurt," he said finally. A declaration of fact. He threw the ball and I caught it.

"You're right," I said. "It doesn't." I wound up and threw the ball back to him—easy, but not so soft as to take the luster off his pride. This time he caught it in the webbing like a little pro. "It's complicated."

"How?"

"Well, in this case I guess you could say empathy's

got more to do with what I feel in my heart than what you feel in your hand."

Sam plucked the ball from his mitt and studied it. He checked out the grass stains and the nicks. There was a seriousness of intent in his face, a decency of spirit, that I prized in him above all other things.

"You mean your heart hurts?"

"If I think yours does."

"You should shake it," he said. "It helps the pain go away."

"You're right. I should."

"You told me that, Dad. Remember?"

"I remember, Sam."

He threw me the ball then, and I caught it.

He said he wanted hot dogs for dinner. Ball Park Franks were his favorite. I kept them in the freezer just for his visits. On occasion he liked to chant the old Ball Park radio jingle, "They plump when you cook 'em." I took a package out now and set it on the kitchen counter, hard as a brick, and reached into the drawer beneath the electric oven and pulled out the nonstick fry pan Donna had given me for Father's Day. A Tony Bennett song was playing on the radio— it was five o'clock, and the Sox game was over and so was the postgame show—and as I opened the package of hot dogs I whistled along as best I could with the music and the singing. Thinking there was just time enough to have a few dogs and some Sprite and then

I'd drive him over to Ruth's and it would be the end of a good day. I switched the burner on.

"Aren't we gonna cook outside?" Sam was sitting on one of the high stools at the pale blue Formica counter, drinking a can of Sprite, his feet dangling almost a yard off the ground.

"No," I said.

"I thought we were gonna cook outside."

"We don't have time. I've got to get you back to your mother's by seven."

"It tastes better outside," Sam said.

"You're right, it does. And we still don't have time."

"And it's funner."

"'More fun.'"

"More fun," Sam said. "It is."

"Depends for who. I'm the cook and it's not more fun for me. It's more work. I've got to go get the grill out—"

"Last time you promised we could."

"No," I said. "Not last time."

"The time before."

"Maybe I did. I don't remember."

"You did. You promised."

"Okay. I did. We still don't have time."

"I really want to," Sam said.

"No, Sam."

"Please."

"You're not whining, are you? Convince me you're not whining."

"I'm not whining."

"Good."

"Dad?"

"What, Sam?"

"Look at the stove."

I looked at the stove. The pan was dry as bone and a thick cloud of black smoke was rising up out of it. "Fuck!" I said. I switched off the burner and grabbed a dish towel and chucked the still smoking pan into the sink, where, with the addition of a little water, it sizzled and popped and finally lay dead.

I turned around to find Sam laughing gleefully and imitating me.

"Fuck!" he said, just the way I had.

I glared at him and he stopped laughing. "You think that's funny?"

"Sort of."

I smiled a little. "You're right. It's sort of funny."

Sam was getting down off the high stool. "So're we gonna cook outside?"

"Looks like it."

"Can I get the grill?" He was full of beans now, standing by the counter, his hands fiddling with the lid of the cigar box that held my keys and junk and change.

"Okay."

I spoke without thinking. Before I knew it, he'd grabbed the spare garage-door opener out of the cigar box and pressed the rectangular white button; then, just as I realized what was happening, he went running out of the kitchen.

I shouted his name, shouted for him to wait. Maybe he didn't hear. Maybe he heard and was simply too revved up to stop. The screen door banged shut and out the window I saw him tearing across the lawn toward the garage. I felt something pop in my veins. In seconds I was out of the kitchen and through the front door onto the lawn, running flat out. I saw him ahead, already closing in on the garage, and beyond him the pale light spilling out of the open carport onto the dark tar drive, mingling almost invisibly with the late-afternoon light. I was gaining on him. He wasn't running very fast. He could have been anybody. There was the white Corsica sitting in the drive, pointing its nose at my own car now exposed to the road but still hidden from him and me. I shouted his name again and he looked over his shoulder and saw me chasing, but just laughed and kept on running—it was a game of some kind, a race, and he hoped to win it. I put my head down and ran harder. Any moment the taillights of the Taurus would come into view and he'd see it parked there and want to know why. I ran as if my life depended on it, and when he was just in front of me I reached out and grabbed a fistful of the back of his T-shirt and threw him hard to the ground.

He tumbled once, twice—it was slow motion to me. First the look of astonishment on his face: it had been a game, a race. Then astonishment evaporated and pain was his universe. It wasn't just physical. One and a half somersaults and he was lying on his back in the grass, the wind knocked clear out of him, his head not ten feet from the driveway. For a moment he stared straight up at the sky (the sky had never lied to him). The tears were starting; everything he believed in was not that way. The old man could not be trusted. Again. There was just my meaty face leaning down over him, my big-knuckled hands held out like clothes hanging on a line to dry, my mouth so full of "sorry"s and the word "forgive." Sorry old man. Then there were just two choices left to him—either curl up in a ball or run away. Sam ran away. While I stood flat-footed on the lawn and watched him disappear into the house.

On the drive back to Ruth's he sat all the way against the door, as far from me as he could. I spoke to him but he wouldn't speak back. He wouldn't look at me. He'd stopped crying before we left my house. It was just his body I had in my car, not any of the stuff that made him who he was. I might have been delivering a package.

I kept talking. I don't know what I said besides "sorry." My hands were shaky on the steering wheel and my thoughts erratic. I recalled that in some Islamic countries thieves are punished by having their hands chopped off. We passed a two-pump gas station that was closed for business, and I saw myself losing my hands one by one, then my feet. I saw myself losing my tongue, and it was not as terrible as you might think. There was all manner of relief for the crooked and the bad, I imagined, but I did not say this to my son, sitting with his head practically hanging out the open window so as not to have to look at me.

We were getting near Bow Mills. Train tracks ran

along the western edge of town. The trains were freight luggers and they ran at odd hours day and night. I looked ahead to where the tracks crossed the road like stitches binding a wound, and remembered the sound of the train passing in the middle of the night, the haunting call of its whistle, how I used to wake to find Ruth already sitting up in bed beside me. I remembered Sam rushing into the room in his pajamas, four years old and climbing into bed with us. Then the house so quiet after the train had gone through, the ghost of the whistle like just a fragment of some dream, and Sam wedged in between us like a pillow, the three of us wide awake and listening. Now as we came to the tracks the red warning arms started to swing and flash, and the bell began clanging and the guardrail swung down. I stopped the car and turned off the gas.

"Train," I said.

Sam said nothing and kept his face right where it was, looking due south out his window. Like that, he'd only be able to see the train after it passed.

"You'll miss it," I said to the back of his head.

"I don't care," he said.

"Yes, you do."

"No, I don't."

The train was coming slowly, just an engine and a few boxcars. The growing density of sound and the earth rumbling under our tires; like a surge of current looking for some place to go, I felt the urge to drive the car onto the tracks. But I did nothing.

"I can't apologize again, Sam. Saying how sorry

I am a hundred times doesn't make it mean any more. It just makes it cheaper."

"I hate you," Sam said.

My head fell back—as if he'd placed his thumb between my eyes and pushed. The train came down on us like a tight fist of storm, roiling the air and entering the heart. Sam put his hands over his ears. He kept them there till the train had passed and the warning had stopped and the guardrail was raised; kept them there, in fact, until he was home and safe again with his mother. At which point he left me without a word.

Ethan

I had to get out of that house.

I showered, shaved. I left the house quietly, no see-you-laters, with two spots of toilet paper stuck to my neck, pinked with blood. Slamming the car door, turning on the engine, I thought how Grace must be listening. How she would have turned to look out her studio windows, which, on purpose, faced away from the road. How the whole point of those windows was to protect her from other people—people, perhaps, like me—the cars coming in, the cars going out. How her room was green and it was cool and it was private and it was hers.

I drove in the only direction that occurred to me; west on 44, then north on 7. Half an hour away, Smithfield College sat nestled between two hills above the town of Great Barrington. It was small and liberal and pretty, and I'd been teaching there for twelve years. I could have driven to it in my sleep. I climbed the hill, rising through leafy green trees, past houses white and gray and brown. A black dog stood at the edge of the road, barking. Then the houses fell back and the trees fell away and the brow of the hill stood clear and green. I passed the entrance sign that declared, "Smithfield College, Founded 1902," and the man-made lake, the eight tennis courts and the playing field, still patchy from the end of lacrosse season. The sun was low, turning a faint orange. A pack of cross-country runners appeared up ahead, bunched like Canada geese. I passed them. The road sloped down the hill and to the right, into a hollow where, for a time, it evened out. The air smelled of pine needles. I passed the red-brick freshman dorms and the Greek Revival dining hall, and the log-cabin student union donated by some alum who'd gotten rich selling mail-order home kits in the Pacific Northwest. My car climbed the second, twin hill and went past the sweet yellow-painted Colonial that housed the registrar and the president's office, and then the tiny white music building with the stained-glass windows in the shape of Arthurian shields that had always felt to me like a holy place in miniature, a divine closet, where more than once Josh had practiced his violin while I graded papers. I parked in the lot behind the red-brick English Department building, adjacent to the heavy-stoned Richardsonian library with the crimson roof, which contained forty-six thousand volumes, two of them by me. There was one other car in the lot, a red Jeep that belonged to an assistant English professor named Jean Olsen. I got out and walked inside.

The lights were off and I left them that way. Downstairs, the student lounge was empty. The low-slung furniture with the rough orange fabric—endemic to such places—seemed to glow in the dusky natural light, as did the posters taped to the walls: Literary Ireland; the Tower of London and the Beefeaters; Barnes and Noble's take on Oscar Wilde, right beside James Michener. At the far end of the room a coffeemaker lay disassembled on a long folding table, like a bomb waiting to be put together.

My footsteps echoing on the linoleum, I went up the stairs to the second floor, into the empty faculty lounge, where the furniture was the same as below but the posters were better and the rows of wooden mail holes looked like a Chinese puzzle. A vending machine hummed and knocked. All down the long hall the doors were closed except for one at the end, where a wedge of light spilled out, breaking into the otherwise unrelieved dimness, and from which I could hear the rapid clicking of fingers on a computer keyboard. I remembered Jean Olsen's Jeep downstairs, and the book-length study of R. P. Blackmur she was writing, and her desperate, decent hope for tenure, and I felt nothing and wished she'd never left her house. My office was three down from hers and I moved quietly. I had the door unlocked and shut behind me, the light on, before I felt the pressure drop and the solitude take hold; the solitude I needed. I'd made it undetected. Everything was the way I'd left it. The window was closed. The six-week-old air was crammed with dust, and the dust entered my nostrils and mouth, it was on my tongue, tasting of death, it was thick on the surface of my desk, on the spines of my books, on the framed pictures of my wife and children.

Sound and movement from the bottom of the ocean: I blinked and raised my head off my arms. The door was open, a person standing in the shadows. A woman. Jean Olsen. I was still hunched over my desk, where I'd been sleeping—not sleeping, passed out. My neck was stiff and painful. I made myself straighten up.

"Should I turn the light on?" Jean asked.

"No."

"Should I leave?"

I didn't answer.

"Then I'll stay until you definitely kick me out." Jean came deeper into the room, plopped herself down on the worn brown-corduroy couch that for thirty years had sat in my father's office at the University of Chicago. "I had a feeling it was you. When I heard footsteps a while ago. I couldn't think of anybody else who'd be here on a summer night."

"Except you," I said dully.

"Right. Except me."

It was like being underwater. I could hardly see her expression in the dimness. Then through the open door I heard the vending machine start up, a faint, motel-like humming. I rubbed my neck and felt the crushing weight inside inexplicably shift from my chest to my abdomen, where it weighed more and hurt more and at the same time felt more remote. If this was grief, I did not understand. I was beyond touching, this life or any other, and while Jean Olsen sat looking at me I tried to remember which drinks exactly could be bought for seventy-five cents and a trip to the faculty lounge: Pepsi, Mountain Dew, Sprite, Nestea, Dr Pepper. . . . Suddenly, the machine fell silent again. And Jean Olsen let the shoes drop off her feet onto the floor, one and then the other.

"You know," she said, "you could really use some air in here."

I said nothing.

"I'm going to open the window a bit, all right?" She got up and cranked open the window half a foot. Evening air breezed in, surprisingly fast. The sound of crickets. Jean sat down again. "And in spite of what you said about the light, I'm going to turn on this little reading lamp right here, okay? I think it would help."

The lamp came on. We both sat blinking. Jean was wearing faded blue jeans and a tank top that showed off her tanned arms. Her face was handsome and strong, her hair cut shorter than mine. She was thirty-one years old, still with the tall, firm, hipless body of a girl athlete. She sat with her knees up, her bare feet comfortably splayed over the worn corduroy.

After a long silence, she said, "What happened to you and your family is beyond awful."

"It didn't happen to me," I said. "It happened to Josh. He's dead, I'm alive."

"It happened to you too, Ethan."

"It happened because I let it happen."

"That's not true—"

"What do you know about it?" I said.

"Nothing," Jean murmured. She looked away. The room was oppressively silent.

"I'm sorry," I said. "Forgive me."

Her shoulders rose in an uncertain shrug. "It's okay." She got up and went to the window, looked out through the finely meshed bug screen that made the night beyond appear washed out, used.

"How's Blackmur?" I asked, as kindly as I could.

Jean gave a thin little smile. "Critical."

"You're smart, Jean. Smart and honest. It'll work out."

"I didn't come in here to talk about me," Jean said. She turned from the window and faced me. "I was thinking after I heard you come in about how you stood up for Larissa and me two years ago."

"I didn't do anything special."

"We wanted to live together in a college *dorm*, Ethan, as faculty advisors and as lesbians, and you made them do the right thing. It was a big deal for us." There was a hardback copy of Henry James's *Notebooks*, edited by Leon Edel, sitting on my desk, and Jean reached out and picked it up. Dust grayed her fingertips and she wiped her hand on the leg of her jeans. She opened the thick book and flipped through the first few pages. Her eyes were on the writing as she said, "I guess I just wanted to come in here and remind you that you're a good man."

Her words did something, had an effect all their own; hidden beneath the desk, my hands gripped one another tightly. My voice was stiff. "I appreciate that, Jean."

"I keep remembering this day last fall," Jean said, still looking at the pages of the book. "I think it was Columbus Day, because the campus felt totally empty. I was walking past the music building, coming up here to do some work, when I heard someone playing the violin. It was really beautiful and I stopped to listen. I stuck my head inside. Josh was sitting on a chair at the back, up on that little raised platform where we have the concerts. He was practicing. There was a music stand in front of him, but most of the time he kept his eyes closed, and his body looked scrunched up and relaxed at the same time, and the sunlight was coming through one of the stained-glass windows and making his face into a rainbow. He was so beautiful, Ethan. And it was obvious you thought so, too. I could only see the back of your head. You were sitting in the last row of benches, grading papers. But every once in a while you'd look up at him and nod."

Jean closed the book. She put it down. She looked up and saw that I was crying. "And I wanted to tell you that I never had a father like that. Most people don't. Most people grow up waiting for their father to come and listen and nod, but he never does. He's too busy watching the playoffs or taking the goddamn lawn mower apart to listen. You listened to him, Ethan. You *heard* him."

I sat still behind my desk. I couldn't speak or otherwise move, and Jean did the only right thing then.

"I'm going to leave you alone now," she said.

Grace

She woke to an empty house. She woke in a fog, with no sense of herself. The dimensions of her life came back to her only gradually. She lay unmoving and felt the walls close around her, rough and cold to the touch.

The clock read 10:45. It was Monday—the day she'd promised herself she would start to do some of the things required of her. There were so many things. Ends to tie up, holes to fill. She shut her eyes and saw Josh's casket disappearing into the ground.

Deep under the covers, she curled into a ball, into her center, seeking a primordial comfort.

Downstairs, in robe and bare feet, she sat at the kitchen table with a mug of coffee. She couldn't eat. Just the sight of a package of English muffins in the refrigerator made her long to be sick. She could imagine starving herself to death without any trouble at all, gradually turning bodiless, then mindless, memory-less, into nothing. Except it would be too easy. She stared out the window at the garden she'd made. Sallie chasing a squirrel up the oak tree.

There were these periods, small pools of under-water time, when Josh was not there for her. When she couldn't or wouldn't think about him and so couldn't locate him, even in memory. *Gone. Already.* While she treaded water, got lost in oblivion. While she was undone by such complicated maneuvers as getting up and sitting down. Undone by English muffins. Over-heard saying, to absolutely no one, "Brushing my hair is beyond me."

She got up from the table, carried the mug to the sink, and set it precariously on top of the tall pile of dirty dishes: it did not fall.

If it falls later, she thought, while I'm thinking about something else, I will not care.

There was a To Do list in her head, comprehensive and written in a nice, fine hand. The problem was remembering it. The lines got broken up, separated, like a sheet of paper ripped into pieces and thrown into a hat at a party, each piece with a different word on it. She could only draw one word at a time, which was useless.

She chose the bathroom first, hers and Ethan's. She went to the laundry room for the cleaning sup-plies and yellow rubber gloves, and put them all in a plastic bucket and carried them up the stairs and down the hallway. She looked neither to the left nor to the right as she went. But she could not ignore it: the door to Josh's room was closed, the door to Emma's open. She walked fast, her stomach reeling, her mind crying out, and then she was standing in her room. Sunlight broke dappled through the curtains onto the hardwood floor, her clothes strewn there, the bed against the wall looking stripped and violated on her side, where she'd thrown the covers off. But not on Ethan's side: he'd pulled the sheets up almost to the headboard, as if to cover any trace of his presence. She had no recollection of his getting out of bed; did not really remember him being there at all, except that he'd been the one who'd turned out the light last night. The tidiness of his side of the bed disgusted her. How contained it was, and selfish. You couldn't tell from it anything about what he was thinking or feeling or suffering.

Now, standing in the middle of the spacious, sunlit room, she ducked her head as though she'd just gone shooting into a tunnel. The bucket fell from her grasp. It banged on its side and clattered terribly, and the cleaning supplies spilled out: Fantastik, Windex, Comet, a sorry old sponge, those yellow gloves shocking as a scream. And she started to cry, sinking to her knees on the hard floor.

Later, she sat on Josh's bed with her feet on the floor, her palms flat on the spread. Everything cold to the touch. Everything neater than it was supposed to be in the room of a ten-year-old boy. She remembered, on that morning eight days ago, walking through this door and telling him he wouldn't be going to the concert unless he cleaned his room from top to bottom, left to right, spic to span—"We'll leave you behind." A mother's idle, love-crippled threat. And how much it hurt now to discover the degree to which he'd listened and obeyed. The room was neat, the bed was made. All his secrets lay tucked away in their secret places. Such a cruel irony that this should be the only room in the house with any order now. As though a bomb had fallen everywhere else. Well, she could exist here, in this room. It was the only place. She could curl up here and let the world outside remain as it was, beyond her, not understanding, not giving a damn—

Far below, the doorbell rang.

No. Go away.

She waited. But then the bell rang again, and like some automaton she stood up. When the bell rang a third time, she went to the stairs. Gravity urged her down them. Then she was at the front door. She was opening it: a police officer, walking back along the flagstone path to his police car parked at the side of the road. He was almost to it when he heard the door open and turned around. He wore mirrored sunglasses and she wasn't sure if he was the same one she remembered from before.

"Yes?" she said.

He took a couple of steps toward her. "Mrs. Learner?"

"Yes."

He pulled the gray hat off his head and held it at his hip. "Sergeant Burke, Mrs. Learner. State trooper, Canaan barracks. I'm the one in charge of your son's case."

Say "police officer," Em.

She said, "I'm Grace Learner." She felt dislocated, pulled from the socket.

The officer nodded. The sunglasses couldn't hide the fact that he was looking at her strangely. *He is trying to be careful and correct,* she thought.

"We already met once before, ma'am."

"Yes, of course."

"I was going to call," he said, "but I was coming out your way and thought I'd just drop by instead. I promised your husband I'd keep him posted on things."

"My husband's not here."

He nodded again. *He'll go away now.* But he stayed where he was, looking at her. Probably expecting her to be properly curious about his news: *He can go to hell.* Curiosity is just another kind of hope, and hope is sick, it is feeling after death. She wanted to knock the mirrored glasses from his face.

"Maybe I should come back another time. . . ."

"It's all right," she said, surprising herself.

She stepped back from the door, and he came slowly forward along the flagstones and into her house. For a moment she saw the beginnings of her face take shape in his glasses, before he took them off. His eyes were gray. Then, looking down, she saw the gun in his holster, its curved grip jutting out from his hip like a bone or a horn, and it reminded her of the gun her daddy had brought home from the war, the gun that he'd kept, along with his old uniform and his medals and the love letters he'd received at the front, in an army trunk in the attic. Where once he had found her snooping.

It was the letters she'd come to look at, but he didn't know that. He'd assumed it was the gun. She remembered the dry heat of the attic and the smell of the trunk, naphtha and must. And how he had taken the gun out from its dented metal box and shown it to her, saying grimly, "This is a dangerous thing, Gracie. A terrible, dangerous thing. I keep it because it meant something to me in the war. But it's got nothing to do with our lives here, honey, and you must promise never to touch it."

She had promised. She had loved him so. And then, years later, after he had died and she had found herself grown and married, one day the trunk itself and all of its contents had arrived from Durham on a truck. Thinking of her infant son, she had stuck it in the barn, and made sure that it was locked, and never looked at it again.

"Would you like coffee?" she asked Sergeant Burke.

"That would be nice, ma'am, thank you."

On the wall to the left of the stairs hung the Arts and Crafts mirror her grandparents had given them as a wedding present. It was a handsome piece, simple and true. She had always admired it. Now, leading the way to the kitchen, she saw herself in it. She'd forgotten all about the ugly robe she was wearing, forgotten the bed-pressed hair and red, swollen eyes. And suddenly she understood the embarrassed expression on the man's face, why he stood with his shoulders slightly hunched, as though drawing away from the sight of her: the ugly, tedious fact of her misery had unmanned him. Not that she blamed him. She almost started to apologize for her appearance but couldn't get the words out. All at once, a crushing weariness.

She poured him a mug of coffee and led him to the living room at the back of the house. An old room, the floor lower at the middle than at the corners, the walls faintly bowed. On one of the walls, a watercolor landscape she'd made in college.

Sergeant Burke sat on one of the comfortable chairs in front of the fireplace, sipping his coffee, looking at her where she sat on the sofa. Then looking past her, down the length of the room and all that was in it, through the far windows of old blown glass. The bubbles and imperfections in the panes transformed the sunlight in some way she couldn't fathom. And she thought: *He is an observer, this man, a professional—a detective, a hunter-gatherer of facts. He will see all there is to see about us.*

"The coffee's good," he said.

"What?"

"The coffee." He held up the mug. "Tastes good."

"Oh." She nodded, tried to smile. "Would you like some more?"

"No, ma'am, thank you."

She stared into the cold stone fireplace. *Cold since when?* A chilly night in early June. The fire crackling.

Reading *The Lion, the Witch, and the Wardrobe* to Emma while Ethan played chess with Josh. Josh had won—he had won, checkmate. She touched her hand to her cheek. "I don't know where my husband is, Sergeant."

He said nothing.

"Is it Monday?" she asked.

"Yes, ma'am."

"Ethan drops Emma off at music camp."

"Probably on his way home right this minute," Sergeant Burke said encouragingly.

She said, "It must be lunchtime by now."

Sergeant Burke looked down at the floor. "It's after three, ma'am."

"So late?" Aware of her fingers slipping off the cliff edge one by one, endless space below. Attached by nothing. *I do not want to fall.* She folded her arms over her chest and squeezed until breathing was a challenge she could think about for a few seconds at least.

"Ma'am," the officer said. His voice was tentative, awkward. "I don't know if your husband told you, but we've got a counselor we work with over at the barracks. Her name's Charlotte Lewis. She's got a master's degree in social work. More than that, she's a nice lady. And, uh, if you ever felt the need—"

"'Need'?" She could taste the word on her tongue like metal.

"To talk. Talk about things."

"With whom, Sergeant? This woman? Did she ever meet my son? Did she ever know him? Could she possibly have any idea who he was?"

Who was this talking? she wondered suddenly. Whose voice coming out of her mouth? *I do not recognize her.*

Sergeant Burke's eyes had left her for the room behind her head. "I know you're upset, Mrs. Learner. . . ."

"Upset?" Grace shook her head. Already the anger was leaving her like water through a drain; she wanted to hold on to it. She was a husk; she'd never been so empty. Her voice was frighteningly calm. "You're wrong, Sergeant. I'm not upset. I'm hardly even here."

His look of confusion then would once have been a kind of victory for her, something to laugh about and describe to friends. Not today. They sat in an awkward, distinctly unprofessional silence as the clock ticked.

I am finished.

Somewhere outside, a car door slammed.

Sergeant Burke stood up. "That'll be your husband."

"Yes," she said slowly. "My husband."

Ethan

Monday morning I got Emma into the car on time, and drove her over to music camp.

We said very little on the way. Perhaps she was still waking up. Perhaps conversation of any kind was simply beyond me. Outside it was hot already and I had the air conditioning on and the windows rolled up, like a city driver or a man on the interstate. Emma sat in the front seat with her sun-browned legs sticking straight out. She'd dressed herself, as always, according to her own sense of fashion: a red V-neck T-shirt and denim shorts, and sneakers with purple stripes and Velcro straps instead of laces. I drove with the radio off. Ten minutes to the center of town, such as it was—general store, mediocre pub, gourmet sandwich shop, pharmacy—and around the little oblong green, past the white houses and the tall white church behind which the birds would have been singing under a single, broad-limbed oak, and eventually to the Sherman R. Lewis Elementary School, where I parked beside a green station wagon.

"Here we are," I said, turning off the engine.

Emma said, "That's Mrs. Wheldon's car."

I didn't know what to say. I reached into the back-seat for her music books.

"Sam Arno's got a black eye," Emma said.

"Does he?"

"Uh-huh. It's totally gross."

"I'm sorry to hear that," I said, and received from Emma a look of disappointment, even pity, at my banality. I handed her the music books. Bach was on top, a selection of pieces for the intermediate piano student. "Do you want me to come in with you?"

"No. . . ." She was staring out the window at the playground, the metal slide shining white-hot under the sun. Something was happening inside her, but I had no idea what it was. I felt my heart sinking.

"Emma?"

"It's okay," she said in a small voice. She pushed the red button by her hip and the seat belt came free, went sliding across her. But she made no move to get out.

I leaned over and kissed her head. "I hope it goes well today."

"Is Mom going to pick me up?"

"Yes."

"Tell her not to be late, okay?"

"She won't be."

"Good."

She sat there for perhaps ten seconds more, saying

nothing, staring at her feet, mustering courage. Then she opened the door and got out.

I watched her in the rearview mirror: a bright shot of red dropping out of my blind spot and into the white heat of the morning. Refracted, she seemed already distant. And then, thirty feet away, I saw her stop.

I waited. She stood dead center in the mirror, her red-shirted back to me, halfway to the entrance to the school. I hoped she'd start walking again, but she didn't. Finally, I opened the car door and got out.

The air was hot and dry, the sun so bright off the pavement it was like being struck in the face. I walked toward her. Even when I was close, she didn't turn around, and I went up and crouched down behind her and put my hands on her shoulders. I felt the tremor in her then, like a live wire run taut, and for a long fixed moment it was as if I were holding her again by the side of Reservation Road, trying to absorb her trembling and knowing that I could not. Gently, now, I turned her around. Her face was red and streaked with tears. Her nose was running. I picked her up in my arms and the music books fell to the ground. Her crying was ancient, fierce, and nearly silent.

She was just eight years old. I knew everything about her, and nothing. After her tears were done, I asked her if she wanted to go home. But she said she was okay. She insisted on going to camp. She was stubborn. Nothing more was said, nothing explained. We picked the music books off the ground and entered the school.

Out of the bright light and heat into coolness and near dark; my eyes were slow to adjust. I held my daughter's hand for guidance. And for a moment there was just blind memory: holding my own father's hand, breathing in the aching stone coolness of the synagogue he used to take me to on Chicago's South Side. A grief temple. A kind of vertigo. Then I was back again in the square high lobby with the gray stone crosses embedded in the walls, impossibly deep. Emma was holding my hand. And the woman standing before us, her hands clasped at her waist, was Ruth Wheldon.

"Good morning, Mr. Learner," she said. She sounded slightly breathless, as if she'd just run up the stairs.

"Good morning," I said.

"Hi, Emma."

"Hi, Mrs. Wheldon."

Ruth Wheldon smiled at Emma. It was a pretty smile, turning nervous at the end; apparently, she'd exhausted her prepared remarks.

"I was just dropping Emma off," I said. "I hope we're not too late."

"Oh, no," Ruth Wheldon said.

I bent down and kissed Emma on the cheek. "Good-bye, Em."

Ruth Wheldon took a hesitant step closer. She was wearing a kind of summer pants suit, all in green, and high heels. "Mr. Learner?"

"Yes?"

"Do you think I could talk to you for a minute?"

I glanced down at Emma, who was staring at her feet. "All right."

"Emma, why don't you go downstairs and join the other kids?" Ruth Wheldon said. "Tell Mrs. Peabody I'll be down in a minute. Okay?"

Emma nodded. She seemed, like me, broken now by weariness, too tired to resist anything. "I'll be done at four-thirty," my daughter said to me—reproachfully, like an adult—and then, music books in hand, she walked to the back of the lobby, turned to the right, and disappeared down the stairs.

Ruth Wheldon cleared her throat. "I want you to know how sorry I am. How very sorry."

The words were ashes in my mouth: "Thank you."

Ruth Wheldon seemed on the verge of saying something more, but didn't trust herself. Her eyes were gleaming even without direct light; perhaps it was tears. She stood looking at the floor, then at me, then high above my head. I knew nothing about her except for the odd clothes she habitually wore and the fact that despite them she was attractive. That her sorrow seemed genuine yet touched me no more than if it had been false. "You probably want to talk about Emma," I said, to make it easier for her.

She nodded gratefully. "I talked to your wife last week."

"I know."

"About the concert Wednesday evening." She paused. "Is it still okay?"

"It's up to Emma."

"Sure."

Her attempt at a smile died on her lips. There was no easy way to do this, and the crosses in the walls weren't helping. Death is death. And I thought of my father in temple, his shoulders slumped, grieving for centuries of pain and loss, only a fraction of it his own.

"I also asked your wife about counseling for Emma, Mr. Learner," Ruth Wheldon said. "If you had any plans in that direction. I don't want to pry. It's none of my business, and the last thing in the world I want to do is to make things harder for you and your family after the tragedy you've all been through. But I'm concerned about Emma. There are times when it's like nothing's happened, and other times when you can just feel her start to crack. I think she's got strong feelings of guilt. She feels almost responsible in some way for what happened, like it was her fault."

"Her fault? That's ridiculous."

My voice, angry and assaulting, echoed faintly against the walls, and made the silence that followed feel all the more regrettable. Taken aback, Ruth Wheldon merely stared at me.

I thought: *I am harming Emma, too.*

"I'm sorry," I stumbled. "I didn't mean—"

"You don't have to explain," she said.

"No. It's just—she's—you've got to try to understand. Emma's the only one who's innocent."

"I don't think I know what you mean."

"Never mind. Excuse me."

"No, please—"

"You think Emma should see a psychiatrist?"

Ruth Wheldon looked miserable now, on the verge of tears. "Yes, I do. Somebody who knows more about these things than I do. A professional."

"Okay," I said. "Okay."

"Thank you," she said.

"Don't thank me."

I reached out and touched her hand. I didn't know why. Then I left.

Around the little oblong green, this time in reverse. White church, white houses. The white heat of morning. All of it a strange reminder now of the blank white light in the empty refrigerator at home: nothing for Emma's breakfast again this morning. I saw the hand-lettered sign for Krause's General Store and pulled in.

Paul Krause stood behind the burnished wood counter, talking to gossipy, bilious old Mrs. Briggs, the school principal's mother, and ringing up her goods. He paused midsentence when he noticed me come in, his mostly bald head swinging in my direction and then quickly retreating. Mrs. Briggs followed his initial look, her ossified neck forcing her body to turn a full hundred and eighty degrees to get me in view. She was not by nature as diplomatic as Paul Krause, nor as genial, and my sudden appearance caused her to emit a breathy "Oh!" of surprise.

"Morning, Ethan," Paul said, with an unmistakable gentleness.

I nodded. "Morning, Paul." I hurried to the back of the store to avoid any contact with Mrs. Briggs.

There were five short aisles of canned goods, boxes of cereal, plastic bottles of shampoo. Along the back, beside the refrigerator and freezer, twenty- and fifty-pound bags of flour and sugar were piled three feet high. A pair of buck's antlers decorated the wall — taken, Paul had once told me, by a much younger version of himself. He had a pot belly now. He swept the place daily, kept it clean. He talked patiently with the Mrs. Briggses of the world. I'd never understood how he made any money, though it was not my business. Chain supermarkets had long ago come to Winsted and other towns.

The door opened. Mrs. Briggs shot a last carnivorous look in my direction and departed. I carried a dozen eggs, a loaf of oatmeal bread, a box of Bisquick, and a glass bottle of Vermont maple syrup up to the counter, where Paul rang them up on the old-fashioned register with the round indented keys and the white-backed number cards that popped, ringing, into the window like so many jack-in-the-boxes. He paused before punching up the total. "Anything else, Ethan?"

We made eye contact. For some reason, I thought about how I'd touched Ruth Wheldon's hands. I turned and looked back over the small store, dark with wood and smelling of flour. "Nothing I remember," I said.

He nodded. He didn't tell me he knew what I meant. He punched in the total and I paid and thanked him and went out.

I was reaching for the car door when my peripheral vision filled with a shape and color that made the breath die in my throat and my head snap up in the direction of the road: it was there, passing right by me. Four doors, dark blue, a reflecting midnight blue. A man driving. I dropped the bag of groceries. It landed on the pavement at my feet with a sickening crash, eggs and syrup blown to smithereens. I saw the neat chrome uppercase letters across the back of the trunk, FORD on the left, TAURUS on the right, and below it the flat blue of a Connecticut license plate. Diminishing fast. Thirty feet, forty feet, a hundred feet and turning left, following 44 west toward Canaan. Gone. I never saw the headlights.

There was no deliberation. I couldn't get the keys out fast enough, couldn't hold them without dropping them on the ground and again inside the car, pounding my open hand against the steering wheel and screaming at myself, *Stupid fucking clumsy fool!* Then the key was turning in the ignition and the car shot backward into the road, which happened to be empty. I turned the wheel hard and the tail slid left, tires shrieking, the nose veering to the right, and I shifted again and the car jolted forward as if rammed from behind. Just before making the turn for Canaan, I glanced at the rearview mirror and recognized Paul Krause standing over my bag of shattered groceries with a broom in his hands.

I was not a good driver. My car swung wide on the turn westward. The guardrail separating the ten-foot bridge from the stream below came rushing up from the side. The back right bumper hit and released, and then the car straightened, accelerating onto a long straightaway. The dark blue sedan appeared at the end of it, distant but there. I locked on it. On him, faint dark blur through windshields. Probably thinking of himself as just an ordinary man, a citizen. He had no idea what was happening. It didn't matter. I would appear in his mirror like a ghost. The red needle on the speedometer was climbing past fifty. Trees whipped by. I felt the ground rushing under me, under rubber and metal, huge chunks of it left in my wake. The distance between us was closing; he couldn't have been going very fast. He was meandering toward Canaan. A day spent antiquing, perhaps, driving his car as if he had the fucking right. I could see the blue of the license plate, the make-and-model chrome. I could feel the steering wheel gripped in my white-knuckled hands and the sweat beaded on my upper lip. And I did not flinch when the rounded blue tail of his car grew larger than life, letters and numbers emerging as if out of a mist. I kept my speed. A thousand feet ahead on our side of the road I could see a gray stone wall.

I was fifteen feet behind him when he finally noticed me. His head jerked toward the rearview mirror, and instantaneously his car zigged to the right, almost onto the shoulder, offering me room to pass. I took it. I stepped down on the pedal and my car surged forward, entering his blind spot on the left, our vehicles no more than a yard apart. Five hundred feet ahead, the shoulder ran out, replaced by the gray stone wall. He was whipping his head to the side, trying to find me. I saw short dark hair and a flash of surprisingly white skin. I was pulling even with him, turning my wheel half an inch to the right, closing the narrow gap between us. The speedometer at sixty, the noise of the two engines all-consuming, pounding through the closed windows, pushing up through the seats. Every stone of that wall coming clear as day. And I turned to look at him. I wanted him to know. I saw the porcelain wedge of his profile and it was strange, so pale and smooth and frightened. Too strange. It gave me pause. Then it crushed me. I felt something crack in my heart, and a sickness start to leak out.

It was a woman. A woman about my age. A woman looking at me in terror, her lips moving soundlessly behind the layers of glass and noise and speed that separated us, calling out for her life.

My foot came off the gas. The car slowed as if it had been shot. She passed ahead of me and kept going, and it was over.

Grace

The front door opened—then silence. He must have seen the car out front, must know she was here with the police, but he did not call out to her.

Standing in the living room, Sergeant Burke cleared his throat.

"Ethan!" she called. Her own voice sounded damped to her, cloudy, like a cataract eye. "In here. We have a visitor."

Footsteps—he appeared under the wide archway with a flushed face, as if he'd just stepped in from the cold. But it was high summer. *Drinking*. A peculiar sense of dread, climbing her like a vine. She didn't get up.

"Afternoon, Mr. Learner," Sergeant Burke said, with a sober nod. He sounded positively relieved to have another man in the room.

Ethan nodded back. "Hello, Sergeant." Then his eyes fell on her and his face darkened. She watched him absorb her robe, her hair, her face. Even across the room she could feel his anger, the black thunder in him—because she was disheveled, because she'd failed to keep up appearances when appearances were important. (*Are they? Are they really? I don't fucking care.*) He was far too private a man to yell at her in front of a stranger; he'd merely disown her with a stare. He turned away from her.

She made herself speak. "Ethan, Sergeant Burke came by."

"Did you find him?" He was looking at the trooper.

"No," the sergeant said.

"Do you have anything?"

"Not much so far. But it's early yet."

Ethan looked about to say something but changed his mind. She could hear the sharpness of his breathing—an exhale like a horse, a boxer throwing a punch. He came and sat down on the other chair, leaving her by herself on the sofa. He did not so much as glance at her. Sergeant Burke lowered himself onto his chair, careful of his gun belt, his eyes scouting them both in carefully controlled movements: *A detective, a professional.*

"We've got the lab work done. That's really what I came by to tell you folks about." Sergeant Burke hooked a finger under the gun belt at his waist and hoisted it an inch. This seemed to relieve him of some pressure. He cleared his throat again. "Mr. and Mrs. Learner, the car that hit your son was dark blue, more like a midnight blue. It's a Ford, we're ninety-nine percent sure it's a Taurus, which as you may know is a model the company started back in 1986. Our lab guys tell us it's one of the earlyish years, but just which year is where things start to get a little fuzzy. Ford used the same paint mix and the same glass and plastic on the Taurus right through '92. So, we could be talking an '88 here, or we could be talking a '92. That leaves a lot of cars in between."

"You're making excuses," Ethan said. His voice was quiet and frightening.

"I'm telling you the facts, Mr. Learner."

"You want facts? A man murdered my son."

"*Our* son," she said. She instantly regretted it. It was a cliché and sickened her. She turned from them both and stared out the window.

"We are tracking down records of every dark blue Taurus sold in the state before 1993," Sergeant Burke said.

"Then what?"

"We try to put together a profile of the suspect. We put the profile into our computers and try to link it up with the sold cars we've traced. There are names there, in some cases addresses. We try to rule out cars that have left the state. There are many ways, Mr. Learner. We are pursuing them all."

"What if it wasn't bought in the state? What if it's been scrapped? What if the son of a bitch doesn't even live in the state?"

"Those are good questions. Real questions. And we will tackle them one at a time."

Ethan got up and walked to the window, stood looking out. "He's going to get away with it," he said. "Isn't he?"

"It's way too early to be talking like that," Sergeant Burke said.

Ethan turned around. The look on his face was chilling.

He was in his study, sitting in the leather chair she'd given him for his birthday, reading. She wasn't surprised to find him there. He had always depended on books. When his father died, she remembered, he'd cloistered himself in this room for days—reading, reading, reading. When depression struck him, as it did, he would turn silent and removed, incapable of focusing on anyone but the characters in his books. Then it would pass. He'd return from his reading as from a private hideaway, without pictures to show or stories to tell. Then he'd want to talk about other things. About them, his family. What was everyone up to? Emma's best friend, Josh's pet turtle, her own watercolors, which she did in her spare time for the hell of it, because she could, because she'd once been pretty decent at it. He could be curious in a human, not just academic, way; he could be kind and loving. She was trying to remind herself. Because this man sitting in the chair reading Henry James for the hundredth time while she stood in the doorway waiting to be acknowledged might have been a different man.

Which novel? *The Ambassadors.* Ah. *My husband.* He looked up but didn't close the book. She was just a temporary interruption, a speed bump on his road home.

"Yes?" he said, as if she were one of his students knocking on his door during office hours.

"You've been drinking," she said.

"And you just look like you have."

"Fuck you."

She wanted him to lash back, she wanted a fight. But he just sighed and looked up at the ceiling. "Sorry," he said. "I didn't mean that."

"Of course you did."

He was silent.

"Ethan."

He looked at her. He took off his glasses and rubbed his eyes and put on his glasses again. He closed his book and set it on the floor.

She watched mutely. This was his private room of ritual and she couldn't interfere. That had always been their unspoken bargain.

I have my own room, she thought, *and I will go to it soon.*

"I went to a bar," he said. "After I dropped Emma off."

"Which bar?"

"I don't know. I don't know bars. Some dive."

"Is that the plan now, Ethan? Start going to dives in the middle of the day?"

"No plan," he said.

"Just see what happens, play it by ear—is that it?"

"That's it."

"What courage! What a hero."

"I knew you'd think so."

She turned away from him. She didn't know what

to do. This hole they were falling into felt like a grievous sin to her, a sacrilege to Josh. Yet it was happening, and she did not know how to stop it.

When she turned back, he was reading again. She felt overcome with the desire to hurt him in return and she stood very still in the room, afraid of herself. She tried to find it in her heart to look beyond it all. To find the man she loved. To see the room as a catalogue of his better nature, its objects touchstones of the past. But it was hard, now. She blamed him.

There, on his desk surrounding the computer, were piles of books from the college library. There were stacks of xeroxed academic articles, too, for a paper he was supposed to be writing this summer on Edith Wharton, and the speckled composition books he used for notes. He wrote with a fountain pen that had belonged to his father. He used sepia-colored ink. It had always seemed to her as if the words came out of him already aged, from another era. His handwriting was knotty and small. She remembered the first love letter he'd ever written her, when they were still students, how hard it had been to decipher. "You'd have to be an archeologist to read this," she'd told him—a response that had pleased him to no end. "Yes!" he'd replied. "Exactly."

"Say it," he said now.

She looked at him. His eyes were fierce with self-hatred.

"Come on. I'm guilty. Say it."

An immense pity flooded her. She shook her head.

"Say it!" he shouted.

But she would not. It would be the end of them as a family—she believed that—and it was not, finally, in her nature to destroy. So she turned and left him there. And his voice, raging and pleading against the walls of the house, pursued her down the hallway.

"Goddamn you, Grace! Why won't you say it? Why won't you?"

Dwight

We met for lunch at Tommy's Diner; usual place, usual table, a corner booth at the back, near the pay phone in case someone called. Every time the phone rang Jack Cutter believed it would be for him. He had that kind of sense of himself. He was forty-two years old, rotund, florid, heart-attack-perfect. A big small-town lawyer. He'd read *To Kill a Mockingbird* maybe half a dozen times, and once told me that Atticus Finch (who seemed to look a lot like Gregory Peck) appeared regularly in his dreams and spoke to him in glowing terms.

In certain respects, it was a regular Tuesday afternoon. Dr. Zinser, my dentist, sat at the table by the register, reading a Dean Koontz paperback and eating a piece of key lime pie. I'd bought my snow tires last winter from the guy at the table next to him. And sitting at the first booth along the wall was a man in a seersucker suit who looked like the fellow in Sheffield who'd sold Ruth and me that wrought-iron chandelier years back. There were a couple of farmers, too, and part of a road crew taking up two booths, their yellow hardhats resting here and there like domed pool lights. And finally, slick and daunting in shades of blue, a pair of state troopers sat in a booth smack in the middle of the place, two seats for themselves and two for their hats. The police barracks were just a few football fields up the road, on the other side of the train tracks that, having limned the edge of Bow Mills, ran by here too, cutting into southwestern Massachusetts.

We'd ordered our food and now time was dragging strangely. I tried not to look at the cops sitting there. Jack and I were old friends and didn't normally have trouble making conversation (he usually made most of it). We'd met at law school, when he was in his last year and I was in my first. I'd called the number on a sale notice for used law books on the kiosk in the student union. They were Jack's books. I was greatly hard up for cash then, but so was he and he'd stiffed me on the price, talked me into the buy with all the verbal mastery of a good preacher. He had a confidence in the sheer wattage of his personality that up till then I'd experienced only in my biceps. It was enticing, not quite real, like hearing a foreign language I wanted to learn but knew I never would; there was something addictive in the idea of it. Two years later Jack was best man at my wedding.

That day he drank too much even for a big man and knocked over a glass of red wine. It stained the white tablecloth like a birthmark. Undeterred, he toasted Ruth and me over the wreckage. It was an elegant, memorable speech, maybe a little unhinged. Lawyers were trained to fix things, he said, but the greatest lesson of all was never to try to fix what couldn't be broken. He said that the love Ruth and I had was the authentic article, the crystal vase, the china cup, the thing whole and perfect and needing only a custodial, loving hand. But not fixing. He said that we lawyers, schmucks like him and me, we must curb our pathological need to negotiate and tamper. We must learn to let well enough alone or risk transforming the sublime into the merely expedient. We had—he was very sorry to say it, but he felt it was his duty—a perverse and even perhaps criminal tendency to ruin what precious little was good in life.

The jukebox switched over and Patsy Cline came on, singing "Crazy."

"You think Cheryl sleeps around?" Jack said. "More to the point, you think she'd bestow her favors on old Jack here? Because, I'll tell you, buddy, I've got a hankering."

"What?" I said.

Jack frowned at the inattention, a subtle and practiced double-dip at the corners of his wide mouth that I remembered him using with some success on the judge who'd presided over my case. "What's with you today? You look ready to blow. Have a beer."

"I'm fine, Jack. Usual stuff. Nothing serious."

"Have a beer anyway. For the hell of it."

"Okay. For the hell of it."

Our food arrived—cheeseburgers and fries— brought by Cheryl the waitress with her stiff black hair and dark-polish nails.

"Who's got the rare?"

"Bloody's for me," Jack said.

Cheryl banged the plates down on the table in a good-natured way.

"Cheryl, sweetheart, a Bud for Dwight here and another for me."

"I don't get paid enough to be your sweetheart, Jack," Cheryl said.

Jack grinned. "We can negotiate." He watched her walk away, her hips breaking the stiff planes of the nubbed pink uniform and shooshing. The diner was long and narrow, with windows all down one side, sunlight pouring in over the booths and shining in the customers' eyes. Jack watched Cheryl walk the length of the room. She picked up an empty coffee cup and a gravied plate and a basket of dinner rolls from a table and dumped them behind the counter. He studied her rear end. "My kingdom for a waitress," he murmured. Then he raised the cheeseburger to his mouth and a quarter of it disappeared. He put a few fries in after it, a wedge of pickle, and added a hearty, pirate's swig of beer. "Amen."

I looked at the troopers sitting there eating. The one facing the sun had put his aviators on.

The food was gone. We were drinking coffee. The pay phone had rung once but it was a wrong number. Jack poked at his teeth and gums with a toothpick. He'd put down three beers to my one.

"How's old Sam doing?" he asked.

"Doing okay," I said.

"The school year go okay?"

"It was okay. Dyslexia's all over the place now. People seem to know how to deal with it."

"He's a good boy."

"Yes, he is."

"You two getting along all right? Everything smooth?"

I'd called Sam five times since Sunday but he wouldn't come to the phone even once. Ruth had said it: "He doesn't want to speak to you, Dwight. Did you do something to him? He won't tell me what, but it must've been something. Goddamn you, Dwight, he looks miserable. I think maybe he should see a psychiatrist."

"Smooth?" I shook my head. "I wouldn't say so."

"Yeah?" Jack said. "Sorry to hear it."

"There've been some ups and downs lately."

Jack nodded. "Vicissitudes." He looked pleased with the word. "That's called being a father, Dwight. You should spend a couple of days over at our place. My kid? My guess is Toby's started smoking a little weed after school. You know, normal teenage stuff, nothing serious. But Barb's acting like the kid's gotten into devil worship. She's going around blasting me for not being enough of a role model. I mean, for Christ's sake. Every morning at breakfast, blah blah blah, calling me a lousy father and worse. Finally a couple days ago I told her either bring on the divorce papers or shut the hell up. I said of course I'd represent myself in court. That settled it. She wouldn't be caught dead actually *paying* for a lawyer." Jack laughed.

The antiques dealer in the seersucker suit stood up to pay. He reached into his pocket and pulled out some change, sorted through it on his palm, plucked out the pennies, and dropped the remaining coins on the table. A quarter rolled on its edge in a wobbling circle before falling flat beside the others. He walked to the register, passing the troopers drinking their coffee. At the table where Dr. Zinser had been eating pie, now there was a fuel company employee, a black man in gray coveralls.

"I don't always trust myself, Jack."

"What are you talking about?"

"I'm talking about Sam."

Jack sighed. "Oh Jesus, here we go." He tossed the toothpick he'd been chewing onto the floor. "It was an accident, Dwight. So said the court and so says I. I'll bet you a grand he doesn't even think about it any more. It's like it never happened. He's a kid and he's let it go. You should do as much. You're the one keeps dragging it around everywhere like some fucking stone. Drop it already. Give yourself a break."

"I can't."

"In that case do something memorable. Throw yourself into a fucking gorge. Sue somebody and hire me as counsel. Fill my wallet with dough. Just don't talk about it any more." He smiled, reached out and slapped me on the shoulder. "Hey. Come on. In America it's called a joke. Cheryl!"

Cheryl was going table to table with the coffeepot. She came over.

"Refill?"

Jack tried to put his arm around her waist, but she stepped away smartly. The coffee sloshed in the pot and almost spilled out.

"What we want here are two more beers."

"Not for me," I said.

"Absolutely for him," Jack said. "Especially and most importantly for him."

He was a little drunk, and I hadn't realized it till then. "Not for me," I repeated.

"Loosen you up," Jack said. "Throw your cares to the dogs."

"Your reputation too," Cheryl said. "Don't you guys work?"

"We don't work, sweetheart. We're lawyers."

She went away to get the beers. Once again we watched her go. Small-town life. She walked behind the counter and set down the coffeepot and bent over the bar fridge where the longneck Buds were cooled by the case. She pulled two bottles from the rack, and then at the far end of the diner the door opened and I turned to see who it was.

It was a state trooper. Just inside the diner he paused. Even with his shades on, I could tell he was looking for somebody in particular. He scanned first the tables and then the booths, stopping on the two troopers finishing up their meal. He nodded and they nodded back, curt, military nods, and for a moment I let myself believe he was there just to see them. Then he looked past them. His chin inched up until there could have been nothing in his sight except Jack Cutter and me. He came toward us. I faced Jack and put my hands flat on the table—the way I'd put my hands on the steering wheel, at ten o'clock and two o'clock, if a cop stopped me for speeding. A gesture designed for innocence. I heard footsteps coming and closed my eyes.

"Two Buds."

I opened my eyes. Cheryl was putting two bottles on the table. The trooper was right behind her. He'd taken his shades off and his eyes were gray. His hair was gray too, at the temples. He was tall and fit. Cheryl turned around and walked off, and the trooper stepped up to our table.

Jack took a swig of beer. "Afternoon, Ken."

The trooper nodded. "Jack. How goes things?"

"All right. Nothing in particular to complain about."

"Glad to hear it." He turned to me. "Mr. Arno? Dwight Arno?"

"Yes."

"I'm Sergeant Burke of the Connecticut State Police, Canaan Barracks."

"What can I do for you, Sergeant?"

"I'm going to have to ask you to come with me."

"What the hell for?" Jack said.

Burke ignored him and kept looking at me.

"Is there a problem, Sergeant?" I said.

"Do you know Stu Carmody?"

"I'm his lawyer."

"Know what he looks like?"

"Of course."

"Then you'd better come with me right now."

"Not till you say what the hell is going on here, Ken," Jack said.

Burke's eyes narrowed. "I'd shut your mouth now, Jack, if I was you. Okay?"

"Where is Stu?" I asked.

"All over his barn."

Grace

Sarah Gladstone's phone messages had turned hysterical. Their big summer "shindig" was on Saturday, just four days away, and she wanted to know where the hell Grace was. The birch trees were all wrong, not really white as promised, and the koi in the new pond looked dark. There were other problems too, but she wasn't going to go into them on the machine. She was sorry for Grace—very, very sorry—but there was nothing to be done about it; this was business: documents had been signed, guarantees made. Grace would have to come over immediately and set things right.

"I don't want to go," Emma said.

They were in the kitchen, Sallie lapping water from her bowl. Emma's breakfast dishes sitting dirty in the sink and Grace looking out the window at the towering sugar maple.

"Please," she said.

"Justine asked me over."

"We'll be back by afternoon. You can see Justine then. Besides, it'll be fun."

"But Justine said—"

"No, that's a lie," she burst out. "It won't be fun. I just need the company." She reached out and touched Emma's hair. "Please, Em."

I am losing it, she thought—*can't listen, don't care if my daughter plays or doesn't play. Pure, selfish need.*

And Emma? The evidence right there on her face as she tried to make up her mind what to do: annoyance, confusion, an unselfconscious anxiety.

Now, finally, a nod: "Okay, I guess."

Grace hugged her. "I love you."

They rode together in the front seat of the wagon—her car, with a hundred and twenty thousand miles on it. An old friend, a relic, an icon; the sort of car that showed she'd had a life, been around, done things, wasn't uptight, had once been fearless. Well, it was a lie. Today she'd made sure to buckle Emma's seat belt herself, and now she couldn't stop looking at it, making sure it was still fastened. *Keep your child safe.* Starting to sweat every time the speedometer crept over thirty-five.

"Why're we going so slow?" Emma demanded.

"We're not going slow."

"We are."

"We're going the speed limit."

"It's boring," Emma said.

Grace looked over at her. "Where did you learn to talk like that? Not from me."

"I'm bored."

Emma brought her feet up on the seat and began unbuckling one of her red strap shoes. Grace watched out of the corner of her eye, listened to the open-mouthed breathing: a pantomime of childish concentration and moody restlessness. When Emma had the shoe off, she held it in her hands for a moment, vaguely satisfied. Then she fit it on her foot again. The rebuckling took a long time. Finished, she stuck her legs straight out and admired her shoes. For some reason, Grace felt like weeping.

"What's the matter?" Emma said.

"Nothing." She blinked, and the tears that had been sitting in her eyes receded.

"Mom?"

"What?"

"Did I tell you about the puppy Justine got for her birthday?"

"No. Tell me."

"It's really little and cute. It's a beagle puppy."

"That sounds nice."

Emma frowned. "Can we get a beagle puppy?"

"We have Sallie."

"But Sallie's so big."

"There's nothing wrong with being big," Grace said, a bit too vehemently. A hawk flew over the tops of the trees, over the road, and rose, circling along invisible currents of wind, toward the hazy, shimmering sun. She watched it until it was above the roof of the car and out of sight. She was angry but didn't know why. "You'll be big one day, too, and prettier than ever."

"Like you?" Emma said.

Grace didn't answer. She watched the road. She rolled down her window the rest of the way and felt the soft, warm air beat against her face and shoulder. And she thought: *It is like North Carolina in springtime.* And suddenly she imagined, for the first time in her adult life, going home to Durham again. Living with Mother again, in the white house with its sundrenched attic. Climbing the worn, polished stairs to her old room. Curling up for good.

Is Emma with me? Or Ethan? Or am I alone?

"Mom?" Emma said.

The lovely, soothing image vanished: gone the fragrant green spring, the white house, the bed of childhood; now she was at the bottom of a well, looking up.

She said, "Yes, Em."

"Justine heard her mother talking about Josh."

"Josh?" Her voice broke a little—she heard his name, like a little fragment falling off a statue. "And what—"

They were passing the sign for Wheaton. The little green sign, as for all Connecticut towns, with the white topographical outline of the state and the name inside: Wheaton. She was gripping the steering wheel so hard her hands ached. She made herself go on. "And what did Justine's mother have to say about Josh?"

"That if he hadn't been playing in the road he'd still be alive," Emma said.

A car passed suddenly on the left, despite the yellow line: a roar of engine, the poison tang of exhaust. Scared her to death. Without planning to, she took her foot off the gas; the car, as if etherized, coasted onto the shoulder and stopped. The engine idled.

Emma was looking at her in confusion.

"Why'd you stop? We're not there."

"No." Grace could hardly hear her own voice.

"Then why?"

"Emma, do you know what Justine's mother meant when she said that about Josh?"

"Meant?"

"What she was really saying."

"No, I—"

"I'll tell you what she meant." Her own poisoned voice: it was like seeing herself from a great height, like watching herself in a nightmare, unable to stop herself. "She meant that Josh would still be alive if your father and I had been more careful. That's what she meant. She meant his death was our fault."

Emma shook her head fiercely. "That's not what she said." She looked certain.

"But that's what she meant."

"No."

"Yes, Emma."

"But it's not true!" Emma cried suddenly. "It's not!"

Emma's face was falling, the certainty of childhood dissolving now like a tablet in water. Grace felt sick to her stomach with regret, but still she could not stop herself. "Yes, Emma. Yes, it is."

She reached out to touch her daughter.

"No!" Emma shouted, slapping her hand away. "Get off me!"

Grace shrank back at once. "I'm sorry—"

"I hate you! I hate you!"

"No . . . please—" In a panic Grace turned the key in the ignition. But the engine was already on; a metallic screech rent the air, and she cried out as if she'd been stabbed. She fell back against the door, sobbing.

Dwight

It was dusk and the school parking lot was full of cars. Inside the building the concert had just started. Halting notes rose to the open windows of the gym like birds trying to escape, sometimes successful, sometimes not, sometimes hitting the panes, sometimes finding air. Children's music. I sat in the Corsica with the windows down, listening, looking out over the playground in the dusk, slowly working my way through a pint of Jim Beam.

Ruth had told me that Sam came tenth on the program, near the end. That meant there was much bad music to get through before then, and much confidence to pull out of the bottle before I could face my son and the other parents and their children. Before I could set eyes on Ethan and Grace Learner and their daughter. They'd been names in the paper, small blocks of print. They'd been ideas and now they'd start to breathe. They'd breathe me in. Soon I'd see their faces, maybe the color of their eyes. It was dusk. I was halfway through the bottle and still not sure it would be enough. A few small kids and a couple of au pairs were gathered around the slide in the playground. The kids took turns sliding down. I heard shouts and laughter. The slide's surface shone in the dusk.

Somebody was playing "Greensleeves" on a recorder. It might have been two instruments; it sounded like a duet. Ruth must have lost her mind to put on a program like this. I wondered what she was wearing. Something wrong for the occasion, probably, something way off, standing in front of the community, all those upstanding citizens with kazoos in their pockets. Embarrassing. Yet beneath the clothes there was that same body I knew. I had tried to stop thinking about it but it had never worked. Too often at night her naked image was projected against the blank wall of my memory, alone or with me, someone like me, joined at the hips, thrashing around like two teenagers in heat.

I put the bottle to my mouth and swallowed, and a little bit of fire rushed down my throat. Everywhere else the light kept draining away. In the playground a boy went zooming down the slide on his rear. Something about him made him go faster than the others; at the bottom he flew off as if he'd been kicked, and landed in a heap on the ground. I heard him crying.

"Greensleeves" came to a weepy close. A fifteen-hanky performance. The applause was hearty, and then Ruth was introducing the next number. I couldn't make out the words, but I recognized the sound of her. It was her public-speaking voice, hauled creaking out of the basement and oiled up for this summer rite. Only Sam's appearance at the end of the set, gleaming trumpet in hand, would crack her composure, turn her back into herself. No one else would know the difference or care.

I had to get going. It was now or never. I put the bottle to my mouth again and tasted how things might be. There was no direction to think in that was totally without consequences, which is just another way of saying that I was alive against my better judgment. I saw how Stu Carmody had understood the human condition as well as any man. Though he too had made a mess of it in the end. He'd wanted to go out of the world neat and orderly, everything tidied up, but it hadn't worked out that way. He'd tried to hang himself in his barn, but the rope was old and it broke from his weight (the police found it on the premises). So he was forced to rig up his shotgun. The irony of which was not lost on him before he blew his brains out. In a suicide note addressed to me he stated that, though he could not remember it, he knew for certain his coming into the world had been a bloody mess, as all births are, and he'd been nothing but a damn fool ever since for thinking he might leave the world any way but how he'd found it.

Grace

Everyone seemed to arrive at once. Cars pulled into the parking lot behind the school, one after another. The doors opened into the soft light and children ran screaming for the playground, where the metal slide shone like a silver waterfall. Parents tried in vain to call them back. In the end they simply watched them go and smiled knowingly at one another.

It was cocktail hour, voices smoothed by drink. They were all there: old neighbors, old friends and enemies. Nothing had ever been forgotten. She got out of the car and stood watching. She saw the first boy begin his descent down the slide.

He flew, laughing the whole way. He seemed to shine, too; like a little god, like a messenger. And she felt the gleaming metal in her heart like shrapnel, and then its swift, painful expansion, how its coldness could become all that she was. She turned away before the boy reached the bottom.

She found Ethan standing on the other side of the car, looking at her, the hood between them like a table.

"What?" he asked.

"Nothing."

"I thought you said something."

"No."

He turned to Emma. "Do you have the music?"

Emma disappeared into the backseat and came out holding a paper folder. "I got it."

"I *have* it," Ethan corrected.

"I know," Emma said. "Mom?"

"What?" Grace couldn't look at her. Because she was afraid of her. This little girl in the white dress and red strap shoes, a red ribbon tied in her blond hair. Ethereal and perfect. A daughter who did not seem to remember telling her mother that she hated her.

"Look," Emma said, pointing. "Tommy Gilmore's going down the slide."

She looked: a pudgy boy rocketing down to the ground.

"Tommy Gilmore's not wearing a white dress," Ethan said to Emma.

"I wish I wasn't either."

"You look pretty. Grace? Are you with us?"

"I feel sorry for Tommy Gilmore," Grace said.

"Why, Mom?"

But she couldn't explain it.

"Let's go inside," Ethan said.

• • •

She saw again the gray stone crosses in the thick brick walls, both church and state. They went up the front steps and into the high wide lobby and she saw the crosses there, too, resolute above the small crowd, and she thought that perhaps this was what she needed, more of this rock-bottom shelter under God. A thick-walled place. Someplace to go. But it was just a school; it was not for her. They were in the midst of it now, other families entering the lobby and milling around, and she felt Emma shrink back instinctively behind the protection of her legs. Grace let her hand fall to her side, a casual offering. Without even a glance, Emma reached up and took it.

"It will be okay," Ethan said softly, out of the blue.

It was a small thing; he might have been saying it to himself. Still, she was grateful.

She felt they were being watched, whispered about. She looked around. And what she saw made her stomach turn over: in the corner Judy Aronson stood in a huddle with Pam and Dick Foster and Mary Ann Lucas and her husband, Tom. They were talking among themselves and shaking their heads communally over the tragedy of it all and darting somber glances at the Learner family in the center of the room. Grace looked away. She wanted to leave now. She and Judy Aronson were friends. Not the Fosters as much, and the Lucases not at all, but Judy Aronson yes, they'd been friends, had had lunch together regularly over the years and had talked a great deal, about real things. And Grace felt the betrayal bitterly, as a sign of what was to come.

• • •

It was almost time for the concert. The gym was on the second floor and people were climbing the stairs. Mothers held tight to the hands of their youngest children as they took each step. A lifeline. She felt her spirit go with them, her body left behind, just bones and flesh. She couldn't make it.

"Grace."

She turned. It was Judy, standing with a hang-dog look on her wide face and her arms out. Grace felt tears suddenly pushing behind her eyes, and a searing anger.

Judy stepped up and hugged her. "Oh, honey. Did you get my messages? I called three times."

"The machine's broken," Ethan said quickly. "Hi, Judy."

"Hello, dear." Judy took one hand off Grace's back and gave Ethan's arm a squeeze. Then, with the same hand, she managed to touch Emma's hair. "And you, Emma."

Emma recoiled. And Grace stepped out of Judy's arms and took her daughter's hand instead. "Yes, the machine's broken."

"I don't know how to say how sorry I am."

"It's all right," Grace said. "It can be fixed."

"No, I meant—"

"Grace." Ethan put his hand on her back. It was a warning and not warm. "Sorry, Judy," he said. "This is hard."

"Don't apologize for me!" Grace said, louder than

she intended. She felt heads turn and the blood rushing to her face. Ethan looked away. Judy looked away. But not Emma. Grace held on to her daughter's hand for dear life.

Judy had recovered and was making her farewell speech: "Now Grace, I want to have lunch. Whenever you're ready, you come over and I'll make something delicious and we'll sit and talk. It doesn't have to be *about* anything. We'll open some wine. I just want to see you, make sure you're all right."

"I'm not all right, Judy."

"Well, we can talk about that, too."

Another hug was not attempted. Grace watched Judy climb the stairs, her graying brown hair cut short and square like her body, a sturdy, no-nonsense frame. The kind of friend you counted on to give it to you straight, not to gossip about you, no bullshit or pity or self-pity, a good dark sense of humor. All washed away now. Her son Aaron was in Josh's class. Judy Aronson was a single mother. No, more than that—she was a widow. Her husband had dropped dead of a heart attack while shoveling snow from the driveway. It was the first thing Grace ever knew about her.

There was Emma's hand again, the faintest shift in pressure. Grace squatted down and looked her in the eyes.

"How are you, sweetie?"

Emma looked at the floor. "Okay."

"Are you nervous?"

Emma nodded.

"I played in a concert once, when I was about your age. Did I ever tell you that?"

Emma shook her head.

"Well, I did. My daddy made me. Just about everyone we knew in Durham was there, and I had to get up on a stage in front of them all and sit at the piano and play. I'd never been so terrified in all my life. But it went well. And I wasn't half as good as you."

She was on her knees in the center of the bustling lobby, holding her daughter. The rest were other people. She kissed Emma on the lips.

Ethan gave a long, despairing sigh: "We'd better go up."

It was just a school gym with fluorescent lighting harsh as a microwave, and rows of folding metal chairs with an aisle cut down the middle. The sight filled her with dread. At the end of the aisle was a low wooden stage, and on the stage a grand piano, a piano stool, a music stand. Ruth Wheldon stood over the music stand, adjusting its height. Over red pumps and a floor-length red dress she wore a powder-blue silk shawl that kept slipping off her shoulders to reveal flashes of smooth, tanned skin. Grace had never seen anything quite like it except at her prom long ago, or perhaps in the horror movie *Carrie*. She felt kind of sorry for Ruth Wheldon. And yet, at the same time, she couldn't help noticing the slender, athletic shapeliness of the woman's shoulders and arms, the curve of her bust, and how her sand-colored hair shone soft even in the cutting light. Men would be attracted to Ruth Wheldon, in spite of her clothes. Grace could see her sitting in an open convertible on a quiet dark road, a man's arm around her, his breath on her neck. It was an image from another time and place, another woman and another man, and she didn't know why it came to her now, and didn't want it anyway. She reached down and smoothed Emma's hair back behind her ears.

"Don't," Emma said.

"It was sticking out."

"Let's sit here," Ethan said.

They sat in the third row, with Emma between them. The chairs were cold and hard. Other families were settling around them, parents talking to their children, boys' voices rising above all other sounds. She would not look. Her thoughts threatened to seize her, take her back in time. She refused to give in to them. She kept her eyes straight ahead—the stage, the piano, the music stand. She had to hold on. She could hear people she knew whispering, gossiping with the impunity of the well-intentioned.

Ruth Wheldon had spotted her and was trying to make eye contact. Then she was walking over, the red dress rustling like taffeta. She was standing in the aisle, row three, her hands held together in front of her in that way favored alike by the very religious and the very nervous.

"I'm so glad to see you all here. Hi, Emma."

"Hi."

"Hello, Mrs. Wheldon," Ethan said.

"Ruth."

"Ruth," Ethan said.

"Are you ready, Emma? We're all looking forward to hearing you play."

Emma didn't say anything. After an awkward moment, Ethan put his hand on her back. "Emma, Mrs. Wheldon asked you a question."

Emma moved her head up and down.

Ruth Wheldon tried to smile. She turned her wedding ring round and round on her finger. "There's a lot going on."

"Yes," Grace said.

"Well." Ruth Wheldon took a step backward; she looked ready to flee. "Emma goes ninth, just before my son. I put her near the end so she'd feel less pressure."

"Thank you," Grace said.

Suddenly Ruth Wheldon reached out and squeezed her hand. "I'm glad you're here," she said. And then she walked back to the front of the room, wiping tears from her eyes.

It was a kind of torture for everyone involved—Grace felt quite certain of that. The method was deceptively innocent. The Starkey twins, Megan and Billy, played "Greensleeves" on their recorders. A sweet, redheaded pair. They might just as well have run their fingernails down a blackboard. Marcia Starkey, the mother, cried her eyes out in the eighth row. One hand dabbed at her mascara with a Kleenex while the other carefully monitored the volume on the cassette recorder on her lap.

The song came to an end, the tape clicked off. There was applause and, afterwards, as she got up from her seat in the front row and walked to the stage, the intense rustling of Ruth Wheldon's dress. She made the introduction, and somebody's little girl walked up to the stage carrying a guitar.

"Jesus," Ethan whispered. "This is a nightmare."

She actually smiled, looking at him over Emma's head: it was so Ethan—the mordant, ever-suffering cynic. For a moment she felt how much she loved him.

But he wouldn't stop.

"I told you we shouldn't have come to this thing," he whispered bitterly. "This was a mistake."

She went cold. "*My* mistake, you mean."

There was no reply. And then, as if on cue, a new song began. A young voice singing high like a reed by a stream. Grace could make no sense of it. It was as if a cord had been cut, and the time that passed then passed without her, though she was sitting at its center. She sensed only how the notes touched the air as shadows will touch light, how all things return to their source without explanation, without shame. There was only one truth: that she lived now on the periphery of a world she once had owned without a thought. Cowardice and darkness surrounded her; courage too, though she could not find it.

Applause. The girl sat down, a boy stood up. Other people wouldn't go away. And with each new performance Ruth Wheldon appeared and disappeared from the stage with an earnest, faintly goofy precision, like a beautiful cuckoo clock.

It was the Dixon boy, twelve years old. He played the clarinet and knew he was good. The way he held the black instrument like a wonder stick, something to throw, or dance with, or make magic with. "A-one; a one, two, three," he said, like a little Benny Goodman, as if he had a quartet behind him, and then launched into "When the Saints Go Marching In" — New Orleans–style, the rhythm all out there and the audience compelled to clap. She took Emma's hand in hers. Thinking that the boy couldn't have known — how could he have known? *Daddy's favorite song.* Joyous and southern was how he'd liked his music, and until the day he died he'd played this song on the phonograph in their parlor in Durham, over and over again on Saturdays, and on Sundays after church, after meals, holding his Grace high off the ground by her wrists and dancing her around the room, making her cry with delight, while Mother called out to be careful.

A sound came from the back of the gym: the groan of hinges. Someone arriving late. A few angry people turned to glare, but not Grace. She had nothing left over for strangers.

The boy played on and the people clapped. And she held tight to Emma's hand, waiting for something to happen.

Dwight

I took a last deep breath and pulled open the metal door at the back of the gym. The hinges groaned, cutting through the music, and in the room's bright light and hardwood shine faces I recognized turned and frowned at me.

Up on a makeshift stage, in front of about fifty people seated on folding chairs, a boy was playing the clarinet. He couldn't have been more than twelve or thirteen and he was playing "When the Saints Go Marching In," his foot tapping and the black flower-like instrument moving herky-jerky in his hands as if being blown around by the wind inside of it.

It was fine music, and some parents in the audience were clapping to the beat. Larry Baylis was clapping, and so was Chuck Zorn. They'd be just off the train from Grand Central. A quick pit stop home for a double martini and a change of clothes, a flip from boardroom chic to catalogue country, and then here to see their children shine before the community.

We'd all been neighbors once. But I'd been expelled, both privately and publicly, and they didn't want me here. I was a good-riddance piece of history resurrected from the dead. Their faces showed disgust, anger, maybe even fear. And then they turned back to the music and soon were clapping again.

I slipped into an empty seat in the last row. A few chairs away a pretty, older woman sat alone. She nodded and smiled at me, and I smiled back. She was a divorcee maybe, a widow, somebody's silver-haired aunt. She was my new best friend. The boy went on with his playing and the saints came marching in. It was New Orleans here, it was Mardi Gras, and the boy moved herky-jerky, and there was a sickening heat in the pit of my stomach and at the back of my throat.

A jazz flourish, a precocious little riff, and the song ended. Applause broke out. The boy walked back into the audience to join his family, the clarinet held easy in one hand as if he'd just smacked one out of the park, and Ruth got up from a seat in the front row and turned to face everyone. Public Speaking 101. She was blushing.

"The next performer will be" — her voice caught and she cleared it — "Emma Learner. Emma will play a prelude by Bach."

At the sound of the name I half rose out of my chair. The whole room was before me and every person in it. Ruth caught sight of me then and her face turned stony, but it was wasted on me: in the third row a small blond girl had stood up. She had on a white dress and a red ribbon in her hair, and it was Emma Learner, and she turned and put her hands in the lap

217

of the beautiful blond woman sitting next to her. They were mother and daughter, there could be no doubt about that. The woman was Grace Learner, and she whispered something in her daughter's ear and kissed her on the cheek full of love, and watching it all I felt a confused stab of regret and shame and age-old longing and maybe even of envy. She was too perfect, too much in the center of a life I never had been and never would be a part of, and from my cheap bleacher seat at the margin of things I could hardly see her through the washed-out memories of the sickly, unstrung housewife who had been my mother.

Then these particular thoughts disappeared. The man sitting next to mother and daughter—a tall, handsome man with small round glasses and black curly hair—leaned down, and it was Ethan Learner, and he kissed his little girl on top of her head.

Emma Learner walked to the stage, where Ruth smiled reassuringly at her and adjusted the height of the piano stool. Then Ruth went back to her seat. Next to her I caught a glimpse of the back of Sam's head, and the gleaming lips of the trumpet held vertical on his lap. There was whispering in the audience before the music started; an ugly adult sound, edgy with gossip. Ethan Learner put his arm around his wife and squeezed her shoulder. And I saw how she gave in to nothing—not the comfort he was offering, not the voices whispering around her—but sat rigid and erect on her chair, looking ahead at her daughter and nowhere else. Pretty soon he stopped squeezing, and then his hand fell off her altogether.

Ethan

She took her place, small before the piano, white to its black, red-shoed feet floating above the pedals. She leaned forward over the keys and stared down at her hands, as if it were all up to them. Then she began to play, and the gossiping fell to nothing.

Trouble came early—a difficult passage. She got caught and misplayed a note, and then another. Grace and I winced for her. But she just gave a breathy sigh of disappointment and played on. There was no way of knowing her thoughts except that for those few minutes she seemed to have left us all behind; as if, for the duration of her playing, there was no such thing as memory. Just her fingers traveling the keys, pushed to their limit, and the long black box ringing out.

She made no more mistakes, and then she was done.

They were still applauding when she came back to her seat. We kissed her and told her how good she'd been. But she would have none of it. She sat straight on the chair while her eyes filled with tears. Her mother took her in her arms, and Emma pressed herself there, burrowing. Her voice came, faint and mumbled.

"What?" I said. "I couldn't hear."

The color had drained from Grace's face. "She said she'll never be as good as Josh."

"Emma . . . ," I began. But I could think of nothing. I turned away. The applause had died out and Ruth Wheldon was walking up to the stage, her long dress whispering. No one in the crowd would meet my eye.

Ruth Wheldon said, "The last performer of the evening will be Sam Arno, on trumpet. Sam will play 'America the Beautiful.'"

Polite applause as a small, sandy-haired boy stood up in the middle of the front row and climbed the stage. Just his back visible, and the trumpet that he carried in both hands like a trophy, its color the color of white gold, its ends sticking out to either side of his narrow body like some piece of treasure he was hoarding, or chained to. His mother bent down to him, whispered something in his ear, gave him a kiss. Then he turned around.

A murmur ran through the first rows of the audience. The skin around the boy's right eye was a patchwork of faded blues and yellows. The eye itself was noticeably bloodshot. Some woman whispered, "My goodness!" It sounded like Judy Aronson.

Ruth Wheldon flushed and looked helplessly at her son, who was staring hard at his trumpet, as if he wanted to crawl inside it. The harsh gym lights offered no sanctuary. "Um . . ." she said, and all eyes in the room turned to her. She tried to smile; impossibly, her color deepened. "You're probably all wondering about Sam's eye," she said weakly. "Well, he was out with his father, Dwight, last week and they got in a little accident. Nothing serious. Actually, he's fine." Her smile withered on her pretty face. She touched a hand to her son's head and walked quickly off the stage.

The boy watched her intently. A serious, sad boy, I would have said. Who had been in an accident. Who had a black and bloodied eye: his father's fault, one way or another. The boy waited until his mother was safely in her seat before raising the trumpet to his lips. "'America the Beautiful,'" he said, his voice high and far away, an undiscovered continent.

Suddenly, hinges groaned at the back of the gym: I turned in time to glimpse a man's broad back disappearing through the open door. Fresh murmurings shot through the crowd. Then the door closed with a bang, and the boy started to play.

We made it home, upstairs; Grace said she'd sit with Emma until Emma fell asleep, so I went into our room alone. The floor littered with dirty clothes, the bed unmade. You could see something had happened here—a terrorist attack, a bloody defeat without a battle. The kind of war for which there is no diplomacy or solution, no thought that could possibly matter. I stepped out of my clothes, leaving them like skins on the floor. Naked, I went into the bathroom and brushed the encroaching coffee stains on my teeth and emptied my bladder and stood for less than a minute under a shower so hot there was nothing left to consider but the red scalding pain. It made me shiver. And afterwards I lay on my back with the white sheet up to my neck, like a corpse waiting to be prepared. Grace's bedside light was on, shining over her empty place. I was afraid of the words forming in my head; "Josh" was a word. I closed my eyes and began to hum to myself. The notes just appeared at the back of my throat, unchosen, familiar: "America the Beautiful." I fell asleep.

I dreamed it was dark in the car. Our car. Driving back from somewhere on a moonless night, my beautiful son singing in the backseat, his voice high and soft and sweet in the dark. We all knew the song, the famous stirring words: "America the Beautiful." But on this night for some reason it was annoying the hell out of me. I hated it. I kept telling Josh to be quiet, but Grace kept saying no, let him. Let him. It was pitch black in our car and I kept saying "Be quiet," and Josh kept singing. And then, still driving, I turned around to yell at him. Nothing there but blackness. "Where is he?" I demanded angrily, wanting to punish him. "Where he always is," Grace answered calmly, sounding bored. Then she screamed, and I turned around.

Just ahead, in the washed-out tunnel of headlights, Josh stood fixed in the road, his mouth open. And I chose wrong. My foot hit the wrong pedal and the car sped up. He was still singing when I ran him over.

• • •

I woke in my house. Sweating and afraid in my own room. Sick with guilt. The room was dark. I reached out for Grace but she wasn't there. And for a long horrifying moment that felt like a tumbling through nothingness, I sensed no other human presence in the entire house, neither heartbeat nor breath, nor family, nor love. It felt like the death of everything I had once believed in and hoped for and been a part of.

I rolled over, peered through the darkness: Grace was there, at the far edge of the bed, curled away from me. Asleep. The sheet carved a phantom across her back, a waterline rising and falling with each breath, and there were shadows in the hollow between her neck and shoulder and around the long sweeping curve of her hip beneath the white sheet. I was chilled, damp with sweat. Now, like a burrowing animal, I slid my body across the bed and found the pocket of her warmth. Her skin emanating heat as if she'd swallowed the sun. He skin smelling of soap and earth and something like wildflowers. I touched her hip and her eyes opened. I pressed up behind her, hard now and curving between soft moons of her flesh, my fingers working down from her hip through the damp triangle of her hair and into her, and her scent rising up, musky and beautiful. She moaned softly. Then she turned, opening her body to me, her pale night limbs unfolding like a butterfly being born. I entered her whispering her name, and felt the horrors of the dream begin to recede.

Then it ended. I saw her eyes change while I was

deep inside her. A going away. Her mouth fell slack under the weight of the words she would not utter. And then she was sand draining through my fingers.

I pulled out, rolled away from her.

"I'm sorry," she said.

"I know."

"I can't."

"I know."

"I can't. I just can't."

"I know," I said.

I got out of bed and went to the window. Looking at nothing, the darkness. There was just a thin new moon in the sky. I heard her go into the bathroom and shut the door. The old leaded windowpane was cool against my forehead. She began to run a bath. I pictured her sitting naked on the edge of the tub, steam rising around her like smoke. In a little while, I thought, she wouldn't be able to see herself in the mirror, and then she would lower herself into the hot water and scrub me out.

I knelt down and put my face to the open window. I breathed in and out, and there was dew in the air, particled and summer-lush. I missed the winter that had passed without my having paid attention to it, the smells of woodsmoke and juniper, my son's footprints in the snow. My son would not be growing up.

Grace turned off the water. Through the closed door between us, I heard the liquid circles of her feet stepping into the bath, and then the rest of her. The white faces of her knees above the clear greenish water. She did not cry for very long.

PART THREE

Dwight

Late one night in the middle of August I got in my car and drove over to Wyndham Falls. I found Pine Creek Road, and drove slowly past the mailbox that had their name on it. It was an old house, handsome, set back from the road, with frowning black shudders. All the lights were out.

I had no plan in particular. It was just a need, no different in some ways from an animal—a bear, say—who comes out of the woods at night to sniff at the edges of the human world, wondering at how close it is after all, and how foreign. What in theory seems like clear boundaries between lives turns out to be something a little more confusing when your face is pressed up against it. I had spent hours sitting in my house trying to imagine this place and the lives inside it. For some reason, in my mind it was always at night. A white house like this one now, on a road called Pine Creek, but with one window glowing bright. And a blond woman standing behind it, looking out at the blackness, where I was.

But dreams are cheap, and most of the time they are wrong. There was no light on at all, there was no woman. I stared through my window at the darkened house, and then I turned the car around and drove back the way I'd come. And promised myself: Never again.

The rest of August went. Like anybody else, I turned out the light at night and lay on the bed till sleep came; or if not sleep, then something like it, some thickening and dulling of the nerve ends. In the mornings I kept getting up and going to work. I had a week's vacation coming at the end of the month but put it off because I was afraid of any downtime at all, when the days would be as empty as the nights. (When Jack Cutter heard I wasn't taking my vacation he was incredulous, even concerned. "Are you sick, Dwight? Are you in love?" I just shrugged.) I was a coward. I kept Donna in the dark, never called her at all. I kept the Taurus with the busted right headlight in the garage, and the door there closed. I watched the summer pass.

The only relevant clock for me had become Sam's bruised eye. It faded to the color of nicotined fingers, the sallowed eye-pouches of old men in bowling alleys. Then it faded all the way back to youth. But this was a different youth, less innocent and sure, even if Sam didn't yet know it himself. By September he was already on his third life (how many would he get?), and he was only ten.

We had our Sundays together. Over the weeks he seemed somehow to have put behind him the fact of my throwing him to the ground. The subject never came up. Which was a relief, of course, but which also made me grieve. Because it came clear to me that my son, with his decency of heart and purity of vision, had gone and filed my most recent infraction within the overall record of my life, where it quickly became part of a pattern and so no longer stood out as worse than anything else I'd done to him. This big-picture view was heroic, an act of compassion that set him far apart from the likes of me; but it required a terrible, adult kind of distance. I wasn't blind. Each time I lost control, I watched Sam take another step back from me, and I missed him a little bit more.

Anyway, the days passed. They passed in bright silence, seen through glass, sealed off—laboratory rats making their way through the maze, oblivious. Same blue sky for everyone; just because I was a murderer the paperboy didn't stop tossing the paper on my drive. And I kept my promise to myself. I went about my business, I kept away. Blond woman; tall, dark man; little girl. If I'd had a lick of art in me, I could have painted them from memory. Painted them over and over, sitting in that gym full of parents and children.

There are books on survivors. I've seen a few. Pictures that show people after warfare, after a pogrom, people minus a leg or arm or eye, the invisible points where they are held together and the equally invisible points where they have been separated forever from their own spirits. Look first in the eyes, where the stories are written in permanent ink. Ethan Learner's arm dropping off his wife's shoulders because she wouldn't look at him. Together, then separate. Add, then subtract.

There would be no Indian summer this year; September was a clear blue chill. In the late afternoon colored leaves swirled airborne over the road through Canaan. And on weekends, pickup football games sprouted on town fields all over the area. Jackets and sweatshirts used for goalposts, swarms of warriors whooping it up, half of them going shirtless in the ancient rite of Shirts vs. Skins.

It was the Skins who perennially believed themselves the bad-ass kings of the turf, racing down the field after the kickoff, screaming for an ounce of Shirt blood; little men in the act of preparing to be big. All my childhood I'd believed in the Skins, wanted to be one, was one. As if publicly showing off the bruises my old man had made earned me the innocent license to hurt. There was no one around to tell me otherwise.

Now summer was over, officially. And whenever possible, I drove from here to there with my windows rolled up, to keep out the voices of children.

Ethan

I began another academic year at Smithfield because I had to. Someone had told me this once, but I'd forgotten who. Or I'd read it—Marcus Aurelius, perhaps, one more lost footnote for me. Not that it mattered. You moved forward. That fall I was scheduled to teach two electives of my own devising: Bitter Pill: Irony and Temporality in James (Late Period), Ford, and Woolf; and Heroic Fiction/Fictive Heroics: Writers After Warfare. There was nothing to say about these courses except that I'd thought them up in an earlier time, as a different man in a different life, and thus the grim ironies they held for me now were wholly unintended, if no longer unimaginable.

The first few weeks of the semester passed. New and old students got themselves settled, class rosters filled in and solidified. One morning I looked up from my spot at the front of the classroom, between the tabletop podium and the blackboard, and saw the young faces gathered as I'd seen them gathered for a dozen years: earnest, quizzical, eager, bored, skeptical. Too early in the year for adoration or resentment. Though not too early, I noticed, for pity. Most everyone at the college knew what had happened to my son. They had read about it in the papers or heard about it in the dining hall. Like sightings of a ghost, they claimed among themselves to have seen Josh on campus in the past, his black violin case slung over his bony shoulders, or claimed never to have seen him. They believed that they knew me and what kind of man I was, what sort of father, or they believed, rightly, that they did not know me and never would.

Twice every day I drove by the Canaan police barracks. And, unable not to, each time I passed I would turn and regard the building—squat, drab, impenetrable, it resembled nothing so much as a bunker in some cheap and futile war—and try to imagine Sergeant Burke sitting alertly at his desk, staring perhaps at the framed photographs of his own family, still in pursuit, supposedly, of the identity of the man whose gray outlines I'd seen inside the car that killed my son. This was an exercise in rage and hope, in constructing a balloon and attempting to fill it with just that mixture of gases that will cause it to rise without also causing it to explode. Rage because after two months there had been no progress in the case. They had found no one; as far as I knew, they suspected no one. Because in their failure to find who had committed the crime Burke and his upstanding colleagues had come to feel like the enemy to me, or at least the only enemy I might ever know other than myself.

And hope? Because in spite of everything the case was still alive. Because blame might still be found, placed, allotted. Because there was at least one man outside of the cave we lived in who spent his days with Josh's name on his lips; who, looking out a car window at the passing roadside on a day leaning toward dusk, perhaps saw my son's face.

It was an evening in early October.

I stayed in my office until six-thirty, hiding with the door shut; hiding in books that no longer smelled right, felt right to the touch, and so no longer gave refuge—as in a house blackened by fire, when the only sensible thing to do is gather up what's salvageable and move on, but you just can't face it, so you stay put, you and your poor family, night after night, wandering the rooms with soot-blackened fingers and damp ash up your noses, saying to yourselves, "It just doesn't feel the same."

By six-thirty the building was empty; even Jean Olsen had left for the stale, canola-fried air of the dining hall. I gathered up my books and walked out to my car and drove across campus. The blue sky was faltering, the days already growing noticeably shorter. Leaves were turning on the trees by the road where it dipped and then climbed past the music building with the beautiful windows and over the brow of the second hill to the gate.

Through Great Barrington, through Sheffield, across the state line and the train tracks. The darkening sky, and everything under it distinct: two crows flying over the phone lines; a man loading bags of fertilizer onto the bed of a pickup; the first sign of pumpkins. The summer was over, it was autumn, and Josh—

He is sitting on our leaf-strewn lawn, smiling, a gutted, grinning pumpkin in his lap and an orange-handled child's safety knife in his fist, the dull, serrated blade streaked with pulp, glistening seeds heaped on a sheet of newspaper beside him. He is seven. He's just carved his first jack-o'-lantern and couldn't be more pleased with himself. I am raking leaves and watching him out of the corner of my eye. He lays down the knife with an artist's air of skeptical yet satisfied completion. Then he turns silly. Giggling, he waves me over, teasing: "He looks like you, Dad! He looks like you!" I pick him up and spin with him across the lawn, around and around, twirling our bodies together like a top, his head upside down, his mouth open—until, crying with laughter, he begs me to stop—

I slowed down. Ahead now, in the dusk, the police barracks appeared—squat and ugly, a spotlight shining from above the front entrance out over the parking lot, where only three cars were parked. Without another thought, I turned in.

Since that first time, the morning after it happened, I hadn't been back. Perhaps because of the unfavorable, even alarming, impression made by my first appearance in the barracks, Sergeant Burke from the beginning had seemed eager to keep our conversations localized, contained. There was the one meeting at our house, followed, for a while, by weekly phone check-ins, always with the same news, delivered in tones of careful military neutrality: Nothing to report yet, we're still on the case. By Labor Day, though, his calls had slacked off and his voice had begun to betray a new kind of frustration. I was phoning him three, four times a week and he was never available to take my calls, he was busy, he was ducking me, using the auburn-haired, small-eyed dispatch officer as a cover.

The place seemed abandoned now. If not for the spotlight shining over the entrance and the stray fluorescent cracks visible at the edges of the metal blinds drawn over the windows, this particular barracks would have looked out of business. The waiting room was empty; the dispatch room was empty, too. Did the police, like regular citizens, go home en masse on the dot of five or six o'clock, leaving the world's troubles on their desks for the next brave morning? Did they too have trouble meeting their mortgage payments? The law in shutdown. As far as I could tell, the waiting room bulletin board was papered with the exact same xeroxed messages as on my last visit: somewhere a dog named Moby was still lost, perhaps dead; somewhere loitered the hooded-eyed fathers wanted by the state for failure to pay child support; somewhere roamed the fugitive rapists and killers.

There was no bell to ring, so I tried rapping on the Plexiglas window, producing merely a padded-cell sound of muted struggle. Then I turned to the steel door marked Authorized Personnel Only and began to pound on it with my fists.

The door opened and I found myself face-to-face with the dispatch officer with the auburn perm and the small eyes. She was out of uniform and disgruntled.

"What do you think you're doing, banging like that?" she demanded. "This is a police station."

"Excuse me," I said. "I need to see Burke."

"You mean *Sergeant* Burke."

"Yes. *Sergeant* Burke."

"Is he expecting you?"

"No."

"Then it'll have to be another time—he's got an important meeting this evening. Or if you want you can talk to the night-duty sergeant. His name's Nichols. He just came on."

"I don't want to talk to Nichols—"

"*Sergeant* Nichols."

"I want to talk to Burke."

Her eyes narrowed to slits and she tugged the zipper on her purple fleece pullover high up under her chin, the metal pulltab getting lost in the soft, jowly flesh there. "Maybe I'm not making myself clear. What you're gonna have to do is call Sergeant Burke in the a.m. Got it?"

"I've *been* calling him. That's why I'm here."

"Sorry."

She started to turn away, pulling the door closed behind her. I grabbed the door.

"You're not listening to me."

The woman whirled around and spoke rapid-fire. "If you know what's good for you, you'll take your hand off this door right now."

I let go of the door. My hand hung in the space between us, restless with the need to do something. I saw her looking at it.

"Step slowly back from the door," she said.

I stepped back.

She took a breath. "There are regulations," she said.

"I don't care." I stepped back farther until the edge of a plastic chair was pressing against the backs of my legs, and then I sat down, as though pushed by a terrible exhaustion.

"Well, I do," she said. "I have to, it's my job."

"What?" She was not in clear focus. I removed my glasses, rubbed my eyes, put my glasses back on. Everything taking a long time. "Have to what?" I said.

"Care." She was looking at me strangely. "About the regulations."

"My son is dead," I said. "What do your regulations have to say about that?"

The exhaustion was too great. I closed my eyes. I had not had a decent night's rest since my son had died. And here, now, in this windowless room, I felt as if I had not slept since being born, and was only now understanding that I would never sleep. I sat in my own darkness, waiting to hear the sound of the steel door closing.

"I remember you."

I opened my eyes.

"You're Learner. Your boy was the hit-and-run."

I nodded—like a dull boy outside the principal's office, or perhaps just a boy beaten senseless. Nobody's father. As the seconds passed, her fingers began to play with the zipper at her throat.

"All right," she said, as if conceding defeat in our battle of wills. "Wait here."

Burke came out into the waiting room still slipping his coat on. Underneath were a blazer and tie, a button-down, and khakis. His short graying hair was combed, and it all looked like dinner at the in-laws.

"Mr. Learner," he said. "I was planning on calling you."

I stood up. There was something abject, almost humiliated, underneath his voice tonight that gave me pause. His gray eyes, usually machine-steady, were restless and wary.

"When?"

"Tomorrow." At this lie Burke glanced at the bulletin board and its paper sorrows.

"Why, do you have news?"

"Information."

"What information? Is it news or isn't it?"

"Why don't we sit down." Burke's hand gestured

like an usher's, and I felt a net of invisible threads of sweat break out on my forehead.

"Just tell me, Burke."

Burke nodded, as if to say that he'd known all along it would go this way and there was nothing to do now but proceed. He cleared his throat. "All right. Mr. Learner, as of yesterday your son's case has been listed inactive."

"What?"

"Standard police practice. After a certain period of time, all unsolved cases get reprioritized."

"Reprioritized? Is this some kind of sick joke?"

"Obviously, we'll still be on the lookout for the perpetrator," Burke went on. "That hunt will be ongoing but indirect, as will any evidence gathering. But I have to tell you that officially the case has been moved to the back burner. And I've been reassigned."

"You can't do that," I said.

"Mr. Learner—"

"No. I'm sorry, you can't do that."

"It's hard, I know that." Burke reached out and touched my shoulder.

"Take your hand off me."

Burke's mouth tightened and he took back his hand. His voice turned a few degrees more officious. "We've got a small force here, Mr. Learner, barely enough men to keep up with all our responsibilities week to week. If we didn't separate the old cases from the new ones we'd be swamped."

"*Swamped?*" I turned to the wall and struck my

open hand against the bulletin board, sending thumb-tacks skittering across the room and papers raining onto the floor. Burke did not move.

"Take it easy now. There was no need—"

"Shame on you," I said.

"I'm a police officer, Mr. Learner, and I'm doing my job the best—"

"You're a son of a bitch and a coward. You've got no guts, you've got no heart—"

"Now you hold on right there!"

"I hope it happens to you, Burke," I said.

Now his eyes fixed on me like two gray stones. "What did you say?"

"You heard me. Your own son. How would it feel? Your own son mowed over on the side of the road and you the one standing here begging for a scrap of infor-mation, a little bit of goddamn human decency, and all you get is nothing, looks the other way, calls ducked, standard practice. Shame on you. I never thought in my life I'd say it but it ought to happen to all of you so you know. So you know what it feels like. Because if you don't know you just don't give a damn, do you? Just doing your lousy job, right? Shame on you. My son was worth ten of you."

Burke's face had gone pale. His hands were balled into fists at his side, and there was a look in his eyes that said he had better remove himself from this situa-tion. And in that momentary expression I saw that he and the police were now finished with me. They'd had enough. My rage, which felt to me still barely even tapped, had wrecked whatever goodwill there'd been, and with it any chance of finding the man who killed my son.

"Sergeant," I stumbled, "I . . ."

He turned his back on me. Facing the Plexiglas window, in the center of which floated his dulled and watery reflection, he began to button his coat.

"We're done here, Mr. Learner," he said in a frigid voice to the empty dispatch room. "In a few days' time there'll be a name in your mailbox. Any problems you have from now on, any questions, any complaints, you take them to the trooper with that name. But not to me. Good night, sir."

He turned and went out through the front entrance into the night, and was gone.

Dwight

And promises get broken, one by one.

At three a.m. one night in early October, I drove over to Pine Creek Road.

Downstairs, a single light was glowing, spilling out through a window onto the rectangle of lawn. From the glimpse I had, the lit room looked empty.

This time I didn't turn around. I parked down the road a way, out of anybody's sight, and started walking back to the house. Wishing I'd had more than two drinks before leaving my house: a couple of stiff ones couldn't touch this roadside darkness. The moon was no moon at all. My heavy footsteps on the road, twigs snapping in the woods to my right, an owl in there lifting off and flying.

I remembered going hunting once with a school friend and his father. It was my first overnight trip, and at the end of a long bloody day we'd made a campfire ringed with rocks and sat around it saying almost nothing, eating our dinner and listening to the fire, drink-

ing Irish coffee out of a thermos. I was fourteen and
my mother had been dead six years. When the time
came to turn in, my friend's father placed his hand on
my head, ruffling my hair. "Did good today, Dwight,"
he said. "You're on your way." We got into our sleeping
bags. Soon, my friend and his father were sound asleep,
their steady breathing like the warm nuzzling of animals in the dark. But I couldn't sleep. Too much had
happened. I'd done good, I was on my way. I lay awake
thinking about the deer I'd killed that day, a poor,
flinching shot, and the blood it had trailed as it ran
frightened through the woods and fell, ran and fell,
and how I'd wanted it to die for my own reasons.

The woods gave out onto the Learner place and
I stopped to get my bearings in the differing degrees
of darkness. A barnlike garage on the near side, with
the stable doors drawn closed. Shrubs around it, and
what looked like an orchard of shadow trees off behind,
toward the house. The place was landscaped, designed,
thought over; even in darkness you could feel the
womanly care that had gone into it. Grace Learner, I
thought. Who designs gardens.

I stayed there at the fringe of it all until my breathing separated itself from me, grew close to regular. I
tried to think of it as just a house. But this was hard,
with me dressed head to toe in black at three in the
morning and the one light shining downstairs, poking
out onto the lawn like a shout; someone was awake.
Though from this angle and distance I couldn't see
inside the room. I let myself imagine it was her.

A split-rail fence ran along front, between the lawn

and the road. Keeping outside of it, well beyond the spillage of light, I went across the face of the house and then over the fence at the point where it came out under the limbs of a huge oak. My old football knee was stiff from the cold. The leaves on the ground smelled damp. The house was twenty yards away.

For a long time nothing moved. The lit room was a stage set waiting for the actors to show up: the high back of a reading chair, a little table with a glass and a bottle of the hard stuff, a tall bookcase sagging with books, a desk with a computer and a lamp, more books. A thinking man's lonely palace. There was a sofa against the left wall, complete with mussed-up blanket and pillows.

And I thought: Ethan Learner. Professor of English at Smithfield College.

It was an empty room. Then it was not empty. He reached for the glass, and I saw that he'd been there all along, reading, hidden by the chair's high back. An arm went out for the glass and then disappeared with it—that was all I saw. Then it became a matter of waiting for the rest of him.

Not long afterwards, he stood up. His back was to me. He shuffled to the desk—not walked, but shuffled like an old man. His dark hair was wild. He wore a heavy bathrobe over his clothes and carried the glass in one hand and a book in the other. He set these things down on the desk next to the computer and moved to the door, where he stopped and raised his hand to the light switch on the wall. I thought he was going to leave, go upstairs to bed and his wife.

Just before switching off the light, he turned to look at the sofa with its blanket and pillows. It was a long look, as if he was seeing himself there, huddled and awake. As if he had stores of pity for the man he saw there, who was himself. Then, deliberately, as if by an act of will, he turned to the window. I saw his face clearly for the first time. Hollowed out. Empty, as the room had been empty even though he'd been in it. For a second I thought he was seeing me. But it must have been his reflection he saw, in the windowpanes, because just then he turned his head away and switched out the light.

Now the night was a tide, simple and black. You could be invisible in it, submerged, of no consequence, not even there. I took a deep breath and stepped from behind the tree and out into the middle of the lawn.

And looked up.

Somewhere behind the dark windows, Grace Learner lay sleeping.

Ethan

We were truly alone now; we'd been cut loose. You
don't realize what an anchor hope is until it is definitively gone and you stand gutted, as though disembow-
eled, with no weight left inside to hold you down on
earth. Hollow, you begin to float. The mind, without
recourse to other people, without ballast, turns in on
itself, rooting out the darkest reaches of the person you
thought you were. Nothing looks the same. It is existence as one long hallucination; existence as daily
riddle—to which, as in a masochist's dreamscape,
every object, sight, sound at first appears to be the
answer, the missing piece, yet in the end turns out to
be meaningless.

The police were gone, out of it. They had shut
down, locked their doors, taken down the shingle.
Leaving us on the outside.

Cowards.

Some things, of course, would go on as before.
The not sleeping. The nights alone on the sofa. The

detective-fiction daydreams ending in a cataclysm of vigilante justice. In the realm of fantasy I was a hard wronged man with a mission. This was a world of bright colors and clarity, quite the opposite of how things stood in real life. Never mind. This would be my story now. So nights I sat in my study and closed my eyes and killed the daylights out of a man I couldn't have identified had I passed him in the street. A nameless, faceless man.

All this was ridiculous, no way to live. And it was ridiculous that sometimes, as I sat gnawing on an impossible future, the past would come back to me in the shape of my father. That brilliant man, that intellectual, who ran from his helplessness and his rage and chose to paint it as a victory. I would find him sitting across the room, in the wingback chair by the window—older, sadder, mumbling still the hypocritical pacifist slogans of his latter days. His moleskin trousers worn thin, his tweed jacket redolent of pipe smoke. Had he been real, I would have taken him by the collar and shaken him. I would have called him a liar. I would have thrown him out.

I want to be clear about this, now. Without hope, the need to punish is the one true religion. Blame must be fixed on some soul other than one's own. Justice must be done. Or else there is only the desert of grief and one's own footsteps upon it—restless, unceasing, as alone as the most distant planet in the universe.

Dwight

It wasn't planned. It was an accident.

Sam had been caught stabbing a pencil into the hand of another boy in his class, sending him to the infirmary. By noon of the next day, I received a call requesting my immediate presence at the school, to meet with Ruth and Larry Briggs, the principal.

I was late getting there. First, I had to excuse myself from a meeting with Jack and Drew Peckham, a local land developer intent upon screwing his three children out of their future inheritance because they'd voted for Clinton in the last election. Peckham was a major client, and Jack was visibly unhappy about my leaving in the middle of things.

When I arrived, I found Ruth already sitting in Briggs's office. He was leaning toward her over his desk and talking intently, but fell silent as soon as he saw me.

The truth was that Larry Briggs and I had never gotten along. He thought I was a thick-bodied lout, arrogant and maybe dangerous, and he'd been over-heard saying as much back in the days after the accident, when Sam had to write his answers in class on a chalk tablet because his jaw was wired shut. A time I had not forgotten. And as for my return view of Briggs, I considered him a misplaced Anglophile in a hound's-tooth sportcoat who thought the town of Wyndham Falls beneath him but had never mustered the imagination to leave. He saw himself as a culturally superior Robinson Crusoe on a barren isle, woebegone, when in fact he was just a plain old narcissist whose own voice sounded like a choir to him because he was incapable of hearing any other. His bitterness over his circumstances he took out on the hides and minds of little boys and girls whose imaginations were exponentially brighter than his own.

Today, Larry Briggs didn't bother getting up when he saw me. I crossed the room and sat down on a chair next to Ruth. By way of a greeting, she said my name once—said it flat, the way you might say the word "tree" if you were out walking in the woods—while Briggs nodded curtly in my direction and said nothing. In the gap made by their silence I heard the sound of children playing in the playground outside. Then Briggs went on with what he'd been saying to Ruth before I'd arrived, went on talking to her as if I wasn't there.

He had a skin-cream tan. And he talked about my sweet son as if he and Ruth were the only two people on the planet who might know anything about him. He inquired, clinically, about troubles at home, about Sam's relationship with Norris. He said that Sam's homeroom teacher, Ms. Throm, had observed of late an alarming level of aggression in Sam, a boy always known for his gentle, shy demeanor.

And Ruth was admirable, I'll say that for her. She was a master thespian, an audience killer. She said no, no trouble at home. She said fine, Norris and Sam got on fine. Her head dipped down, her hair let loose, her pretty nose and hazel eyes looking on the verge of being crushed by worry for her son, who had already been through so much. She said she couldn't speak for what went on between Sam and me, that wasn't for her to say. Of course, Sam's relationship with his father was a complicated business, she guessed everyone knew that.

Here Briggs nodded sympathetically and said oh yes, he did know that, certainly. He said, like a shrink, "Go on, Ruth."

And here Ruth smoothed her skirt over her thighs—it was a little tweed skirt, in a sickly shade of green—and told Briggs about the summer Sunday that Sam went to my house and came home different. She'd never been able to find out what happened, but something had, because she'd noticed a change in Sam since then, and so had Norris: troubled, at first afraid, then increasingly sullen, now possibly aggressive. Something must have happened. Because how was it otherwise that a boy might go from gentle and shy one month to jabbing pencils into the hands of other boys the next? She was beside herself, my ex-wife said. She was at a loss.

That was the end of Act One: the diva had sung.

Ruth caught her breath and looked at me. A hard look, driven by scrutiny, not love, not generous enough for hate. A look that made me remember hitting her that one night, hitting her with my fist, the plate shattering on the floor and her going down with it. The memory was like a car coming at me in the dark, blinding me with its lights, and I flinched, there in the office, my head turning away from her. Now I was looking out the windows of the school. And I saw how the sky today was of a blue to make you afraid: a gemmed hardness without compassion. Every bad thing that had followed my hitting Ruth shone clear on its surface.

I decided to get out of the room while there was still time. I stood up.

Ruth said sharply, carelessly, "Sit down, Dwight. We're not done here."

I was standing above her, looking down. Maybe, staring at my knees like that, my ex-wife forgot, for a blissful moment, what kind of man I was. Maybe she simply thought she was home talking to Norris. It wasn't Norris, after all, who carried his temper tucked inside his gut like a bomb. And it wasn't Norris she saw now, as she raised her head and looked into my face. I watched the old fear come roaring back into her eyes. Her back stiffened and her mouth drew a line.

I took a step away from her: because she was right about me. Dead right. I could feel the adrenaline in my arms, the bunched muscles, the big hands itching for trouble. With no more effort than breathing, I could picture doing every one of the bad things her mind was accusing me of doing.

I started for the door.

And now Larry Briggs came jumping out of his chair. Larry Briggs: his cheeks pinked with outrage, barking at me that he knew all about my "history" and wasn't surprised one iota—this was just the sort of behavior he'd expected from me. He wagged his finger at my back as I disappeared through the door. And never even guessed just how lucky he was to be alive.

Grace

She sat on the grass by the playground watching the second graders running wild. She counted fourteen of them, and they were screaming and scampering through the sections of giant plastic tubing and slipping down the slide and swinging on the swings; at least two had fallen and were in tears.

She checked her watch. On the top floor of the school, Emma was sitting in a room with the child psychologist, "working through the trauma of death." And in the face of such incontrovertible wisdom—such method, technique—what could she have done but take her hat off and bow down? Then retreat. *Put myself out to pasture where I belong*. Here on the grass, staring after other people's children, seeing how it was done: family life. She had known once, had done it herself.

In the playground the teacher, Mrs. Poor, was applying a Band-Aid to the knee of a Korean girl with pigtails who was crying. A tiny, bright spot of blood was visible on the girl's pale skin. And Mrs. Poor was saying soothing, meaningless things like "Now, now" and "There, there."

To the east, past the tennis courts and the playing field, woods began: the leaves there a mottled tapestry of ocher, crimson, rust, persimmon. In a week or two the hills and shallow valleys would be iridescent, as though on fire. The thought filled her with a fleeting rush of hope, a feeling she tried to hold, tie down, but it slipped from her grasp. A few weeks—what had two and a half months changed? Time was not the promised balm, wonder drug, heal-all: Josh would never be alive again. *I am stone, Lord, not flesh as you once promised, and all the days to come will work their hard weather on me, until I am carved with the loss of him. . . .*

She crossed her arms and hugged herself. Did it functionally, like someone reading from a manual— here is what you do for pain. And without surprise she saw it again: a blond girl walking across a lawn carrying a pitcher of iced tea. Smelling the wet grass and hear- ing the glass-and-china crash of human collapse, of death in the making; then turning and finding Daddy on his back by the pool, a strange man pounding on his chest and Mother screaming, pleading for God's com- passionate intervention, as if He might actually hear, as if He lived in the house at the end of the drive. . . .

And she wanted to scream: *How does one get through it, survive?* And now, almost calmly, like a faint echo, an answer: *One does not.* And now another: *It is too much to bear.*

Why couldn't they see that?

She'd grown up believing what was said around
her—said on Sundays and holidays, said with bourbon
glass in hand and naked, grasping hope in the heart;
said, bending down, to blond little girls who have seen
love collapse and die by the pool: that there is virtue to
be mined in pain, oh yes, that all human tragedy is
part and parcel of God's plan, a way for the soul to
reach through darkness toward the light of salvation.
Then why was Mother screaming so? Then why was
Daddy on the ground? A good man, a doctor, a vet-
eran of a war neither he nor anyone else had understood; a survivor of so many things. The world ever
after his death cold, a monstrous experiment. *This is
what children know, for they are the prophets of loss*.
And now it had happened twice. Now Emma too
might grow up afraid, crippled by the belief that it was
love that was aberrant; that the seed from which life
grew was not Josh's birth, not his curious spirit and
passionate probing intensity, but his death, his murder. And who could blame or sincerely contradict her?
No one. No one who would not lie.

Grace lay back on the grass, curving an arm across
her eyes so that she would not have to look at the sky,
which, immense and blue, frightened her now. She
heard a sound escape her lips—not quite a moan, but
something new, untranslatable.

And then, abruptly, she sensed she was being
watched—a feeling like being touched by a shadow
on the end of a stick. She sat up and looked around.

A big, powerful-looking man, broad in the shoulders and chest, stood at the edge of the parking lot

about twenty feet behind her. He was dressed in a blue suit and a white shirt unbuttoned at the neck. A tie hung loose from the collar. She got to her feet. Her heart was pounding, which shamed her; she wanted to be neither angry nor afraid, yet for some reason she was both.

"Yes?" Her own voice sounded brutal to her. "What do you want?"

The man looked at her before speaking. He seemed to be studying her. She took a step back, then regretted it.

"Are you Grace Learner?" he asked, finally. But it sounded like a false question, as though he already knew the answer.

"What do you want?" she repeated.

He said nothing.

"And you were watching me. Why? I don't know you."

"Don't be afraid." His voice was gravelly, quiet, and sad.

"I'm not afraid. I'm angry. I want to be left alone."

"Don't be angry."

"Who are you?" she demanded.

Dwight

She asked me who I was.

She kept looking at me. A woman in grass-stained jeans and scuffed hiking boots, a red-and-black plaid shirt, a down vest unzipped. Blond hair barely kept together with a rubber band. A dry yellow leaf hanging off one shirt sleeve. Her face was pale, her eyes wide and blue and stunned. A woman who had disowned her beauty, spat on it, and here it was still trailing her around like a too-faithful dog. Her face said: Get off, don't want you, don't give a fuck. She didn't look like somebody's mother. More like a patient recently out of shock, lost now. Like someone whose only real desire in life was to crawl back to the trauma ward—a far-flung country, quiet, the one place on earth where she'd felt safe. She wanted to get back there, but the map had been burned. Leaving her outside the school, forced to listen to the cries and laughter of children.

I opened my mouth to speak.

But what came out was just my name. It meant nothing to her, might have been the start of a song; I might have been somebody else. She stood there looking at me, sniffing the air as if she could smell the copper taste in my mouth. And in her face I saw this, too: she thought she was the only one living outside the town walls. She didn't know that I'd spent my life there.

I looked away, and then I walked away.

Grace

Late October. The sky was the blue of heaven; the leaves died on the trees and fell to earth.

She stood at her worktable, account and appointment books spread open before her, her hands flat on the tabletop, which was canted thirty degrees to ease the strain on her arms and back during the long hours of drafting; whose surface she had long ago smoothed with a sheet of milky green contact paper, now marked with a decade's worth of stray pencil and ink marks, like the hieroglyphs of a civilization forever lost. She hadn't drawn a thing in months. Hard even to remember what it felt like to put pencil to paper, to figure and design, the goodness it had imparted to her life. And so within a short time, a kind of free-fall from the sky, her art and mind had become shadowed like everything else; a penumbra of feeling and desire, a distant reminder of a once great light.

The books open on the table were conclusive: her career, if not already dead, was grievously wounded.

259

Of the four jobs she'd been hired to do for August and September, all had been aborted; there had been awkwardness, unpleasantness—return of payments demanded and given, orders canceled. Her reputation among clients and suppliers was damaged. Not even communal pity could mask the fact that she was seen as someone who could no longer be trusted, who might not recover.

She wanted to care, but could not. Knew she should care for Emma's sake, but could not. Knew that it probably should have meant something to her when Ethan came home, as he had last week, and announced in a drained, nearly robotic voice that he'd decided not to take his year-long, half-pay sabbatical the next year, because they would not be able to afford it.

With a sigh, she closed the books. She felt dirty and stale, wanted to wash her hands and face. A wastebasket sat beneath the worktable—an old present from Ethan. It was woven of reeds from the river Liffey, and he'd been unabashedly proud of it on the day he'd given it to her, full of stories of its provenance. Why, Joyce himself had . . . She could not remember. There was Molly Bloom at the end of it all, saying yes. Yes. And Grace thought, *I cannot remember what that feels like.* Why say yes? She took the books now, accounts and appointments, and dumped them in the wastebasket. Then she went around the studio throwing open the windows, hoping the brisk air would cleanse her somehow; it did not, though it carried to her the scent of apples from the two trees out back, as clear as if she were holding a bushel of them in her arms. This, anyway, was something. She breathed in deeply.

She heard the phone ringing and she went to it; Mother had said she might call. Mother who was very concerned, these days, about Emma and "the shrink." Afraid for Emma. Constantly making not-so-subtle comparisons between Emma and Grace, the original bereaved child, the little blond girl who'd lost her father. "Well, just look how you turned out," she'd said hopefully last week. "You turned out just dandy, didn't you? In spite of everything."

Grace didn't feel dandy. She felt as if someone had cut out her heart with a spoon.

The phone sat on a table in the corner of the studio. She reached it on the third ring. "Hello?" But there was nothing, just dead silence. And then a click. She put the receiver back down, thinking, *All right, Mother.*

She knew what her mother really thought, what she wanted: that Emma should come down to Durham and live with her for a while, until things got "cleared up" at home. But this was wrongheaded, Grace wanted to argue, based on the misguided assumption that things would ever get "cleared up" at home. Cleared up by whom? The police? She had never believed in them. They had gotten nowhere and then they had quit. They weren't even good liars.

The phone rang again, startling her. Her hand was

still resting on the receiver; she felt the vibrations within like a tiny SOS. She picked up.

"Hi, Mother."

But it wasn't Mother—she sensed that immediately. The silence on the other end of the line was heavy and male and, somehow, distinctly not southern. A chill passed over her skin.

"Hello?" she demanded. "Who is this? Hello!"

The line went dead.

Dwight

In my office late on an afternoon without meetings or purpose; paid by the hour with no hours to fill. Where small-town meets small-time.

Time to think.

I kept my door closed. Sat behind my desk as if there was a client present, requiring my full attention. But there was no one. The yellow pencils and the pencil sharpener. The two photos of Sam. The phone. The quiet.

Half an hour passed like this. An hour? Maybe, possible. I'd called her twice, heard her voice, hung up. Now, in my mind, I was still on the line with her, still trying to get the words out. Tell the truth. But I couldn't do it. I saw my mouth moving, shaping the words, but no words came out. The call was over.

She wouldn't have understood anyway, I told myself. And so I promised myself, once and for all, to just let her go.

• • •

Then the day got worse: the door opened and Donna walked in.

I straightened myself on my chair but she wasn't fooled—she knew my schedule these days, its time gaps deep as swimming holes. And she was not enamored of my sense of industry, among other things. She stood just inside the doorway, hands on her shapely hips and a look, somehow, of both resentment and relief on her face, like a rich investor who's decided to pass on that phony tax shelter once and for all. We hadn't slept together since mid-July. After Josh Learner died, I stopped calling Donna. And when she called me, I made excuses that became less believable by the week. There was never a big scene. Eventually, she just stopped calling, and the ice that formed between us at work grew so thick we could barely see each other through it.

I fingered my tie. "What is it, Donna?"

"I want to talk to you. That's what it is."

Before I could respond, she closed the door. I got up, extending my hand out over my desk to the straight-backed chairs. "Have a seat."

Donna said, "Don't use that voice with me, Dwight. I'm not one of your clients."

I nodded: she was right. I stepped out from behind my desk and went to her and tried to give her a kiss, but she put her palms on my chest and pushed.

"You're a son of a bitch," she said.

"I know."

"And you look like shit."

"I know that, too," I said.

"Goddamn you, Dwight."

"Yes."

We sat down on the two chairs. I hadn't managed to kiss her, and I had the sense of yet another package of long-diverted trouble finally arriving on my doorstep. I almost never sat on these chairs. They were more uncomfortable than seemed likely. For a fleeting moment I thought of poor Stu Carmody sitting here, talking to me about the outer limits of his pain and his life, looking for a flicker of compassion. I said, "I think I know why you're upset, and I'm sorry."

"You *think* you know why I'm upset?" Donna said, her voice rising. We were sitting just a foot apart. She reached out and took my jaw in her strong fingers and forced me to look her in the eyes.

I didn't last long before I looked away.

She shook her head in a slow, disgusted way, as if she might spit. "You don't know," she said. "You don't really *know* anything, do you, Dwight? You may think you do, but that doesn't count."

"You're right," I said, not looking at her.

"So what's that?" she accused me. "You throw in the towel, don't even try? 'Oh, I'm real sorry, everybody, but, you know, everything in my life's just shit. So I guess I'll just leave it that way, 'cause it's easier.' Well, that doesn't work for me, Dwight. It's not even fresh. You've pulled it on me too many times. I've got feelings for you, sure. I've never been coy about that. But that doesn't mean I plan to spend my life waiting for you to grow up."

Donna stood up, pressing some moisture from her eyes with the heel of her palm. I stayed sitting and life-less. She looked down at me with something like pity in her face.

"Don't expect me to be here for you when you hit bottom."

She turned to go. She was reaching for the door-knob when the door opened and Jack Cutter walked in.

I got up then. "Goddamnit," I said. "This is my office. Doesn't anybody fucking *knock* anymore?"

"Not me," Jack said calmly. "Hello, sweetheart," he said to Donna.

Donna hurried past him without a word.

Jack looked at me with mock concern. "Don't tell me: trouble in paradise?"

"Shut up, Jack," I said.

Down the hall the washroom door slammed shut.

"Well, well," Jack said.

It seemed like a friendly visit for about the first ninety seconds. Then that was over, like a pretty little detour that leads into a swamp, and Jack got to the point. As he talked to me, he went and sat on my chair, so that I had to look at him from the wrong side of my desk. He was wearing a candy-striped shirt that fit tight as a drum across his medicine-ball gut, and bright red sus-penders for trim.

His message was almost clear. He said he wasn't too happy about my performance of late. There were a couple of things. First, there was the Carmody case.

"I've been keeping this to myself for a while, Dwight," Jack said. "But now with this other stuff, I think it's just as well—"

"What other stuff?"

"I'll get to that in a minute."

"Tell me now."

"In a minute," he said sharply. "Now listen to me. I happened to get a peek at that pretty little suicide poem Carmody wrote, and I'm telling you, you were clearly implicated."

"What are you talking about?"

"You knew all along the old geezer was going to off himself, and you didn't tell me?"

"What if I did, Jack? What does it matter? The man was sick. He had a right to some privacy."

"Not on this one he didn't. Not from me. I don't give a shit about his privacy. I'm the guy responsible here, and the rule is I know everything that goes on. That's how this place works."

But Carmody was just the tip of the iceberg. There were other things that wouldn't do. There was my general condition at work lately, which was singularly unimpressive, even for me. There was Drew Peckham, who was so incensed that I'd left my meeting with him early, he'd told Jack he never wanted to set eyes on me again.

"Drew Peckham's our biggest client, Dwight."

"And Sam's my son. You know why I had to be at school that day."

"That kind of trouble's bad for business, Dwight," Jack said.

"You think that's trouble?" I said. "Because Drew Peckham's got his ego bruised? Believe me, that's not trouble."

Jack said nothing. He shook his head and hooked his thumbs under his suspenders: a backroom pol playing at farming.

Abruptly a shiver of panic started swimming up my insides. "What's going on here, Jack?"

Jack said, "That's exactly what I'm trying to get at."

"Are you firing me, Jack? Is that what you're doing?"

"I'm just trying to clarify the situation."

I stood up. I put my hands on the desk and leaned in on him, inadvertently knocking over the pictures of Sam. They fell flat on the blotter, face down. "Are you *firing* me, Jack?"

Now Jack was standing too. His hands out front of his stomach, ready for one thing or another. A big man, suddenly unsure. He was red-faced and already breathing hard. "Have you forgotten?" he said slowly. "I hired you when nobody else would touch you."

"That's right."

"I'm concerned, Dwight. That's all I'm saying."

I let a few seconds pass. I took my hands off the desk and straightened up. Our faces close across the desk, our eyes locked. I could smell his sour breath.

I reached down and replaced the pictures of Sam, back where they had been on my desk.

That afternoon, alone in my office, I sat looking out past the jungle gym to the field. The summer daisies were all gone, and the grass had thinned, though it was still green. I hadn't seen a single kid on the jungle gym since Labor Day. The field felt empty—even now, with a couple of truant boys tossing a football back and forth.

Now, for a little while, I tried hard to recall this same scene from a year earlier: my sitting in this square room, staring out at the jungle gym and field, the daisies gone with summer and the grass thinned, a couple of boys still hanging around, tossing a ball. A bucolic scene, almost. Just a year ago, Dwight Arno had been a human being. He'd made mistakes, sure, but he hadn't killed anyone. Certainly not a child.

I tried hard to get the memory right, but a year is a long time. Images get distorted.

Now the boys were leaving the field, going home for cookies and milk, or down the road to Fanelli's for double shots with chasers. There was no way of knowing. There was just the present, unfolding, and the dark truth of the just-happened, not yet recorded by history.

The field was empty.

Ethan

"Please," Emma said.

I sighed. "All right. Sallie can come, too."

Emma sat in the backseat with her arms around the dog, as though they were lovers and I their chauffeur. She had stopped complaining about Sallie—too big, not cute enough, too much hair, same old dog. Now she never liked to be without her. She was far ahead of her parents, I thought, her world boiled down to just this: one arm for Sallie and the other for Twigs, the stuffed giraffe, holding tight to their soft, comforting, uncomplicated bodies as all around her the floodwaters rose and people went under. It made better than good sense. One arm, one half of her heart, for a living mortal soul, and the other for a creature who would never die.

We left Wyndham Falls behind, and Emma began to hum to herself and the dog: I looked in the mirror and saw her sitting practically on top of Sallie, her chin resting on the furry oblong dome of the dog's head. Humming a made-up song. The long muzzle poking out. The dog not minding.

Then she caught my eyes in the mirror and stopped humming.

"Don't stop," I said. "I like it."

But she remained silent, holding on to Sallie. And I thought, with a sinking sensation, that I had no idea where she was, or what she was thinking.

"Emma?"

"Are we lost?" she said abruptly.

"Lost? Why would we be? We're just going to Mrs. Wheldon's."

Emma shrugged. "I just thought . . ." She turned back to Sallie. A moment later, I heard her whispering to the dog: "I was just *checking*. I was just *checking*."

"We'll be there soon," I said, mostly to myself.

She made no reply. She began to hum again, faint as a breeze. I did not understand. It was as if, somehow, between front and back seats there had sprung up an invisible partition that muffled our voices and made us unreal to each other. Loneliness had crept over us like a cloud.

I drove on. And then, just as arbitrarily as she had begun, Emma stopped humming. I heard the sound of her seat belt coming unbuckled. She leaned forward, grabbing my seat back with her hand so that I felt her fingers in my hair. "Yesterday . . . um . . . Mom was taking me over to Justine's and she got lost."

"Lost?"

"I mean *really* lost. And she's been there like a hundred times."

"Well," I said—inanely, professorially—"that happens. Sometimes even familiar things can start to look strange."

Emma just shrugged.

"Like words," I went on, feeling too great a need to explain myself. "If you stare at a word long enough it almost always starts to look misspelled."

"Even when it isn't?"

"Right."

"Then how do you know when it is and when it isn't?"

I paused, groping for an answer. "By knowing, I suppose. And trusting what you know. Sometimes that's the hardest part."

We were entering Bow Mills. A village more than a town. A prosperous-looking place, overtaken in recent years by weekenders from the cities. A place where successful men "dressed down" and "relaxed" by mowing and tinkering and watering. As now, on a Saturday morning, passing a rotund man pushing a leaf-blower across his expansive front lawn. And another, dressed in a multi-striped track suit and a down parka, hosing down the four-wheel-drive in front of his three-car garage.

I slowed down, peering through the windshield at the little green road signs. "Look for Larch Road," I said. "That's where Mrs. Wheldon lives."

"Dad!" Emma shouted.

Just ahead, two boys were tearing out of a blind driveway on their bikes. I slammed on the brakes. The tires squealed and my right arm swung out and clamped over Emma, trapping her against my seat back. The car came to a halt and there was a scrabbling sound as Sallie was thrown forward onto the floor.

"Emma!"

"Sallie!" Emma cried, pushing off the weight of my arm so that she could attend to her dog.

The boys made expert, skidding turns onto the road shoulder and rode on.

"*Sallie,*" Emma breathed with relief, as the dog climbed back onto the seat.

My heart was pounding. The two boys rode off without even a glance back at us. They were racing each other and laughing, standing high off the saddles as they pedaled, as though they were running through the air.

Then I heard my daughter, stroking the dog and whispering: "Poor Sallie. Poor, frightened Sallie."

I got us moving again. I found Larch Road and made the turn. A yellow sign announced that it was a dead end. Ruth Wheldon had said to go to the end of the road and the house would be on the right.

"We're almost there," I said.

Emma was looking at me in the mirror. "Is Mom sick?"

I looked away. Trying to recall what it was I had told her just fifteen minutes ago. About trusting what you know.

"What do you mean, sweetie?"

"Is Mom sick?" she repeated patiently.

Ahead I could see where the road ended. We were not far.

"No, she's not sick, Em."

"But she's not okay, either?"

The Wheldons' mailbox was green, with a duck painted on it. I turned into their driveway and parked.

"No, Em," I said. "She's not. She's sad and unhappy. She misses Josh."

There was silence. I was afraid to look at her.

"So do I," Emma said. "I miss Josh."

"I know you do, Em."

We sat in the car staring ahead through the windshield, as though we were still moving, as though we were going somewhere.

"Okay," I said. "I'll wait for you out here until you're finished."

"Okay."

"Do you have everything?"

"I guess so."

"All right, then. I'll see you in around an hour."

"Okay."

There was a long breath of stillness. And then in her high voice Emma said, "Sallie, *stay*." She opened the door and got out, carrying her music books. I watched her. She started toward the Wheldons' front porch. Then she stopped, as if she'd forgotten something, and came back, walking all the way around the front of the car to my side.

I rolled down my window. "What is it? Did you forget something?"

"You forgot to bring a book," she said gravely. "For waiting."

• • •

We stayed in the car for a time, Sallie and I. She didn't complain. Dogs, after all, sense better than humans the high-frequency emanations of personal misfortune; they will not leave you, but neither will they press you on the issues. Having made their sympathies known, they will circle you, waiting for you to look up.

When I finally looked up, what I saw was Norris Wheldon stepping out onto the porch. A man I hardly knew. A man who like his wife seemed to favor brightly hued clothing in all circumstances, all kinds of weather. At weddings no doubt, perhaps even at funerals. Today there were checks and plaids and greens and reds; conceivably, he was wearing golf shoes. He came to the edge of the porch and peered out at the driveway, shading his eyes with his hand against the bright autumn sunshine, stooping a bit. Spotting me inside the car, he began waving as though we were old friends, saying something that I couldn't understand.

I opened the door and got out. Norris Wheldon had stopped saying whatever it was he'd been saying, and in the air now like a faint scent I heard the muted buttery notes of a piano—scales, played by a little girl's fingers.

"Hiya," said Mr. Wheldon, waving.

I opened the back door and Sallie jumped out, trotting directly to the bushes in front of the porch, where she peed long and hard.

"Well," said Mr. Wheldon, looking on. He had stopped waving at me for the time being; in fact, he appeared subdued by the raw act of nature he was witnessing. He stood with his hands on his hips, arms akimbo, staring down at his bushes. "She certainly needed to go," he said mildly, when Sallie had finished.

"Good morning, Mr. Wheldon."

"Norris." He was smiling now, good spirits regained. "Call me Norris. You're Ethan, am I right?"

I told him that he was right.

"You know, Ethan, Ruth felt terrible having to cancel out on your daughter's lesson this week. Making you come over here for the makeup and all. But I'm the one who made her. She had the flu. It's just started going around, you know."

"Coming over here was no trouble," I said.

"I mean, leave it to Ruth and she just keeps on giving her lessons, fever or no fever. That's how much she loves her students." He shook his head in admiration.

"Emma's very fond of her," I said.

"Well, it runs two ways, I can tell you. You've got a sweet little girl there, Ethan."

"Thank you."

I thought that would be the end of it. But Mr. Wheldon stood on the porch nodding his head as though on the verge of saying something more.

"Sallie!" I called out before he could speak. "Here!"

She came trotting over. I got the leash from the car and attached it to her collar and held her loosely at my side.

"You must be darn glad to have her," Mr. Wheldon went on. "I mean, personally speaking, I've never been one of those people who thinks an only child's the way to go. Doesn't make sense, if you ask me. Life's just too rough and tumble for that. I mean, you never know what's coming one day to the next. There's got to be a backup, is my feeling. A backup every single day. But then maybe that's just my business head talking—I'm in insurance, you know."

I told him that I knew.

"Yep. I'm an insurance man. And you're a professor, Ruth tells me? English, that right?"

"That's right."

"I don't read a whole lot of made-up stuff myself, Ethan. Being in my line of work, I mostly try and stick to the facts, you understand. Of course on my good days I do like to think it takes a pretty creative mind to fit the right policy to the right person. 'Norris,' I tell myself, 'these are people's lives you're dealing with. Their hopes and dreams. The big stuff. You can't just go in there and expect to put two and two together and come out with four. It doesn't work that way.' You know what I mean?" He peered at me, waiting for me to say something.

But I had nothing to say. I felt like an immigrant who did not speak his language, whose heart and mind were still back in the old country, no matter this dumb body standing here. After a long, awkward moment, I shook my head. "Excuse me," I mumbled. "I'm sorry." I opened the car door.

"Hey, Ethan, hold on a sec!"

I looked at him.

"No offense meant."

"I know," I said.

"Then come up and sit on the porch. I won't be bothering you. I promised Ruth I'd do a little lawn care before golf."

He seemed to take my silence as an assent; descending the porch steps, he walked around the side of the house, out of sight. I stood where I was, unable to decide even the smallest thing. Mr. Wheldon returned a minute later, carrying a long-handled rake. He gave me a thumbs-up sign. "Ruth hates the sound of those leaf-blowers," he said, as though an explanation were required. "And the fumes give her a headache. Why don't you and your dog relax on the porch? When my stepson comes down I bet he'll fix you a cup of hot cocoa."

And with that Mr. Wheldon began to rake his lawn.

There was a cane-backed rocker on the porch, and I sat on it, rocking. I had never planned on being here. This might have been my nursing home: the dragging, rasping sound of the rake being drawn over the beleaguered grass and dead leaves; piano notes played and held suspended in the air like dust motes in sunlight; the hospital tones of Ruth Wheldon's encouragement to my daughter. A crow cawing in someone else's yard. Sallie settling at my feet, releasing a breath like a god's sigh of contentment, rolling over to sleep.

I must have dozed off. Rocking. Tired all the time.

I must have dreamed this: Josh sitting on a chair in the music building at Smithfield, playing late

Beethoven. Playing not to me, but away from me, to the organ that is like the face of a temple. All I see is his back, the dark curls of his hair, the bow slashing the air above his turned left shoulder, the fragile neck of the instrument. How thin my son is. How, as the music moves from mere melancholy to wretchedness and finally to blasphemous outrage, his body begins to shut down, to hunch and curl like a pill bug closing to protect itself. As though I were watching him change under a microscope into a man, and then beyond manhood into old age. He is shriveling up. As I look on, the bow disappears. And then the violin. The music has stopped for good. And in the silence I call out his name, but he doesn't seem to hear; he's grown deaf. It's no longer possible for him to turn around, even if he wanted to. And I begin to cry. Josh is small as a baby now, curled into a ball, rocking and rocking on the chair. . . .

And rocking, I woke up.

A boy was standing on the porch, not five feet away, staring at me.

I felt my face with my fingers: tears.

"You were crying," the boy said simply.

His voice was high but serious. He was small, sandy-haired, wearing denim overalls over a sweatshirt. I recognized him, though he looked younger without a discolored eye. I couldn't recall his name.

I dried my eyes with my fingers. "I guess I was having a bad dream," I said.

He nodded, as if he understood.

Sounds were returning: piano, a steady raking, a dog barking in the distance. I looked down at my feet and there was Sallie looking back at me.

"That your dog?" the boy asked me.

I nodded.

"What's its name?"

I told him.

"Is she nice?"

"Yes."

"I had a dog when I was little and I liked her a lot too," the boy said. "She was a mutt named Boggs, after Wade Boggs, my favorite player."

"Did she die?"

"Yeah. She got run over by a car. When I was like four. My dad helped me bury her. I can show you the place if you want."

The sound of the raking ceased; the boy and I turned our attention to the front lawn, where Norris Wheldon stood, leaning on the rake like a cane. His face shone with sweat. He waved when he saw us regarding him.

"Took a little snooze, didya, Ethan? Hey there, Mr. Boggs," he said to the boy. "What say you fix our guest here a mug of your special cocoa?"

"No, thank you," I said, loud enough to be sure he heard me.

"You're the boss," he called back cheerfully, and resumed his raking.

"*He's* not my real dad," the boy said to me in a confiding tone of voice.

"Your parents were divorced?"

He nodded.

I noticed the way he was looking at Sallie. "Sallie doesn't mind being touched," I said.

He approached her slowly, getting down on his knees on the porch. She wasn't afraid of him, and he ran his hand from her brow down her long muzzle to her nose.

"My dad drove over this dog on the road," he said, watching his hand as he stroked her. "It was an accident. During the summer. I was asleep when we hit it but Dad said it was black and we killed it. He felt really bad about it. Me too. I got a black eye when we hit it. All my mom said was that's why we can't have dogs any more. Because they're always getting run over."

He didn't look up at me. He kept petting the dog. And I closed my eyes. I was seeing a car hitting a black dog, crushing it, passing on. The dog left by the side of the road like a piece of trash.

I opened my eyes. There was just his sandy hair washed in daylight. His living bones. His hand smoothing a dog's head with tender affection. His unknowing love. There was his face so clear and young without the badge of bruised eye. He was on that stage with his trumpet.

Now he looked up, right into my eyes.

"Is it true you're Josh's dad?"

"Yes," I said. "I was."

"Are you still sad?"

"I'll always be sad."

"Till you die?"

"All my life."

He looked down again, running his fingers through Sallie's soft coat. She was his antidote to what he saw before him, in me: a pain that never ends. He could not imagine it.

Grace

With no work to do, it was hard to tell the days apart. It was November, she knew that much. Every day, it seemed, colder than the one before it. Leaves piling up on the ground. Her garden dying like a country gone to war.

It was an afternoon, today: and she walked slowly around the house, the garage, assessing the devastation. She did not want to miss anything. Apples were rotting on the ground beneath the trees. She went past the little garden shed where she kept her clippers, all her tools, to the beds of roses behind. They needed clipping back, but she would not do it.

It is the breaking of a pact, she thought. *The love of God turned upside down.*

You thought and dreamed and planted, you tended, getting on your knees in the dirt. You watched and waited, tried through experience and luck and empathy to discover what each living thing required to grow and thrive, and then you found some way, any way, to provide it. Because the living thing would not be there but for you. Because it was you who chose.

She walked on. Beyond the roses were the hostas: she saw that they were finished, too. The full green leaves and aubergine-colored stalks of summer had collapsed under the weight of their own decomposition; there was the odor of rot. She turned her head away.

Sallie trotted ahead of her, up the garden path to the west of the house. Under a carpet of fallen leaves the slab pathstones were invisible. The leaves rustled and crumbled under the dog's four paws and her own two feet. Everything alongside the path was dead and discolored. And though she had expected this, it still came as a shock. Tiny Rubies dead. Dead Crater Lake Blues. Silver Brocade. Rust and ocher leaves everywhere, like something strewn at a funeral. *I have not been here in so long,* she thought; *I have not even looked.* It was a world made and then let go. Here at the top of the path where the land leveled out, where she had carried Josh and planted, she once believed, his spirit . . . well, the perennials were finished, too.

She stopped walking; she had seen enough.

How long she'd been outside she didn't know, but she was chilled to the bone; it was afternoon, perhaps four o'clock, the light already starting its decline. She felt as if she had been far from this place, trudging over some former battlefield—Ypres, or Verdun—the boundaries invisible now, grown over with weeds, the past a horrible buried joke.

She went inside.

Climbed the stairs, past Emma's room, found the door open, took a peek inside: empty. Emma not home from school yet. Time enough then to lie down in her own room for a few minutes, curl up, close her eyes; time enough, she thought without much hope, to try to shed the skin of memory that had deadened her these last months and kept her from feeling. She understood: *I cannot go on like this.* She started down the hallway. But then she saw the door to Josh's room standing not quite closed, and she halted. It had been closed earlier, she remembered. It had been closed, as far as she knew, for a long time. The very sight now— just a few inches of boy's blue carpet, bathed in steel-like tones from the windowed light—made her irrationally afraid, as if it signified the presence of an intruder in her house. *Stop it*, she told herself, trying to master her fear. Which worked, sort of; she pushed the door open the rest of the way. Then heard her own intake of breath, and stood as if frozen in the doorway.

"Oh, my baby," she whispered.

It was Emma. Huddled on the floor, crying, among the shards of Josh's smashed violin.

Emma began to cry harder, to wail, pieces of the instrument she had shattered clenched in her fists. And now Grace did not hesitate. Fragments of antique shellacked wood crunched under her feet. She swept Emma up off the ground and carried her to Josh's bed.

Dwight

Another Sunday came, and I decided to take Sam to the Chatham Fair.

There were clouds blowing in from the west but they didn't look serious. Otherwise it was a fine November day, strangely mild. Sam wore overalls and a Red Sox sweatshirt I'd bought for him, and a pair of Converse sneakers no different, really, from the pair I'd had as a kid. He rode up front with me in the Corsica, fiddling with the radio to try and find the Patriots game, even though I'd told him it was still too early in the day. No matter. I drove with one arm resting along the top of the seat back, just above his head. It felt to me as if my arm was floating above him like a guardian weapon, ready to be called to use.

We crossed into Massachusetts and a little north of Stockbridge caught the pike heading west, and soon we were in Columbia County. We'd crossed two state lines in the course of an hour's drive, an experience common to any jaded Northwest Cornerite but a fact still astonishing to my son, who twice said to me, over the fuzz of radio static he'd managed to fix on the radio, "You *sure* this is New York, Dad?"

What could I say? I was sure. Ruth and I had been to Europe on our honeymoon, the only time for both of us. Three weeks in a tin-box Fiat, crossing whole countries as though they were towns for the taking. We made love outside a ruined castle in the middle of France, with yellow flowers poking up between our legs, and Ruth repeating the words "Knights Templars" to herself and laughing like a happy, beautiful drunk. The Knights were the ones, supposedly, who'd built the place and disappeared, leaving it to us.

A country fair.

Prize vegetables and prize pies, a million-plus apples, a pumpkin the size of New Jersey (though still smaller than the blue-ribbon bull), a sheep with a permanent, a politician in a booth. Always, a politician in a booth, talking. Carnival rides. A demolition derby.

After the Ferris wheel and the bumper cars, a pellet-gun sharpshooting contest and an almost-won stuffed warthog, we ate foot-long dogs and cotton candy, followed by a hunk each of fried dough. I drank a couple of beers and tried too hard to make Sam smile.

We were doing all the right things. But something was missing, or broken. Sam had always liked fairs, but today he seemed to stare at his feet a lot and not to care about winning or losing the games he played. He didn't seem to notice when, late in the afternoon, the politician got caught by a photographer with his tongue down the throat of a pretty young girl behind the livestock pen. And he didn't seem to mind that all afternoon the clouds kept blowing in from the west, gathering over our heads.

By four-thirty it was raining. We were already halfway toward dark. With a foolish, desperate grin on my face, I turned to Sam and asked him one more time what ride he wanted to go on next, what gun he wanted to shoot at what target, what food he wanted to eat.

He said he wanted to go home.

There are some scenes that never end, they just keep getting replayed. The walk to the parking lot, the leaving, the long drive home.

On the way back, Sam tried again to find the Patriots on the radio, but we'd bookended the game with our coming and going, and it was over. All he found was more static—for a trumpet player he had a high tolerance for noise pollution—and I got irritated and pushed his hand from the radio dial and fixed the station myself. Sam said nothing, just retreated into the shadows of his seat. And for the next half hour, like a student who's studied too hard and too long for the test, I sang diligently along with Merle Haggard and Conway Twitty, as we recrossed the state lines that held, this time, no traces of astonishment for my son.

Then we were in Connecticut. Sunday almost over. And past the twang of the music, I heard the ring of another failure in my head.

Back at the fair, I'd bought Sam a caramel apple on a stick. I didn't know exactly why I'd bought it—he hadn't really wanted it. I guess I'd wanted him to have something to take home, just one thing clean and normal and fresh-grown to show his mother. He hadn't even taken a bite of it since we'd left, just held it loosely in the fingers of his right hand like a thing of no interest that he was honor bound to deliver.

Now our tires were bumping over the rail tracks north of Canaan, and in the silence just afterwards I heard a little thud on the floor by Sam's feet. It was all shadow down there, but I knew what had happened. He'd let the apple drop. I could picture it in my head, the gluey caramel stuck to the floor carpeting, never to be gotten out. The day gone like that.

I took a deep breath and told him not to worry, it didn't matter.

He didn't say anything.

And all the while I was driving. My hands, not my mind. Tracking the route to my former home, paying attention, seeing with fingers. Muscular memory. While I got lost in a mess on the floor, the police barracks must have gone by, my dentist's office, Tommy's Diner. And at the familiar sight of a narrow tree-lined road heading off to the left, my hands must have known what to do. Instinctively, all on their own. The rule of the body is to take all shortcuts. The rule of the mind too, even if the mind doesn't know it.

I took the turn to the left.

Here, it was like night. The tar blackened and slicked with rain. The few wet leaves still on the trees

giving off no color, as if they were turned in on themselves, on strike. A pathetic, faded yellow line. Everything worn down, shut off.

I switched on the headlights. I slowed down a
little, careful of the water on the road. Recognition
hadn't hit me yet. It was just a road, a shortcut, and I
was still mourning the day, licking my wounds. I'd
have my son home soon, and safe from me.

There was a sharp turn ahead, curving to the left. It
was like seeing a face remembered from childhood.
You do not forget. The first turn curved left and, at this
speed, flowed seamlessly into the second turn, which
was sharper, turning to the right, a curve of beauty and
horror. Where the second turn straightened, there was
Tod Lovell's gas station. It was open for business. The
red neon sign hadn't been turned on yet, or it was broken, but inside the building a light was on. And a man
was sitting in there, doing nothing.

I took my foot off the gas. Like a voice calling, like
the pull of the moon on the ocean. The car slowed as if
it was dying right under me, and I steered it over by the
two round-shouldered pumps and turned off the engine.

I saw the man inside the office get up off his stool.

Next to me, Sam shifted restlessly. He'd been quiet
for so long that just his moving felt like a shout. He
said, "Where are we?"

I didn't answer him.

The pump jock was at my side. He had a goatee
and pimples. I rolled down the window and told him
to fill it up.

Sam said again, "Where are we?"

I didn't answer.

The pump jock came back, a look on his face as if I'd cheated him. "That'll be six and a quarter."

I gave him seven and rolled my window back up. I started the car and drove off, picking up speed past the spot where Ethan Learner would have found his son among the weeds and scrub brush. We were almost out of the clearing when Sam shifted suddenly in his seat as if he'd just woken up.

He said, "This is where we killed the dog."

I didn't say anything. I held on to the wheel and drove, watching my mistake unfurling like a perfect, huge wave. Sam said impatiently, "Right, Dad? The black dog. This is where we killed it."

"I killed it," I said. "Not you. Don't you ever forget that."

"But it was here, right?"

"Right, Sam," I said.

I drove on. Where the trees opened again there was fog lying low over acres of pasture and stone walls. Somewhere behind the fog would be a farm with a silo like a prison guard tower.

Sam said, "Dad?"

"What?"

"What road're we on?"

I said, "It's the shortcut, Sam."

"No. I mean what's it called?"

I stared straight ahead. The fog was growing thicker, turning in slow white circles over the road, blinding me. I slowed down.

I said, "It's called Reservation Road."

Ethan

I slept in our room that night. Not since September had we shared a bed like husband and wife. The first night on the sofa is like the first anything, I suppose: without experience or memory of such a thing, there is no notion of it being anything but a singular, enclosed moment. Certainly not a pattern, a habit. Then a week passes, a month, and before one knows it the sofa, with its humid sheets and creaky springs, has become the way things are. I was brushing my teeth in the downstairs bathroom when Grace entered and inquired, in a neutral voice, where I planned to spend the night. We regarded each other in the mirror above the sink. Her hair was down, washed and shining, and she was wearing a white cotton nightgown; I had the sense that she had made herself up for me. Perhaps I just wished this: standing there at the sink, five feet from my wife, my back to her, I felt her presence like a sudden caress. Heat rushed up through my body. I turned around to face her.

"With you," I said. "If that's what you want."

"Yes," she said, and went out.

The bedroom, when I reached it, was dark. I paused in the doorway to allow my eyes to adjust. The bed, with its white covers, appeared like a kind of ghost ship, faintly yet richly glowing. I made my way toward it, driven by a combination of nervousness and instinct. It was like being a teenager again, only infinitely more somber. I could smell her floral shampoo, the cotton scent of her nightgown. Her blond hair held on its crown some unbegotten light, her face luminous beneath it. I crawled into bed beside her. Our legs touched and retreated. We lay in silence, hearing our breathing like whispers in the darkness.

"I've been thinking about him," she said. "All the time now. Remembering. All these things, Ethan. All these things and no one to tell them to."

"Tell me something you remember," I said.

She was silent. We lay staring up at the black ceiling, our thoughts, like our bodies, parallel and separate. I wanted to ask if she could ever forgive me, but I was afraid. Then, her voice enveloping us both, she began to speak.

"It was the summer we rented the cabin up by the lake," she said. "You'd promised Emma you'd take her out on the canoe, so Josh and I went for a walk up the dirt road. I told him to go on ahead if he wanted. For about fifty feet he ran as fast as he could. Then he just stopped and stood staring down at the ground. It was a turtle, sitting there in the middle of the road. I don't know what it was doing there. It was almost midday, hot and dusty. And he bent down and picked this turtle up and put it down in the bushes by the side of the road, so it wouldn't get run over."

Grace paused; she reached out and found my hand beneath the bedcovers.

"He was our son," she said. "And he didn't know— he didn't know—how I was back there watching him. Back there in the road with my hand over my heart, loving him so much just for picking up a measly old turtle. He put it down where it would be safe. And then he stood there until I caught up with him. He took my hand, Ethan. And he didn't know. It was just another day to him. But it's what I remember."

Time moves slowly in the darkness. Long into the night, Grace went on holding my hand. I rested my head on her breast and, for the first time in many days, managed to sleep.

When, some time later, I awoke, we were no longer touching; Grace lay on her side of the bed and I lay on mine. If I had been dreaming, I had no recollection of it. My thoughts were the same as they had been while I was awake.

I got out of bed. And quietly, while Grace slept, I dressed in the dark and went downstairs.

Grace

Her eyes opened in the dark: she blinked, blinked, trying to make sense—not of a dream but of a dreamlike
movement around her. Something told her to lie still.
She saw Ethan's back, shadowed, leaving the room.
There was the urge to call out—"Where are you
going?"—but she suppressed it. She had an instinct
about it anyway. She thought she knew.

They had been happy that summer, the four of
them, in the tiny rented cabin by the lake.

Happy. She saw Ethan laughing, young. She saw
herself. She remembered the day they had met, fifteen
years ago, looking up from her desk in the dorm room
and finding this handsome graduate student standing
in the doorway—tall, thin, high-cheekboned, dark,
intense. He wasn't looking for her but for her room-
mate, who was out; he had found her by mistake, but
once he found her he would not stop talking. He was
all hands when he talked, nervous energy, his long
fingers gesticulating, playing some harmony only he

could hear. He was like a beautiful idea being worked out right in front of her, and she remembered feeling as if, from the very moment he began to speak to her, he were asking her to participate in the process of creation, inviting her inside himself, telling her, with his expressive wandlike hands, that what she thought and believed and was, mattered.

Now, in the silence, she heard his car start up. The tires on the drive, his leaving.

Dwight

That night, for whatever reason, I couldn't sleep. I watched the Thursday late movie on TV—about a man who terrorizes his ex-wife and daughter, till the ex-wife finally kills him with a carving knife. I read a few pages of a book about the Yankees-Dodgers Series of '49. I stuck some dirty clothes in the washer and set it spinning. I considered calling Donna in the futile hope that she might change her mind about me for one more night.

In the end, though, I gave up the pretense of doing anything worthwhile. I got the bottle of Jim Beam down from the cupboard and poured myself a drink. Then I poured myself another. I was afraid. My skin felt hot, my lungs shallow. I kept telling myself that this was just another night in a long black parade of nights stretching out into the unknown; life was going to go on, I kept telling myself, maybe for a very long time. But this was not comforting. I had never known a night that seemed so long, without purpose or end.

Ethan

The roads at that hour were empty, not a living soul. I drove through Canaan, turned west for fifteen minutes to Salisbury, and followed my headlights up the short winding road to the top of Mount Riga.

It was a summer colony of plain unheated cabins dotting a strip of land between two lakes. The warden's cabin stood nearest the road. I remembered him from that summer four years ago—a tall man with a high forehead and a glass eye. I remembered his cabin as I did all the colony: a place of vivid simplicity, the weathered wood set off against the green of the surrounding grass and trees, and, in the background, the lake's dark but sun-dappled blue. Now my headlights shone over it as they might over an abandoned car: shuttered, it had no windows, no face. The wooden gate in front was drawn down, blocking the way. I stopped the car, pulled a flashlight from the glove compartment, and got out. The night was cold, the air laden with unborn snow, the moon obscured by clouds—not a breeze stirring, not a sound save for the brief ticking of the engine as it cooled. I zipped up my coat, pulled on gloves. Switching on the flashlight I set out on foot along a dirt path, around the wooden gate and past the warden's empty cabin.

Cabin number four was on the water. I approached it from the footpath, shone my light on it at first from a distance, and it was hazy, blurred, and dark. As I drew closer its form grew more distinct, like a memory emerging from the murky remnants of a dream. I came to the front door and it was locked. The windows were shuttered. I ran the light over the door, and there was the name I remembered: "Hyacinth," carved into the wood—as inexplicable as "Rosebud." We had not owned this place; we had spent a single summer here and then never found our way back. We had been visitors. I tried the door again but it would not open, and then I walked around to the lake side and up the two steps to the uncovered porch. The rear door was locked, too, the window closed up. But someone had left a folded beach chair leaning against the railing. It was covered with rust. I unfolded it and sat down facing the still, black water.

Time passed. And I stayed awake and remembered.

A diving float sits in the water like a square white cake. Josh is six; everything he attempts is an event. He spends entire days on the float—diving, climbing out, diving—and I spend my days watching him. His naked shoulders and hopeful resolve. His certainty that the rest of life exists simply to get the dive right. He bursts from the water with his back arched, face turned up to the sun. . . .

But then, one day, the diving abruptly stops. He is standing on the porch when I wake up. It is barely past seven and I emerge from our room and say good morning to him, and like a child prophet he points down the lake and says: "Swans." That is all. I join him on the porch. And there, by the water's far edge, floats a pair of those majestic birds. Josh tugs on my arm. "Dad, can we go look?"

We climb into the canoe, Josh in the bow. I insist that he wear a life preserver. At first he tries to paddle, but the paddle is too long and heavy for him, and in the end he has to put it away; only my paddle eddies beneath the polished blue surface of the water as we glide along. The sun is ahead of us, low but already hot, turning that end of the lake into a mirror of sky. The swans float upon it. I watch my son on his knees from behind, finding something poignant and indelible in his hands gripping the gunwales, the slope of his shoulders, the tilt of his head to the water. We pass in front of another cabin, on whose porch a man is doing deep knee bends. And then, as though caught in the moving silence of a dream, we find ourselves nearing the swans, who at this moment are feeding, their necks extended and their heads hidden beneath the water.

"It's running away," Josh whispers.

Sensing our approach, one of the swans has raised its head and is swimming briskly for the far bank. Its partner remains behind, feeding complacently.

"It doesn't see us," Josh whispers.

We have drawn within ten feet of the feeding swan. I am in awe and can only imagine how my son must feel: the bird is a pure, godly white. The curve of its neck where it disappears into the water is thrilling. I open my paddle to slow our pace as the canoe drifts closer. The feeding swan does not move, does not even raise its head.

"Dad," Josh says.

Something in his tone sends a warning: he sounds suddenly close to panic.

"What is it, Josh?"

He does not have time to answer. Drifting, the canoe bumps the great white bird from behind, toppling it: and the bloody, headless neck rises from the water—

A frog splashed the water's edge and I started. The night was cold and black. The onyx surface of lake rippled, broke to shadows and random glimmers of light. Pale breaths steamed from my nostrils. I put a hand over my mouth and smelled old leather, my father's glove.

PART FOUR

Dwight

It finally began to turn light outside. It always does. I stood at the window, watching it happen.

A Friday morning in November, and I was thinking about my son. Remembering when he was a little boy just learning to talk, the feel of his arms hugging my neck as I carried him around the house, his grip tightening on me whenever he grew scared or happy. Not so long ago in years, and yet a thing so decidedly past it seemed to live in its own time, back beyond my reach.

Outside, now, it looked like snow coming, and winter behind it; it looked cold. And I stood trying to make a plan of some kind, trying to make some sense. But I was too tired to do much. The long night awake had left me spent.

There's no point in stating the obvious, but I will anyway, for my own reasons: not getting caught isn't the same thing as being free.

While I was away from Sam those years, kept from seeing him, reduced to a pen pal, all I could think about

JOHN BURNHAM SCHWARTZ

was getting back to him. By hook or crook. You come
back on your knees if you have to, find whatever house
is empty, take the job that will take you. The pieces of
your life are a jigsaw puzzle—no more, no less—and
you set about fitting them together again, always keeping in your mind the image on the puzzle box that got
incinerated while you were living elsewhere: the image
of your life as a bruised yet still decent enterprise. Without which, it must be said, you are finished.

Now I found the clicker, opened the garage door,
stepped outside the house into the new morning: gray
sky tinged with winter, a sludgelike cold in the bones.
Not a good day for courage or making plans. I walked
across the lawn to the garage. The car was there, midnight blue body dulled by a coating of dust, the broken
headlight, the history. And in the opposite corner, by the
worktable, a file cabinet. I went to it, opened the bottom
drawer, and pulled out a folder. Inside the folder was a
copy of my last will and testament—a document I'd prepared myself when Ruth and I got married, had updated
when Sam was born, had revised after the divorce, and
had updated again just last year. It's a lawyer's job to
always be careful, never to be caught short. Now, standing in the garage, I read it over again.

In the event of my death, all that I owned, minus
debts payable, was to be left to my son. Whether he be
good or bad, sweet or angry, happy or frightened,
whole or shattered; whether he love his father and
mourn him or be thankful that he is gone.

306

Ethan

The night was over.

I stuck my head in Emma's room and listened until I could hear her breathing. Then I went down the hall, undressed outside our bedroom, and stole inside. All was still, early-morning dark, Grace a long raised shadow on the bed, the white pillow luminous around her face like a halo. I slid into bed beside her. She stirred, turning toward me.

"Ethan?"

"Shh. Go back to sleep."

"You're freezing."

"I'm all right."

There was a pause. I lay staring up into the depthless air and saw imposed on it, floating as though on a night-black sea, the white diving float.

"Did you go to the lake?" she asked.

"Yes."

• • •

"A little more," Emma said.

She was seated at the kitchen table, spoon in hand. I stood beside her pouring milk into her cereal bowl.

"A little more, *please*," I said.

"A little more, *please*."

I heard footsteps and looked up. Grace entered the kitchen in flannel bathrobe and slippers.

"You're spilling!" Emma said.

I had not stopped pouring; I looked down: a small puddle of milk on the table. Another night of sleeplessness had left my senses dulled and jittery. "I'm sorry," I mumbled. "I'll clean it up."

"I'll do it," Grace said. I felt her fingers graze my shoulder as she passed to the sink for a sponge. Emma and I watched her wipe up the mess I'd made.

"Thank you."

Grace did not smile, but I could see she was trying. She'd brushed her hair. She seemed awake in some way she had not been in a long time. I could not remember, I suddenly thought, the last time the three of us had all been present for breakfast.

I asked her if she wanted coffee.

"I can do it," she replied. She went to the counter and poured a mug for herself and brought it to the table and sat down next to Emma. I sat, too. The room was silent save for the ticking of the clock on the wall. Emma had put down her spoon and was staring at her mother, her face caught in an expression—a kind of wordless, intimate, brave questioning—that made her seem years older. And then Grace reached out and with her finger tucked a few loose strands of Emma's hair behind her ear. "Eat your cereal, sweetie. It's almost time for school."

From outside, through the doors and windows battened down against the bitter early cold, Sallie's barking reached us, faint yet vibrant, like a favorite voice remembered from childhood.

The sky was the color of old pewter. And the dog ran streaking over the grass and the unraked leaves.

"It's winter," I said.

After breakfast, I got Emma bundled up and took her out to wait for the school bus. Sallie joined us at the edge of the road, wagging her tail. Emma stroked the dog between the ears and talked to her.

"Sallie, you be careful when the bus comes."

The bus appeared up the road, a yellow streak against a background of gray and brown. I looked up at the sky, imagining it snowing soon, the snow gathering over our road and trees and house and barn.

Emma said, "How much did Josh's violin cost?"

I looked down at her. "It doesn't matter," I said as gently as I could.

"But how much?"

"Your mother and I don't want you to worry about that," I said. "All right?"

She was silent. The school bus, driven by Mr. Peoples, passed us slowly, on its way to turn around a bit farther down the road; Emma was the final pickup. I looked up and saw children's faces, some still sleepy-eyed, behind the closed windows, and then the bus turned around, red taillights flashing, the warning beeper sounding as the wheels reversed. It came to a stop in front of us and the doors opened with a whoosh.

"Bye," I said. I bent down and kissed her. "I love you."

"Bye," she said, already looking past me into the bus.

She climbed on. With a thrifty nod of his head, Mr. Peoples closed the doors. He waited as Emma walked down the aisle and found an empty seat in the middle of the bus, on the side nearer to me, next to a sandy-haired boy. I recognized the boy. And then the bus shifted into gear and slowly began to pull away.

Emma never did look back. But Sam Arno did. He turned full to the window and waved at me—unsmiling, painfully serious, a shy boy looking as though he wanted to talk.

I watched the bus until it disappeared. And though the boy was gone, I was still seeing him like an after-image burned into my mind: my son's age but not my son. Fair where Josh had been dark, but small like him, serious like him, asking questions of the world in the same unmade voice. Hearing him now, seeing him as he stood on a stage in a school gym holding his trumpet, looking as though he wanted to crawl inside it, his bruised and bloodshot eye caught under the bright lights for all to see. And his mother with him, embarrassed, helpless: "You're probably all wondering about Sam's eye," she was saying. "Well, he was out with his father, Dwight, last week and they got in a little accident. . . ."

A cold wind gusted, sending dead leaves scrabbling along the road edge around my feet. I ducked my head against the chill. Sallie trotted off, came back, and poked my thigh with her muzzle; she wanted to go inside now. I checked my watch and with a feeling of vague consternation discovered that it was later than I'd thought. Fridays I had a full schedule—a ten o'clock and a twelve o'clock followed by office hours after lunch and a faculty meeting at five. I went into the house to gather my books.

Grace was upstairs in the shower; a distant thrumming came from the hot-water heater in the pantry. In my study I filled my briefcase and then stood at my desk bent over a blank sheet of notepaper. I wrote "Grace"—and then I paused, the pen hovering just above the paper, as I tried to decide what else to say. I saw the three of us sitting at the breakfast table . . . but at this instant it all felt too momentous and pressured and I could not seem to find the right words. It was the Arno boy again, trespassing on my thoughts, as if with that long look through the bus window he had in some impossible way attached himself to me. Finally, in frustration, I scrawled the rest of the note—"Back for dinner. Love, E."—and grabbed my bag and hurried out to the car. I glanced up at our bedroom windows to see if she might be watching, but I saw no one. And then I drove away.

I made it through Wyndham Falls, on the road to

Canaan. But in my eyes now as I drove was neither the day ahead nor the hard tarnished sky but Sam Arno's face, looking back at me through glass. A boy in an accident. In a car. A boy bounced around in a car like a pinball—"He was out with his father, Dwight, last week . . ."—at the whim and mercy of his father.

I was entering Canaan now, a town I knew. I turned right at the blinking yellow stoplight, north onto Route 7, and in a minute or two I saw the little green road sign ahead on the right. It was Reservation Road, heading off to the east. I slowed down. I was still seeing him: Sam Arno on the porch, awash in light, petting a dog, telling me a story. But transfigured now, a dream figure whose eye had healed as if by magic. A boy too serious, too quiet, too old and too young for who he was. A boy my son's age. I wanted to take him in my arms, hold him like my own.

He was speaking to me.

"My dad drove over this dog on the road. It was an accident. During the summer."

The road ran off to the east, a shortcut to nowhere, a gash in a dark wood. I took it now. Onto black tar, between trees naked of leaves, past a swamp buried in bramble: leave this day behind. Ahead just a memory waiting like a lost love and the young unmade voice calling out: "I was asleep when we hit it but Dad said it was black and we killed it. . . . I got a black eye. . . ."

The turn appeared ahead. The first of two. It curved to the left, and I took it speeding faster than I'd thought and as the car swung around into the second, sharper, rightward turn I heard the tires bite the road and felt the sudden centripetal acceleration and straightening as Tod's Gas and Auto Body emerged from the clearing like a nightmare vision. I braked suddenly. The car went skidding and screeching past the two gas pumps to where the weeds and scrub brush began and came to a halt.

I left the engine running. It had happened here. I got out of the car. My breath thin, drops of sweat streaking my glasses, the air cold and bitter. It had happened here. I turned from the roadside where Josh had lain with his chest crushed and blood pooling in his mouth, and looked past the two pumps, back along the narrow two-lane road. The car had come from there. And it was still summer.

Dwight

Two o'clock rolled around, and I was still at home. Sitting in the den like a resident catatonic. Hearing the phone ring three separate times and the answering machine pick up, and Donna's voice saying my name, first as a question, and finally as an insult. I let it all flow by. I just couldn't do it.

The day was like a mirror of itself, or maybe of me: it kept passing, and yet it stretched ahead too. Endless. In it I was nobody and nothing, just a pinpoint ship on a gray horizon, a faceless mirage. I wasn't coming any closer, wasn't coming into focus. Something had changed, skipped away when I'd thought I had it marked and fixed. I felt weak and small. And I remembered, for some reason, a day, I must have been eighteen, when I left my college dorm and drove over to North Haven to see my old man. I didn't call ahead. We hadn't spoken in months, but from an aunt in Meriden I'd heard he'd had some heart trouble and was hoping to see me.

The day was sunny and warm, full spring, and I drove through the familiar streets, the cramped, aluminum-sided houses and weedy yards and chain-link fences and cracked pavement. At the end of my block kids I knew were playing whiffle ball. There was Mrs. Grimaldi standing on her lawn in a cheap house-dress, holding a rust-stained parasol. She waved and I waved back. I had a stitch in my side, sweat starting down my face. I kept going slowly. Ahead, parked on the street, I saw my old man's brown Le Mans, and then his house, the house I grew up in, the front door light dangling off its wire, an upstairs window taped over with cardboard, everything gone wrong since my mother died. In the yard the grass stood a foot high, spotted with dandelions. He was sitting in the middle of it all, on a bent deck chair, like a sick king on a broken throne, a shriveled old man, stooped and small, not yet fifty. We watched each other closely as I drove by. It was the last I ever saw of him.

I got up from the sofa, went into the kitchen. In a juice glass I poured myself a bourbon and drank it off. I poured myself another and left it standing on the counter where I could look at it. Then I reached for the phone and dialed the office. Donna picked up as I knew she would.

"Cutter and Trope," she said.

"Donna."

There was a pause signaling recognition, then a little suck of breath. "Jack wants to know where you are," she demanded.

"Home," I said.

315

"I've been calling. Where the hell have you been?"

"Home."

"Liar. Listen to me, Dwight. You've really managed to piss him off this time."

"I'm calling in sick. Tell Jack he can go fuck himself."

"You're not sick."

"You have no idea."

"Dwight, listen to me"—abruptly her voice had turned to a whisper—"I can't keep covering for you."

"Then don't. I never asked you to."

"That's right, you didn't," she said coldly.

"In fact," I said, "I recommend we all start telling the truth around here. The whole truth and nothing but the truth."

"What are you talking about?"

I brought the glass to my lips and finished what was in it.

"Nothing," I said.

"Dwight?"

"Absolutely nothing."

"Are you okay?" All of a sudden a note of concern in her voice, a sign of care. I wished that I was with her.

"No," I said. "I'm not okay. I'm sick."

She let out a sigh of frustration. "Dwight, listen to me! Just pull yourself together and get in here. I swear Jack'll fire you this time. He's just looking for a reason."

"Well, if he does, he can go fuck himself."

There was a silence. I set the glass down on the counter again; empty, it made a hollow ring.

"Donna?"

"I can't do this any more," she said. She sounded suddenly on the brink of giving up.

"Donna, I'm sorry."

"No, Dwight," she said sadly. "I'm the one who's sorry."

And she hung up.

I stood with the receiver against my ear, as if she was still on the other end of the line, talking. Then I put it down. Something had been set in motion, but its image was fuzzy, blurred. Only courage makes things clear, and I couldn't seem to find any. I walked through the house to my bedroom. I pulled shirts off hangers, grabbed underwear and socks and pants out of the laundry hamper, filled two duffel bags with clothes and set them aside. From the table drawer I took out the thick packet of Sam's letters. And then, as if it was an island surrounded by sharks, I crawled to the center of the big round bed and curled up, hugging the letters to my chest.

Ethan

Inside the school the bell was ringing, closed in, far-off: two-thirty. I got out of the car. I'd been waiting since noon and my legs were stiff. In the meantime the parking lot had filled. Clusters of parents stood by, waiting for their children. I nodded to the ones I knew, smiled, looked away. Between us the yellow school bus, nose pointing toward the road, Mr. Peoples sitting at the helm with a newspaper spread over the wheel. A scene typical, yet strange today, ominous, it seemed to me: the world holding its breath for a little boy. Stillness and waiting and the gray, wintering light. And now from within the building, bell silenced, the first distant yells and thundering of footsteps.

This was not knowledge but an inkling, demanding confirmation. I would have it. That morning, from the gas station on Reservation Road I had gone to Smithfield; somehow, I had made it through my ten o'clock, lecturing innocent young souls on the false heroics of humankind as represented in our finest literature. What I said I have no idea. When it was over, I left a note on my office door claiming sudden illness and drove over to the elementary school to wait.

It was not feeling yet; that was still on the outskirts. These two and a half hours in the car were not about feeling. I sat in a kind of trance, as if awaiting a judgment preordained, from on high, words that would simply confirm what I had always known to be true. What would happen afterwards was as far from my capacity of thought as the moon.

Mr. Peoples, like a rabbit sensing a fox, lifted his head and sniffed. He folded his newspaper and squared himself on his seat: they were coming. A wild throng of children burst, walking and running, from the doors of the school, a sea of moving color and deafening noise, heading for the parking lot. A hundred of them or fifty. Taking a few steps forward, I spotted him near the front of the pack, dressed all in denim, carrying a plastic instrument case like a burned-out salesman. My heart had begun to pound. I called out to him.

"Sam!"

Hearing his name, he halted in midstride, forcing the moving line of children to part around his body. He turned and I raised my hand in greeting and though he didn't smile I saw recognition lift his face. Stiffly, awkwardly I waved him over. In no time at all he was standing before me, his open face silently questioning, the instrument case—a trumpet—hugged to his chest between the blue nylon straps of his backpack.

I was sweating. My throat was tight; my voice when it came sounded like something squeezed from a tube. "Hi."

"Hi," he said.

"What are you doing?"

He shrugged. "Goin' home."

I nodded, crossed my arms over my chest, cleared my throat; leaned back against the trunk of my car, hoping to appear like a man who might do such a thing naturally, without motive or guile. "Do you want a ride?" I said. "I'll drive you."

He paused, looking from me to my car, studying us both as though for some sign of the warnings his mother doubtless had given him about strange men and cars and offers of rides. His clothes were baggy and too thin for the weather; inside them he floated, a small, pale body. Finally, almost sorrowfully, he shook his head. "I'm not supposed to."

"I understand," I said.

One by one, I saw children climbing onto the school bus beyond him. He will go now, I thought. Deep in my chest, like the first blind step into quicksand, the stirrings of desperation.

But then, suddenly, Sam set the trumpet case down on the ground. "So . . . um," he mumbled, "are you here 'cause of . . . ?" Suddenly out of words, he looked down.

"You mean Emma? My daughter."

He nodded.

"She should be out any minute," I said.

"You gonna drive her home?"

"Maybe."

"Is she sad, too?"

"What?"

"Because of Josh."

"Yes," I said. "She's sad, too."

"I think she's nice," he said.

"Thank you, Sam."

I glanced above his head again. The bus already half full of children. I could see them through the rectangular, metal-framed windows, backpack-humped bodies moving along the aisle to empty seats, sitting down, until just heads were visible and it was all a puppet show.

I looked back at him. His gaze had wandered. I cleared my throat and said his name.

He looked up at me. Immediately I focused on a spot on his forehead, any place but his eyes.

I said, "I took Sallie for a walk this morning."

Silence.

"Remember Sallie?"

"Your dog?" he said.

"Right." I tried a smile now but it froze on my lips. Hopelessness, frustration, somewhere behind it shame. I could feel the sweat beginning to slide down the side of my face. I made myself go on. "And while I was walking her I started thinking about the conversation you and I had the other weekend. Remember, Sam? Because we talked a lot about dogs."

"I remember," he said.

"And about how you were asleep in the car with your father, and when you woke up he told you he'd hit a dog on the road and killed it. Remember that?"

JOHN BURNHAM SCHWARTZ

Sam nodded. "A black dog."

"That's right. And I was just wondering if you remembered when that happened."

The boy said nothing, turned now and glanced back at the school bus, saw it still filling with children. The shouts and games of others. His feet shifted under him, a restless tic. Finally, he turned back to me.

"During the summer," he said.

"I know. I mean what day."

"July. After the all-star break."

"Can you tell me what day it was?"

"Sunday."

There was no particular inflection to his voice. It was just a day. He had no idea what it meant. I felt a tingling in my arms and fingers as if from a mild electric shock.

"Are you sure?"

He nodded. "We were coming back from the game," he said. "My dad got box seats. The Sox beat the Yanks. Mo Vaughn hit a slam in the sixteenth. He's my favorite player after they traded Boggs to the Yanks."

"Can you tell me what time it was?"

He shook his head. I ran the sleeve of my coat across my brow; it came away wet.

"Was it dark?"

"When I woke up it was."

"Right after the accident?"

He nodded. "I got a black eye against the door. A shiner."

"You were sleeping low down in the seat?"

"Yeah."

I took a step back from him. I was seeing it again. The car coming from the left in the darkness. The one dark shadow behind the wheel, the orange pinpoint of the cigarette. Nothing else. But a boy there this time, asleep and invisible.

"Sam?" I said.

He was looking at the bus again. It was nearly full. At the sound of my voice he glanced at the trumpet case by his feet. His feet shifting again, as though he had to pee.

"Um, I gotta go, Mr. Learner. Mr. Peoples gets really pissed off if we make him wait."

"Sam," I said.

I knew what I was doing: just his name once and he went still. His name that I'd heard shouted twice on a dark road as the father drove on. Just his name now in a stern man's voice, a father's voice, the one that demands an answer. He looked up at me like a guilty son.

I said, "I want you to tell me the name of the road where your father hit the dog."

Minutes seemed to pass, while I looked on hardly breathing.

And then, finally, he nodded.

"It's the shortcut," he said, as if reciting a fact he was proud to have committed to memory. "It's called Reservation Road. My dad told me."

Suddenly, the bus motor roared to life. Mr. Peoples pressed the horn. Sam reached down and grasped the handle of the trumpet case, hoisted it up, and hugged it once again to his chest.

"I gotta go now, Mr. Learner," he said, already moving toward the bus. "Bye."

"Good-bye, Sam."

I watched him climb on, move down the aisle, find a last empty seat. Soon he had become a face like all the rest, seen at a distance through glass; he might have been anyone's. The bus shifted into gear.

I saw Emma then. Sitting at the back of the bus, her blond hair like a sun spot in a thundercloud, her face flush to the window in confusion and distress at the sight of me. Somehow, we had missed each other, and now it was too late. I called out her name but the bus didn't stop. It pulled out of the parking lot, turned west, and disappeared down the road.

Dwight

Around six that same Friday evening I drove over to
Ruth's. By that hour it was dark. The porch light was
on, and two cars I'd never seen before were parked
in the drive next to Ruth's green wagon and Norris's
pale blue Mercury sedan. It looked like a dinner party.
I sat in my parked car for a minute or more, forehead
touching the wheel, my hand groping blindly for the
glove box and the pint bottle inside. I got hold of it,
lifted my chin, and drank. As I did, I found myself staring directly into the lighted window of Sam's room
upstairs, but I didn't see him.

Walking across the grass, I heard their voices, rau-
cous and probably juiced with a martini or two, and
caught a glimpse of them through the living-room windows. They were sitting around the fireplace. Some
guy was laughing like a horse. It all looked pretty cozy.

In and out, I was telling myself, in and out. You
know why you're here. Just get in, get your son, and get
out. I was on the porch, caught by that light I'd hooked

up so long ago. I was knocking on the door, thinking how the source of things always seemed to get lost in the shuffle of events and the passage of time, that was just how things were.

It was Norris who opened the door. My bad luck. He was wearing a green blazer and a yellow button-down and his face was glowing like something dipped in oil.

"Dwight!" he greeted me. This was not enthusiasm. More like shock, what you might say if you found a man standing naked in your bedroom closet.

Intending to defuse matters right away, I leaned in close and spoke softly. "Norris, listen. I need you to do me a favor."

"It's Friday night, Dwight," Norris said, recovering his usual bouncy tone. "What're you doing here?"

"I need to talk to Ruth."

"Why're you whispering?"

"Just go and get Ruth for me, Norris. Would you do that? I need to talk to her."

Norris looked at me. He seemed to be considering, in his insurance-man's way, the validity and cost of my claim. Finally, he shook his head. "Sorry, Dwight, I don't think Ruth would appreciate the interruption just now."

"Norris," I said, "it's important. I wouldn't be here otherwise. Just go and get her for me."

"Actually, Dwight, we're having a little dinner party here. Kind of a major shindig, if you want to know—"

Norris stopped talking and looked down. I'd taken a fistful of his left lapel.

326

"Listen carefully to me, Norris. I want to talk to Ruth now. Okay?"

"Okay, Dwight. I get your point." Norris's face had turned a deep pink. "But I want you to know I don't appreciate this. I'm going to hold it against you, in fact. Here in my own home, I mean. A man shouldn't be touched by another man in his own home."

"In principle I agree with you," I said.

"Norris," Ruth called out from the living room, "who's that you're talking to?"

"Nobody, honey!" Norris called back over his shoulder, a little too cheerily.

In a minute we heard the sound of her heels against the wood floor coming toward us.

"Now you've done it," Norris said to me under his breath.

"Norris . . . ," Ruth was saying as she reached the door. Then she saw me and her face fell about a foot. "I should've known."

"Ruth, I need to talk to you."

"Forget it."

"Ruth, listen—"

"No, you listen. This isn't your house. You can't just show up here any time you feel like it and demand to talk to me. I've got a life. We've got people over. So good night. If you want to talk to me you can talk to me Sunday. Move, Norris."

Norris stepped aside briskly and Ruth started to close the door on me.

I grabbed the knob and stopped the door halfway. "Listen, Ruth . . ."

She kept pushing but the door wouldn't budge. "Are you drunk?" she demanded.

I shook my head.

"Goddamnit, Dwight, let go of the door."

"I need to see Sam, Ruth. I need to see him."

"You want me to call the police, Ruth?" Norris said hopefully.

Ruth waved him away. Still pushing on the door, she said to me through clamped teeth, "You can see him Sunday."

"No."

"Goddamnit, Dwight!"

"Ruth," I said, "I can't wait till Sunday."

Maybe it was something in my voice: all of a sudden she stopped pushing on the door and so did I, and she eyed me through the opening with angry but considering eyes. Then the door gave another couple of inches and I saw the long red dress she was wearing, the same dress she'd worn at the concert back in August.

"Norris," she said, "you'd better go back to our guests. God knows what they must be thinking by now."

"But Ruth—"

"Don't worry about me. I'll be fine." She leaned over and kissed him on the cheek.

"If you say so," he said reluctantly, and went back into the living room.

To me Ruth said, "You've got one minute." She stepped out onto the porch and closed the door behind her. The night was cold and she rubbed her arms to warm herself.

"You want my coat?" I offered.

"The only thing I want from you is an explanation. And it better be good."

"I'm going away, Ruth."

She stopped rubbing her arms and looked at me.

"I'm leaving the state," I said.

I'd expected the news to shock her, maybe even sadden her, but there was none of that. She merely nodded, looking me in the eyes with an unsettling directness, as if she knew right then all that I was about and all that I'd done.

I looked away.

"It's time for a change," I said lamely. "Things around here have gone kind of stale for me." I paused. "Things aren't really working too well."

"You mean your life," Ruth said.

"Yeah."

She was rubbing her arms again. They were slender, light-catching arms, just as I remembered, and I took off my coat and slipped it over her shoulders.

"Thanks."

I tried on a smile. "Any time."

"When time's gone by, Dwight," she said, and the loaded seriousness of her tone dragged the sad little smile right off my face, "and you've found yourself another life and haven't been around here for a while, I want you to remember how tonight I never asked you what kind of trouble you're in. I want you to remember that, okay?"

"Okay, Ruth."

"What you have to live with is your own business. That's between you and your conscience. But Sam's my business. He's our son. And that's how it is. And you remember that."

I said that I would remember that always, and it was the truth. And Ruth leaned back against the porch railing, her hair shining in that light, and let out a breath like a sigh, like a hand letting go of what it had long been holding. What fell away was me.

"You came here for Sam," she said.

I nodded.

"You want to go up and see him?"

"I want him to come and spend tonight in my house," I said. "That's the only thing I want. I want just for once to wake up in my own house and find my son there with me. That'll be enough."

Ruth shook her head. "No."

Her voice was firm, and I felt some last small hope start to crumble. "Please, Ruth."

"Why should I? I mean, would you, if you were me? I doubt that. It's Friday night and you've had a drink or two. I know you, Dwight. I know all about you."

"It's my last chance," I said.

"That's your own doing, and you know it."

She stood looking at me for a long moment. I saw a nugget of hard black pity in her eyes that hurt as much as anything she'd ever said to me. Then she turned her back on me and stared out into the cold night, her breath painting the darkness beyond the reach of the porch light.

"I remember waking up every morning believing you were going to change," she said.

The wistfulness in her voice caught me by surprise, struck a wound somewhere in my memory: I remembered too. More than anything I wanted to put my arms around her now. But I did nothing.

"I'm sorry, Ruth. You know I am."

"Yeah, well," she said abruptly, turning around to face me again. "What's past is past." It was as if she'd just woken from a bad dream. She lifted my coat off her shoulders and handed it to me. "Thanks, Dwight, but no thanks."

I put my coat back on. She turned and walked to the door, stopped there, and looked back.

"I'll fix up an overnight bag for him," she said. "He can spend tonight at your place. But it'll be the last time."

She went inside.

Ethan

I drove home that afternoon with the man's name in my mouth. Spitting out the vowels and consonants to myself, over and over, like a diver, alone in green watery light, murmuring to himself at the end of the high board.

The car grew stifling. My muscles ached from their own pent-up tension. I rolled down the window and let in the cold gray air, wood smoke and metal. More than ever it looked like snow.

What do you do with a truth like this? Where do you put it? Ideas don't help. Ideas are nothing. Facts are what matter. Facts were what they'd made of my son in the newspapers, facts were the only language of the police—telling me his history based on his vital statistics as noted in their ledgers. Telling me what they didn't know and what they wouldn't do.

I saw them sitting at their desks with their guns at their waists like substitute souls, and their eyes were heavy-lidded with indifference. And they did nothing.

It was, finally, a message any fool could have figured out.

You gather your own facts. You take a memory, a shadow in a car at night, your son's broken body by the roadside. You take a man's name. You put the facts together. And when you have the facts together, you place the man's name on your tongue and you hold it there against indifference and forgetting, against murder and denial. You do not let it go. You take responsibility for what will happen. You do it yourself, because no one else is going to.

Grace had put her car in the barn, which in bad weather we used as a garage; she must have felt snow coming, too. I left my own car in the driveway.

They were sitting, mother and daughter, at the kitchen table. I appeared in the doorway like a stranger, a visitor happening by chance upon a scene of settled domesticity. Grace had made hot chocolate, arranged some cookies on a plate. Anyone could see that she was trying hard. The kitchen was warm, its lights burning brightly. But Emma looked as if she'd been crying, and there were lines on my wife's face that I had never seen before.

"Ethan. What are you doing home?"

"I, uh . . ."

"You were at school," Emma put in accusingly.

"You went by Emma's school?" Grace said.

I nodded dumbly. The room was warm and bright.

"Are you all right?"

"I have a terrible headache," I mumbled. "I think I'll lie down."

I retreated to my study, closed the door, sat on the wingback chair. I wanted to be alone, to think, but exhaustion wouldn't allow it. I had not slept in so long that now, when I most needed an agile, focused mind, the feeling was of being trapped under an all-encompassing weight, like being buried up to my neck in sand. Time seemed to be running away from me, never to be caught.

There was a knock. Perhaps I said something, because Grace entered, bringing Tylenol and water. I thanked her. She was about to leave. Then at the door she paused.

"Did something happen today?"

"It's the headache," I answered.

She looked at me with a steady gaze. She seemed about to ask another question, but in the end she said nothing and left the room.

Outside, it grew dark, afternoon passing into evening. A bitter wind rose up, rattling the windows, as I sat trying to convince myself of things already decided and things not yet decided.

And then another knock, this time Emma, carrying a dinner tray. The tray was heavy for her and she gripped it fiercely, as though it were an animal trying to leap away and she would not let it. Knife and fork slid, clattering; the glass of water rocked but did not tip over. I took the tray from her.

"Thanks, Em."

"You're welcome," she said soberly.

"What time is it?" I glanced at my watch. "Eight-thirty. Almost bedtime."

"I know."

"I'm sorry about this afternoon. I was confused."

"It's okay."

"I'll be up to kiss you good night."

"Promise?" she said.

Before I could reply she was gone.

In a little while I went upstairs. She was in her pajamas, in her bed, under the covers. Twigs was with her, tucked under an arm. Sallie lay on the floor in the corner. I sat down on the edge of the bed. Her eyes were bluer than I had ever truly noticed and they were gazing up at me, fixed and knowing.

"Are you sleepy?" I said.

She shook her head.

"Well, try. Close your eyes."

Her eyes remained open, staring at me. "Will you tell me a story?"

"Not tonight."

"Please."

"Okay." I waited, not knowing if anything would come to me. Then slowly I began. "Once upon a time there was a man," I said, "and he was silly. A silly man. But he had a beautiful daughter and—"

"And a son?" Emma broke in.

I paused. Like falling into a bottomless pool of sadness. "What?"

"And a son."

"Yes." Her hands—her pale hands with the already chewed nails and the ragged cuticles—were beautiful, resting atop the bedcovers; I placed my own hands over them, feeling at the wrist the faint beat of her pulse. "And a son."

"And then what happened?"

"The man was cursed," I said. "One day he'd run into a goat on a bridge and the goat had put a curse on him. He could never go to sleep before his daughter did. He had to stay up until he was absolutely positive she was asleep. That was the curse."

"Is that what made him silly?"

"Yes. Silly and cursed."

"What else?"

"Nothing. That's the end."

"That's a terrible story," Emma said.

"You're right."

Again, now, a pause, or more like a hesitation; we sat looking at each other until, oddly frightened of myself, I glanced away.

"Well," I murmured. "Time for bed."

"Dad," she said, "your hands are shaking."

I looked down. "Are they? I must be tired."

"Time for bed."

I tried to smile. "You're right."

"Good night," she breathed.

"Good night, Em. I love you."

"Love you, too."

She closed her eyes. I kissed her, once on each eyelid, and got up. At the door I switched off the light and stood staring into the new darkness until I thought I could see her blond head. And then I went out.

At the end of the hallway, just outside our bedroom door, Grace was standing, already in her nightgown.

"Are you coming to bed?" she asked quietly.

I finished closing Emma's door. "In a little while. There's some reading I want to do first. You probably shouldn't bother waiting up."

I thought she would turn away, but she stood where she was, looking at me.

"Are you sure?"

Her eyes were fixed on mine with a poignant intensity; she was looking at me, I thought, as if she knew everything. A sudden physical weakness ran through my body, a debilitating need for her comfort and touch, and in my mind I saw a fantastic sequence of images in which she reached out to me and told me not to go.

"Good night," she said.

I went to her and kissed her. "Good night, Grace."

Then I let that go. The warmth of family, the fantasy of retreating and forgetting. I went downstairs alone.

I waited two hours in my study. This was the hardest time. The night drew later, darker, the house silent save for its cold-weather noises, creakings and hummings and knocks. I sat there and felt the anger come back. Sat rigid on that chair like something frozen until the house itself was forgotten, a discarded shell.

I saw that there was no choice any more. The frustration was like a physical wound which, quickly fading, leaves a red scar of despair. It had hurt a long time already. But now that I knew who he was, it had become unbearable.

I got up, moved about. Ran my hand reflexively over the spines of my books. Sat down again and put my head in my hands. I felt exhausted and terribly frightened but also resolute and not alone; my son, and the man who'd killed him, were in every thought I had.

Then it was later. I went outside. The sky was black with a lining like smoke which was the clouds full of snow; the moon was gone. I walked carefully across the hard, frost-covered ground. Up close, the barn was a shadow mountain, ominous and unfamiliar, and with outstretched hands I felt my way around the side to the narrow door. Hinges cried out. Stepping inside, I smelled the traces of dung and hay, ghosts from another era, and over it gasoline, an automobile in the cold. I switched on the light. A single bare bulb floating high up among the rafters, my breath already rising toward it, dissipating.

On the far side of the barn, beyond Grace's car and the empty space for my own, along a wall of junk, lay the army officer's trunk that had been Grace's father's. Her private shrine to his memory. Looking at it now, its coating of dust and negligence, finding it locked, I remembered the day it had arrived by truck from

North Carolina. Our first summer here. Josh was an infant. We had the mover put the trunk in the barn. "What's in it?" I had asked her. "A few of his things," was all she would say. She had seemed moved almost beyond words, alone with herself and the still undiminished pain of her father's early death. I left her to go through the contents alone, and then, later, I went through it myself, in secret: a West Point blanket, moth-eaten, faded gray and black; a mess kit; a leather valet of tarnished military medals, cuff links, studs, a gold watch; a shoebox of letters with old stamps, the glue dried to nothing, the stamps like dead flies in an attic. And in a dented metal box, a revolver, army issue, property of Captain Avery Spring. And bullets.

Dwight

I fixed up the spare bedroom for him, the one that had never been slept in. The one that had been waiting for him to come home to. And while Sam stood there looking around at the bare ugly walls and such, the criminal lack of posters and Red Sox memorabilia, I tore open the package with the brand-new nightlight that I'd been saving for months just for this occasion, and plugged the thing into the wall. It made a world of difference, if you ask me. Bingo, a motel becomes a house.

Practice saying it, while you can: "Welcome home, son. Here's your room, son." And then remember that rehearsals don't count.

He changed into his pajamas, went into the bathroom to brush his teeth. And my heart was beating hard just from knowing that he wasn't going anywhere but was settling down for the night, right here. Then he came out of the bathroom and told me that the sink was too tall for him to reach. I offered to lift him up myself but he didn't want help. He was ten years old and wanted something to stand on.

Well, I would have gotten him anything he wanted that night. I looked around the house for a couple of minutes but there was nothing for him to stand on. Which wasn't much of a surprise. Because it was an empty, useless house but for him. Because the only footstool I had was sitting out in the garage, coated with dust.

I told him to hang on, I'd be right back. I went to the kitchen for the door clicker in the cigar box.

Outside, the air was cold, the sky heavy; it felt as if any second it would start to snow. I walked across the lawn. Yellow light painted the drive in front of the garage. I went inside. The car was there as it had been, but this time I kept clear of it. I stayed to the left side, where all the stuff was—the junk and sports equipment and tools, the bearable memories. I found the footstool underneath the stray lid of a plastic trash can. It was made of plywood stained a fake cherry color and didn't look strong enough to hold my weight. It looked poorly homemade. I couldn't remember how I'd come to have it, or if I'd ever tried to use it. But I thought it would do fine for Sam, and I picked it up and walked out of the garage with it, making a conscious effort not even to glance at the car. As if, on my boy's first and only night in my house, I might be able to keep these histories separate, his and mine.

Back inside the house, I found him in his pajamas sitting on the gray leather sofa in the den, watching the eleven o'clock news on TV.

"I'm waiting for sports," he said.

What could I say? I didn't give two cents for the state of his dental hygiene or his bedtime. He was my son. I sat down beside him and fit my arm around his shoulders.

Grace

She woke dreaming of suicide.

Snow on the ground; glorious sunshine; the light a series of explosions that leaves her dazed. In her nightgown, doorway of the house, she stands staring at Ethan, who stands in the middle of the yard, his hands, slit at the wrists as though gilled, outstretched toward her as if for an embrace, his blood pouring onto the snow in two steaming, red rivulets. He says nothing.

Now, beyond Ethan, something moves: she sees Josh running across the white ground for the road. She wants to call out but is unable to make even the smallest sound, merely raises her hand in an ambiguous gesture that goes unnoticed. Josh comes to the fence and goes over it. He reaches the road, white also, and runs into it just as a yellow school bus drives by. The bus blinds her like a sun and she looks away. When she looks back he is not there. The bus has passed, never stopping, and there is no sign of him. Mutely

JOHN BURNHAM SCHWARTZ

she falls to her knees in the doorway of the house. She
sees Ethan, on his knees too, arms still outstretched,
face drained of color. His blood has melted the snow
around him; there the earth is bare and damp, red-
rimmed like a wound. But in front of her the snow is
white and thick and she reaches out and buries her
hand in it. The hand disappears. The cold comes like
a burning. And then a sound—

She woke shaking. The covers off her. The room
dark but strange, luminous, dream light, and in her
mind, held like a note that goes on singing itself long
after the song is over, the sound.

She hugged herself, lay thinking, *What is it?* Like a
door closing. A door—

And then, from outside, through windows, an
answer.

She was on her feet before her body could catch
up. Stumbling across the room to the window—one
to the left, northeast-facing, view of the driveway. First
thing she saw was the snow everywhere, in the air
thick and sinking, still and downy on the ground. A
world transfigured. Her dream but at night. And then
his headlights came on, reaching out from the driveway to the road, catching in those beams the continu-
ous, fragmented falling of the heavens. As if during the
night the sky itself had broken. A wave of fear rippled
through her, the need to stop him from leaving, her
hands, panicked like the newly blind, scrabbling up
along the panes to the window lock, grasping with
cold dumb fingers, straining. With a wrench it gave.
And she threw open the window with all her might.

344

It was his taillights she saw, receding up the road like a pair of bloodshot eyes, blurred by the falling snow. Too late. She wanted to scream to him but didn't. *Control yourself*, she demanded silently, to no one, and sank to her knees. Her heart was a small animal fighting for its life. Snow blew in through the open window and landed on her bare shoulders.

In the end, she got to her feet and went down the hall to Emma's room.

She was surprised by the amount of light; the snow outside the windows made everything visible. She stood in the doorway taking it all in: the dog in the corner; the thin chill coming from the frosted panes; the smell of washed flannel sheets; the girl asleep at the far edge of the bed, the covers in disarray. *Emma*. On the ceiling roamed a teardrop pattern of shadow. She took a few more steps, and then she was standing by the bed. She could hear her child's breathing, see the life there, real and within reach. *Not a dream*. And she felt better, less afraid, rooted, somehow, in time and place. Her mind suddenly alight with the words she used to know and believe: "Now I lay me down to sleep . . ."

"Mommy," Emma breathed.

The blond head moved, turned toward her: awake.

"I'm here," Grace said.

And she lay down with Emma to wait.

Dwight

My eyes opened. I was lying on my back on the leather sofa in the den, still in my clothes, hands tucked between my legs for warmth. A baby curled up. I couldn't remember falling asleep, or why, or dreaming. For a few seconds I couldn't remember anything. The gray light more like darkness than light, a kind of glow in it. I sat up and saw through the windows the snow falling quiet and steady, the world all covered over with white, and then I remembered that Sam was asleep, in my house, actually here, in his own room down the hall. And I believe I smiled to myself, thinking maybe, after breakfast, I'd take him sledding.

Then the refrigerator started up, came to life humming, and I looked toward the kitchen.

Ethan Learner was half in shadow but I could see him. I didn't make a sound. He had a gun in his right hand and as I looked on he cocked back the hammer.

"Are you Dwight Arno?"

I must have nodded. Fear had turned me hardly

conscious, able to think only about Sam. Sam here, asleep, here because I'd wanted it, begged for it, down on my knees to Ruth. Whatever else happened, I had to get this man and his gun out of the house before Sam woke up.

"Mr. Learner—"

"Be quiet." It was all he said. His voice soft with a kind of lunatic calm, out on the fringe somewhere, as if not knowing itself how scared or angry it was. He came closer, passing in front of a window. His round glasses turned to silver dollars and then went gray again. He stopped about five feet away, the gun pointed down at the middle of my chest. "Move slowly," he said.

I got up, my bad knee cracking as it unbent. My body a roadside breakdown, veritable junk. But then it happened, I felt it: a slight pause in him as I drew myself up, a shift in his makeup, inside hesitation, as if he'd lost the tune he was supposed to sing. Doubt sticking its head into the room: I must have outweighed him by thirty pounds.

I could see the gun better now. Big, serious, maybe antique. It looked like the army gun my old man had kept in his bedside drawer, memento of his days with a purpose and a team, days surely gone; a weapon kept, during his long slide to nowhere after my mother died, under no lock and no key, as if just waiting for me to get my hands on it. I'd taken that gun out just once, sneaked it off one night while he was passed out drunk, carried it burning hot in my pocket down blocks and through alleyways and across abandoned factory lots and out past the edge of town, where, fear-struck more than tough, I'd blasted a can of Schlitz into the after-world. I knew the sound, the kick, the kind of hole a gun like this one made in tin or paper. The rest was just a good guess. The bullet enters the body, expands in the blink of an eye, blows a hole out my back the size, say, of a walnut, which happens also to be the size of my shrunken heart.

"Where's your coat?" Learner said.

"Over there by the door."

"Let's go get it."

I felt the gun graze my back as I went by him. There were things I thought to say but they were all about my son asleep down the hall, nothing he'd want to hear. So, moving for the door, I said nothing. *Get my coat*, I was thinking, *get out of this house*. In an hour or two Sam wakes up alone, sees the snow out his window and thinks maybe about sledding, wanders down the hall into his old man's room and finds the round bed unslept in and the bureau drawers emptied and the duffel bags stuffed with clothes, feels the first twinges of confusion. Then a check of the rest of the house and the discovery that Dad has skipped out. Again. This would be the worst part, and my heart ached for him. But he would get over it. One day. He had already survived worse from me. And he would be safe, not in danger because of me. He knew how to use the phone, knew his own number; eventually he'd call his mother—

"Put it on," Learner said.

My coat was on a hook by the front door and I put it on.

"Okay," he said, "let's go."

I put my hand on the doorknob. It was my own boy I was thinking about, not his. Last night. My own boy asleep on the couch, the TV droning on, my arm around his shoulders: I pick him up and carry him to his room, his head lolling, his feet sticking out, and tuck him in. First time in my house, last time in my house; he never wakes. And now I was leaving him again. The snowy cold blowing through the crack underneath the front door. I thought what a cheap-shit house this was and how sorry I was to ever have lived in it. I was turning the doorknob when I heard Sam, faint but clear, calling me from the other end of the house.

"Dad!"

Learner froze. "Who's that?" His voice when he finally got it out was a panicked, whispery mess.

I couldn't answer.

He jammed the gun into my back. "Answer me."

"My son," I whispered.

"What?"

"My son."

"Where?"

"In his room."

"Oh, Christ," he said. Sweat had suddenly appeared in tiny glistening beads all over his forehead.

"He's just a kid," I said. "He doesn't know anything."

"Shut up."

"Dad!"

"Let me go in and talk to him."

"No. Shut up."

"Dad!"

"If I don't go to him he'll come out."

"All right," Learner said weakly. "Go."

He steered me with the gun—the muzzle hard and nervous in my spine, leaving a mark—pushed me ahead of him, back across the den to the hall, down it. We stopped outside Sam's door, which was partway open. From the hall I saw just the edge of one window, the strange gray-white morning coming in around the shade, beneath it the tiny glowing bulb of the night-light. I stepped inside the room. Sam lay on the bed with the covers kicked off, wearing nothing but his underpants and a long-sleeve T-shirt. He was still sleepy, his hair mussed, his eyelids thick. I put a smile on my face and said, "Hey, sport."

"Where were you? I woke up."

"I can see that," I said, not answering his question.

"What time's it?"

"Too early for you to be asking."

"You got your coat on," he pointed out.

I'd forgotten I was wearing it. "Yeah, well, it's snowing outside and real cold in here." I sat down on the edge of the bed before he could say anything else. "As a matter of fact," I went on, "what do you think you're doing on top of the blankets? You catch a cold over here and your mother's gonna let me have it. She'll never let you come back." I took a handful of the blankets and lifted them up so he could slip under. A waft of his smell came rising up with the warm, trapped air.

"Listen to me, Sam, okay? I just want to check something. You know the phone number at your mother's house?"

He didn't answer right away. Then he nodded.

"You sure?"

"Yeah."

"Tell it to me."

He told it to me.

"So if you needed to, you could call her and get her to come pick you up here?"

He looked me in the eyes as if he sensed something. Finally, he nodded again.

"That's my boy," I said.

I heard Learner then, a noise so soft and invisible it wouldn't mean anything unless you knew what it was: weight shifting from one foot to the other on the carpet. It made me hate his guts. I leaned over and put my arms around my son, half lifted him out of bed. He weighed next to nothing. I kissed his head and told him that I had to go into the office to work on a crisis—a legal problem involving someone very important—and that if I wasn't back by the time the cartoons started on TV he should call his mother and have her come over and get him.

I let him go. His head dropped back on the pillow. He didn't say anything, asked none of the obvious questions. Just kept looking at me. Till I stood up, tugging at the covers so they fit under his chin.

"You got all that?"

He nodded.

"Good. Go to sleep now, son."

For me, he made a show of closing his eyes. I turned for the door.

"Dad?"

I stopped but didn't look back. I was staring through the doorway at the outer half of Ethan Learner's left boot on the powder blue shag carpet. The rest of him was hidden.

"What, Sam?"

"Can we go sledding later?"

"Sure we can," I said. "Now go back to sleep."

I went out of the room, closing the door behind me. Learner was there, and his gun too. He was sweating, pale as a ghost, and unable to look me in the eye.

Ethan

Call it a travesty, a terrible joke. Call it a mistake beyond reckoning.

Who can describe it? A boy's singular voice. A father's. A conversation about nothing—cold and phone numbers and sledding—that left me, there in the hallway, crippled with shame and guilt and longing. Left me weak.

This was the fatal habit of Polonius: to stand in the shadows listening, peering at life with half an eye, letting others take the risk of living and despising them for it. A gun loves this kind of coward the way a crutch loves the lame.

And then the conversation ended, and he came out of the room.

Outside. Snow again, falling feather-soft, a white like the Ice Age. Cold, cold air. He walked ahead of me. A powerful man, his back, all by itself, massive and intimidating. The truth was, he frightened me. Had he turned around even once during the walk up the road to my car, it might have all been over. Perhaps, silently counting our footsteps away from his house, we were both still thinking about the boy in his bed, covers pulled up. Asleep or awake.

"Where were you? I woke up."

The voice like an echo that would not die.

But he didn't turn around. He let the moment run until we were past the point of hearing. He never looked back, and I began to hate him again. He walked ahead of me as I'd ordered him to, taking for granted, it seemed, the potency of the weapon in my hand, if not the exhausted man who was supposed to use it; I watched the deep, patterned prints of his work boots in the fresh-made snow, laid out behind him like a series of messages. Otherwise he gave no sign of anything, was stoical as a saint, uncomplaining and righteous as a soldier. His back broad and straight, his head already sprinkled with snow but held high—tough, haunted, undissuadable, ridiculous, tragic. He cut a figure. But guilty of murdering a boy? He wasn't saying. He was saying nothing. Doing what he was told. Leaving the talking and explaining and suffering and living to the people who claimed victimhood, who had been left gasping in his wake.

Dwight

It was an old Honda Accord, not well cared for, parked about a quarter-mile up the road. The snow made the walk longer. When we got there he opened both doors on the driver's side and then stepped back with the gun pointed at my chest. The gun was shaking; he no longer seemed able to hold it still. He asked if I had gloves and I nodded and he told me to put them on.

"Now get in."

A breeze was blowing falling snow into the car and onto the seats. I slid behind the wheel, looked immediately for the keys but they weren't there. He closed my door. Then I heard him get in behind me and the other door close, and the keys landed on my lap. "Drive," he said.

I drove past the mailbox with its blood-red flag laid down, past the bankrupt house, out of Box Corner altogether, away from my son. And while Learner gave me directions road by road, turn by turn, I prayed hard to a God I'd never properly given a shit about to look after Sam, please, to see him back to sleep right now, to follow him through all the troubles to come. Too late now. We were heading west on 44 toward Canaan and the headlights were pushing ahead into the fading dark of the road, and Learner's breathing warmed my ear like an animal's shallow pant. The road was wet under the tires, gravelly, and the snow fell onto the windshield in already melting particles, and the heater blew air as the wipers squeaked and clicked. Otherwise quiet. Anything I might have thought to say to help my case was a sick joke next to the facts of the matter, and I ruled against it. Despite the breathing he was calmer here in the car where the world was smaller, shrunk down to just the two of us and the gun, which he kept anxiously pressed against the side of my head. In the mirror I saw steam gradually climbing the lenses of his glasses, though he did not seem to notice it himself.

Outside Canaan, we came up on a pickup with a plow blade hitched to the front doing the roads, and Learner stuck the gun into my aching head good and hard, but when we were past the truck he eased up again, as if he didn't have the nerve. When I checked back in the mirror I thought I saw for the very first time a man who, glimpsed unawares, was just about as scared as I was.

Ethan

I took him to the mountaintop. The wooden cabins, the lake; time of memory, of summer, my son's life. A beautiful boy diving off a white float. The only place I had thought of—the lake at sunrise mirrored silver, at sunset the world on fire. And still my son dives, gets out, dives again.

I would make this man see all that he had failed to imagine. Would push his face deep into the beauty and the regret that he had never known existed—the sun on the lake and the breeze in the cattails and the canoe in the water and the father and son together and the horror of the bloody, headless swan—until this man could not breathe, until he was suffocated by his own emptiness. And then he would be dead, and I would leave him there.

The snow came down from a whitened sky. It fell on the tops of the pines alongside the road up Mount Riga, and much of it never made it to the ground; on the level crown of the mountain, though, the snow

357

had covered everything. Shallow drifts clung to the steep sides of the gabled roof of the warden's lightless cabin, in front of which stood the closed wooden gate.

I told him to stop the car and get out. The footpath leading to the other cabins was gone, whited out, and for several moments I stood there disoriented, the past snowed under. But then I found where I thought the footpath must have been, and with the weapon again at his back I marched him—no other word—toward the lake. I thought he might protest or plead, but he did not. Other than movement there was no evidence of spirit or feeling in him. If he was afraid, he did not show it. Even self-concern seemed beyond him: his head lowered against the falling snow, he trudged ahead like a blinkered packhorse. Countless snowflakes dropped down his gaping collar and landed on the exposed skin of his nape, but he made no move to cover himself. He did not seem to care any longer what happened to him, and so was without needs of any kind—no crime to which he felt compelled to confess, no contrition or remorse to express for the saving of his soul. He'd be gone soon, it would not be long now; and once he was gone, it would be the lot and daily torture of his victims to determine the extent of the damage done by him in the years generously referred to as his life. That would not be his problem. For he was evolution's latest miracle: reduced to nothing, he had nothing to lose. He had been, in the final sum of things, just a transient, passing through without regard for life.

We came to cabin four, which looked not as it once had, but like a shack, a doll's house, dressed over in white. Behind it the lake, the water at this hour, in the newfound winter, blackened, dimpled by falling snow. Swans gone. The white cake fallen or eaten. Not the place we had ever come to. Not the memory I had hunted down like a starving man. Not my son nor his death nor any reason why, but a mystery of unsung grief, forgotten memories, signs lost in weather.

Dwight

It was a cabin no different from any other. For too long he kept me out front of it, staring through me as if I wasn't there, while the snow came down on us like confetti. A single word carved above the door—"Hyacinth"—and behind the cabin nothing but the lake.

Then suddenly he had the gun aimed at my face and was saying, "Walk around the side of the cabin."

His voice was quiet, the gun steady. I could feel it happening now. I tried to think of something to say to him, but there was nothing. No big speech. No fear any more, just tiredness. I lowered my head and began walking around back of the cabin.

You dream what you're able under such circumstances; you dream your limit. I found mine where I'd left my son, in his room, in bed. I hoped he was asleep. I had the blankets in my hand and felt the warm trapped air rising up from his body.

Halfway around the cabin, Learner's foot caught on something—tree root, shrub, rock, I didn't know—and he stumbled forward. He gave a grunt. He had lost all control over his feet, and his gun arm came down and his shoulder collided with my back, and what happened next was no more than pure instinct: my elbow jumped back and I smashed him in the face.

He was on his knees, moaning softly, his hands covering his nose, which was bleeding and probably broken; his eyes lost in a blind squint of pain and disorientation—I saw his glasses on the ground in front of him. The gun sitting in the snow three feet away. He might have tried for it, but he didn't.

I didn't think twice. I picked up the gun and put it in my coat pocket and stepped around him, heading back to the path. This, too, was instinct. But then I took my time. I made a point of not looking back.

The future lay before me, I might have thought. All of a sudden, and again. Sundays on the ball field with Sam, meat on the grill. A bright movie sequel with all the old characters and my son as the star.

Except I couldn't see it. Couldn't see him.

Ahead, through the scrim of falling snow, there was just this: two other cabins by the lakeside, white covering their rooftops. And they were no different, it seemed to me, from the one Learner had tried so hard to reach, like a piece of the past he'd wanted to hold in his fist as he struck me down. For his own reasons.

Somewhere beyond it was his car, and the road back down to Salisbury. That was all.

I walked a little way, and then, thinking I heard him behind me, I stopped and turned around.

He was still there. I saw him through the snow, by the little two-bit cabin on the lake. And he was weeping. On his knees in a cold white world, on all fours like an animal, his face buried in his hands which were buried in snow. Around him the splatter of blood. A man humped on the ground as if in the aftermath of a prayer so full of loss that in the end it had left him broken.

I stood looking at him, unable to turn away. The sky falling down white. Maybe it was a kind of dead reckoning, my own position fixed at this point in time according to the one true and immovable thing, which was a man on his knees. I had taken from him everything there was to take, and had wanted none of it, had hoped and tried to avoid it, had regretted it deeply. But I had taken his boy just the same. And so now I went back to him.

Ethan

There is a kind of failure that defies understanding. No map can be drawn of it. The best one can do is to shout into the darkness behind in the hope that some distant echo will return to illuminate even partially the road chosen, the wrong turns made, the hubris and misguided love and circumstance that brought one to this place where there is no light at all, no road ahead and no turns to contemplate, nothing to think about that is not already buried and past. Somewhere back I had misplaced my son, had lost sight of his memory, which was the one truth that remained after his death, and had instead followed something false, which was not worthy of him.

I heard him walk away, his footsteps heavy and plodding through the snow. He was disappearing. From my hole in the ground I witnessed none of it, but kept my eyes shut tight, my bleeding, numb face in my hands. I could not seem to stop weeping, could not even imagine it. My only dream then was to never get up.

The footsteps were already close when I heard them again. I was too beaten to feel any surprise at his return, nor was I afraid any more; it was with a great force of effort that I raised myself off my arms at all. Then I was kneeling upright and he was standing there. My head swam with dizziness, and my eyes, useless without my glasses, struggled in vain to focus, but he remained just a massive, blurred figure, like some vague totem looming over me. His arm, hazy and thick as a fencepost, outstretched toward me, his brown-gloved hand not three feet from my face.

"Take these," he was saying.

His hand came closer. The snow fell upon it and now the thing in his fingers shot off tiny facets of light like a coin held and turned under a lamp. It was my glasses. They were small and insignificant-looking on the leathered palm of his hand, and he held them as though afraid of crushing them, with his fingers spread far to the sides. I reached out and took the glasses and they were as cold as if they'd been frozen. I put them on, fitting the curved wire earpieces around my ears. Where the nosepieces touched my face, the swollen bridge of my nose felt as if it had been sawed in two, and I breathed in sharply through my mouth, my head afloat again in a sea of dizziness. Then the pain retreated to mere numbness and I could see his face.

"I was going to leave you," he said.

He reached into the pocket of his coat and pulled out the gun. I felt no clenching of muscles, no fear; all that was gone now. In his hand the gun was the color of smoke and looked darker and strange and more like a machine. I simply stared at it.

"But I ran once, and I didn't get anywhere that I can see," he said. He looked at the ground. "Where would I go?"

He let the gun drop from his hand. It fell onto the snow between us and we both looked down at the spot where it lay. The barrel was pointing at him.

"I've got a son," he said. "Ten years old like your boy was. That doesn't seem fair to you, and it's not." He paused, his breath turning white in the cold, the snow falling silently onto his shoulders and head. He stared past me at the lake. "And it's not fair that I've been a poor father to Sam, failed him a million different ways and kept failing him, while you were a good father to your son. I don't know you, but I know that you were a good father to him. And I know it's not fair. It is not right."

His eyes returned to the ground between us, the gun there. He remained absolutely still. He seemed for the moment almost complacent. Yet beneath the dark stubble on his cheeks the muscles in his jaw stood rigid with effort.

I said, "You took his life like it was nothing and then you went on with your own as if you had a right."

"I was afraid."

"That's not good enough," I said.

I picked up the gun. Slowly I got to my feet. My gloves were stiff with blood, and through them I could feel the metallic cold. My knees too were wet and numb from the snow and no longer felt as if they belonged to me. With my thumb I pulled back the hammer. Then I was standing, holding the gun aimed at his chest, my finger braced against the trigger.

He stood motionless, his breath pluming the air.

Then he nodded once.

"Yes," he said.

Now he seemed to be waiting for me to pull the trigger and be done with it. Not tranquil, but resigned, expectant. It could not have been mistaken for an act. I tried to avoid looking him in the face, but I could no longer help it; though neither of us moved an inch, the silence and the passing seconds seemed somehow to be pushing us together. His eyes, set wide in a broad, weather-beaten face, were brown and surprisingly soft, and I saw the pronounced dark circles beneath them.

I let the gun drop to my side and turned away from him.

And then for a long time nothing happened.

I saw the cabin, and the lake, and it was a place in winter.

I saw his son sleeping in his bed.

"I want . . ." I said, and saw only the snow.

He stood there looking at me.

"The police . . ." I said then, but it sounded like

nowhere at all. I put the gun in my pocket and left it there. "Will you tell them what you did?"

After a while he said, "Yes."

Then he was silent. The snow fell down on him and stayed. His feet shifted, and he raised his gloved hands in the air as though he were giving himself up to me.

"No," I said. I saw him with the police, and it meant nothing, changed nothing. "No." I was shaking my head, seeing his son awake now and standing in the cold, empty house.

I began to walk.

He called after me. "Where are you going?"

I stopped and turned. "Go back to your son," I told him.

Dwight Arno said nothing. His hands dropped to his sides and for the first time I knew he was afraid. I walked out to the path. I did not stop. I left him there on the mountain, in the snow, alone.

ACKNOWLEDGMENTS

For shelter, support, nourishment, care, wit, wisdom, friendship, forbearance, and always sound literary judgment, my love, gratitude, and particular thanks to William and Paula Merwin, Alan and Louise Schwartz, Jane Kramer and Vincent Crapanzano, Margaret McElderry, Matthew Schwartz and Karen Levesque, Ileene Smith, David and Jean Halberstam, Ann Arensberg and Dick Grossman, Timothy Dugan, Amanda Urban, Robin Desser, Heather Schroder, Pico, and, above all, Aleksandra.

ALSO BY JOHN BURNHAM SCHWARTZ

BICYCLE DAYS

When Alec Stern arrives in Japan, he discovers a land of opportunity. For only in Tokyo could an impressionable young man fresh out of college find, in one stroke, a new job, a new family, and a society that lavishes attention on Japanese-speaking *gaijin*. Yet, even as Alec claims a place in this new world, he is haunted by memories of the one he left behind—a world once infinitely secure but which disintegrated with the breakup of his parents' marriage. In this incandescently observed novel, John Burnham Schwartz introduces readers to one of the most appealing protagonists in contemporary fiction while enchanting them with the keenness of his eye and the aptness of his voice.

Fiction/Literature/978-0-375-70275-4

ALSO AVAILABLE:
Claire Marvel, 978-0-375-71915-8

VINTAGE CONTEMPORARIES
Available at your local bookstore, or visit
www.randomhouse.com.

COMING SOON FROM JOHN BURNHAM SCHWARTZ

An imaginative tour de force
based on the dramatic real-life story
of the reigning empress of Japan

The Commoner
A NOVEL

Just as Arthur Golden took us into the exotic
world of the geisha, John Burnham Schwartz
ventures into a realm of Japanese society unknown
to westerners. In *The Commoner*, he explores what
happens when an ordinary woman marries into
one of the most cloistered and powerful families
on earth to become Empress of Japan. It is an
extraordinary portrait, rich in dynastic intrigue, of
one woman's unprecedented rise to power as well
as the story of an island nation's wrenching move
towards modernity.

NAN A. TALESE
DOUBLEDAY Available January 22, 2008, wherever books are sold • www.nanatalese.com